RISK

A THRILLER

KATHLEEN MORRIS

Dunraven Press

Ebook Edition ISBN 978-1-7379866-6-9

Paperback Edition ISBN 978-1-7379866-5-2

Hardcover Edition ISBN 978–1-7379866-7-6

Dunraven Press August 2022

Cover Art and Design by Tabulanis

BOOKS BY KATHLEEN MORRIS

The Lily of the West

The Wind at Her Back

The Transformation of Chastity James

Fallen Child

Risk

RISK

I seduce you.
I lure you into the abyss.

-Unknown

If money go before, all ways do lie open.

-William Shakespeare

1

———

lagstaff, Arizona

Grace took a sip of her whiskey. "That's the worst band name I've ever heard."

Jack Wilder gave her that lopsided smile she loved. "I know, babe, but they're not that bad and the money's really good."

"They better be spectacular because with a name like the Lone Star Scoundrels, sounds like a bunch of asshat crackers about to rob a bank or rape your Granny and steal away with her dandelion wine instead of making decent music. We're going to get booked in every chicken wire dive bar across the country. I don't know about you, darlin', but I'm about done with this shit."

Grace sighed and propped her cowboy boots on the empty chair at the table. There were a lot of empty chairs in the club, if you could dignify this concrete block no windows shithole by calling it a club. So many places just like this one, sticky floors and tables, the grime hidden by the dim illumination of neon beer signs, dinky stages and archaic sound systems unless you brought your own, were rampant in this country and this one was no different than all the rest.

This was their second and last night booked here with the Mavericks, and it didn't look as though it was going to be any more successful, crowd-wise, than the first. The Mavericks' label didn't have much of a tour manager, and the Mavericks' own manager didn't have much of a clue about bookings or drumming up local publicity. There'd been no radio station interviews or promos, no record or music store publicity, rich territory that every indie band worth its salt had learned to mine, except for these doorknobs.

They'd signed up for a four-month tour with Barry's band, the Southern Mavericks, a country/rock fusion band that Grace called 'confuckfusion' after the first show, trying desperately to pump up the on-stage live performances to sound as good as the studio record they were promoting, which so far hadn't happened and likely never would. The label, some bottom feeder from the Muscle Shoals area, had given the Mavericks an old RV and their manager had wrangled $150 a day for gas and food out of them, little of which she and Jack had seen unless you counted the occasional cheeseburger or burrito if they showed up to the same fast food restaurant at the same time. A hundred fifty bucks a day didn't go very far split between gas for that monster RV and six people.

The label had booked Jack and Grace in as opener, intermission filler, and much-needed backup vocals and steel guitar. She and Jack had needed the money, and the winter season had been pretty flat in Nashville despite their efforts, so they'd agreed, thinking that at least they'd get some national exposure and be able to try out their songs to national audiences and see how people reacted. Grace had insisted she and Jack drive along alone in her old Explorer and twice now they'd had to cram people in to get to the next town to find a mechanic when the RV broke down, which had been no surprise to her.

The only perk was when she wasn't needed as a backup vocalist, she ran the merch table, selling the Mavericks' new

CD and t-shirts, which gave her a chance to highlight her and Jack's seven-inch EP, and their own t-shirts as well. Barry had been hesitant on the last but she'd insisted and he'd caved. As for Jack, he'd insisted he and Grace get at least four songs a night at most of the shows, openers or midway. So far, and Grace smiled whenever she thought about it, they'd outsold Barry two to one in merch and Wilder & Grace was getting a buzz that the Mavericks weren't, even without the label. She and Jack were a striking pair, his long blonde hair an exact opposite to her dark curls, a fantasy something for everyone couple, especially compared to the testosterone-laden city cowboy Mavericks, who Grace also referred to as the one-shot goodbye mama bros.

Jack looked at her with those pale blue eyes, lips curving in that way that made her bones melt. The man had the face of a Botticelli angel, too pretty for this world until you noticed the thin pale scar that ran down the left side of his face from the eyebrow to his jawline, but Grace loved that scar as much as the rest of him. And, he was no angel, she could certainly attest to that.

"Grace, it's not like that. It's a studio deal, in Nashville, probably two or three months. Me on lap steel, and it's Hi-Top Records and Joe pays great, you know that. It'll be a nice break for you, you can write and I'll bring home the money."

Well. "Why didn't you say that in the first place?" She leaned over and kissed him. "Hell, maybe we can even get the house on Brown Street back."

"Maybe."

She loved the Brown Street house and Jack did too. Since the night they'd met at the Bluebird two years ago, they'd been together and had moved into the little house three days later. They'd made their album there on the recording equipment they'd scrimped to get, and some borrowed from friends all over Nashville. It'd turned out great, only five songs, but they were both proud of it and they knew it was good. They'd had to give the house up when they went on this tour.

They'd stored their equipment and the rest of their stuff in Jack's dad's garage when they left. Hopefully, they'd be able to set up again when they got back. They'd been getting a little buzz back there when they'd played at the Orchid and the Bluebird, and the crowds had been very receptive. They were known in Nashville but not known enough to even get a low slot at the Opry. Grace didn't care, she and Jack had set their sights much higher.

One of the issues was the music they wrote and performed wasn't standard country. They knew they needed that "niche", something people could identify with, but for them it was elusive, perhaps because it was something completely unheard of. What they created was a mix of all they both loved – a melancholy mix of bluegrass, folk, roots, country and truly a sound all its own. They wrote their own, and had even worked up some old Townes Van Zandt covers along with some of the Appalachian folk songs they'd heard, some from Jack's dad Barnett, some from people they'd visited out in the hollers and played music with sitting on their porches, drinking moonshine into the night.

All they needed was money for an album and the endlessly expensive promotion and PR that went with it. Sometimes the frustration nearly drove Grace crazy and knew it did Jack too. Wilder & Grace were destined for more. Certainly more than this stupid tour which was proving to be more costly than it was profitable. She was anxious just to get it over with.

Jack left to talk to Barry. Jack wanted to make sure they weren't just the opener, playing a few songs while the crowd filed in, getting their drinks, yelling hellos and not even listening to who was on stage. They needed a middle slot, too but it only happened half the time. It was a shit move, and one Barry pulled all too often lately, among other things. Grace always changed out her good mic for the one Barry used and she always took it with her when their set was over so she'd be sure to see it again. Barry made a lot of promises and often broke them. Grace was sick of it.

Truth be told, she was sick of this whole damn tour and couldn't wait to get back to Nashville. The label had paid them a flat fee of $3,000, half up front and half when they returned, the only smart planning they'd done. If she and Jack had the other $1500 right now, they'd probably walk.

"Hey gorgeous, Jack abandon you?" Mike Nelson, the Mavericks' bassist and at least to his way of thinking, a ladies' man, plopped himself down beside her. "I keep tellin' you, babe, I'm the man to take up any empty space you got."

Grace snorted. "Don't keep calling me "babe". We talked about that, remember?"

Mike rolled his eyes. "Oh yeah, so you want me to call you Grace or maybe Whitney, like you're one of the guys? But nobody would ever mistake you for one of the guys."

She sighed. "Doesn't matter. I'm not in the mood right now, Mike."

He grinned. "We can always fix that."

Christ. What was with these dudes? She'd known better than to travel in their RV, which smelled like an unwashed locker room and usually rocked long after closing with the band groupies that wanted to get off with a hot musician, no matter if the booking was in a city or some small town. Still, losing your virginity in a rusty RV to a tool like Mike Nelson wasn't exactly Robert Plant and Led Zeppelin at the Beverly Hilton back in the day. Apparently, those girls had watched "Almost Famous" way too many times.

She took her boots off the chair. "No worries, the next ex-Mrs. Nelson will be by in about an hour and if she's a smart high school junior, she'll have a fake ID and a case of starfucker desperation, so you'll get lucky."

"Oh babe, you're killing me here. Oops, sorry *Whitney*." Mike's laughter followed her as she walked across the sticky wooden floor to the bar, the neon beer signs glowing through the smoky air. The no smoking rule wasn't exactly followed here but at least the drinks were free at Max's, although the food guaranteed a close relationship with a toilet in the morning if not ptomaine. She'd stopped by the local Safeway and put some stuff in their cooler this afternoon as usual, in case there were no late fast-food joints open. They'd learned the hard way.

The bartender smiled. A friendly guy, he knew his job well, refilling her glass. "You good, Grace? Hope you guys get a long set tonight. You two are the best thing in the whole show."

She shrugged. "Thanks, but it ain't like I'm singing La Boheme at the Met, now is it, John?"

"You got that right, girl, but with a voice like yours, you could be." He pushed the glass towards her. "On me. I can say I knew you when. I got hopes for you and Jack. Have a good show."

Grace perched on a barstool and watched as Fred set up his drum kit at the back of the small stage on the Persian carpet he always insisted upon using. He was a good guy and she liked him. They'd already brought in all the gear and Mike had gone over to make sure everything was to his satisfaction, propping his bass up on the Ampeg and arguing as always with the sound guy the minute they started the "check, checks".

She glanced up when Barry and Jack came out of the back room. The look on Jack's face did not bode well. She slugged the whiskey. Just a few more shows, she told herself. We can do this.

2

———————

Grace jerked awake when Jack stopped the car and turned off the engine. They were in a parking lot literally in the middle of nowhere. A neon sign that said "Diner" was the only illumination in the ink-black sky. The lights were on inside, and it looked like one of those places that catered to lost souls and night travelers and they always made Grace feel unaccountably sad. She glanced over at Jack, who sat staring blankly out the windshield.

"Where are we?"

He shrugged. "I don't know, somewhere east of Flagstaff. Holbrook was the last town I remember, could be in New Mexico. Come on, I need coffee and you probably do too."

He'd been angry and non-talkative for hours now, even before the show, insistent upon driving into the night as soon the show was over, somehow wanting to put space between them and the Southern Mavericks, and not for the first time. True to form, Barry had bowed to the lamebrain manager who'd brought in a dismal local band to open, pre-empting her and Jack from even a crap opening slot, and then Barry hadn't even given them a middle slot in the show. They'd only made thirty bucks from a T-shirt and one CD from some lovesick girl who'd followed Jack around all night and that was barely enough for gas to get them to the next booking in Albuquerque.

They'd packed up their gear and left right after the show and Jack hadn't said a word, just started the car and drove through the night towards the New Mexico border. Grace thought the best course was to say nothing because if it was possible, she was even angrier than he was. She'd fallen asleep just to stave off the argument they were destined to have after a bad night and there'd been way too many of those lately.

The waitress brought coffee and a plastic-covered menu to their booth beside the window overlooking the parking lot. Grace looked idly at the menu. Her stomach growled but the hollow feeling she had wasn't really hunger for food, but for something entirely different, a chance at a dream they deserved but wouldn't ever get, especially doing what they were doing right now.

"You want anything?" She waggled the menu at Jack, who shook his head and stared out the window. She looked around but far as she could tell, there were no other customers, not even at the counter. The place was as empty as their future.

"Fuck this." She got up and went over to the waitress who sat behind the counter doing a crossword. Her name tag said "Fran". "Can you do a BLT, Fran?"

"Sure, hon," the waitress gave a weary smile. "It's pretty good, too. Be out in a minute."

"Thanks a lot."

She plopped back down in the booth. Jack looked up.

"Sorry I've been so...you know," he said.

"Me, too." She sipped her coffee. It was surprisingly good, not tasting like it was the dregs from back a few hours. Fran was good at her job.

"It's just, man, I'm so damn tired of this shit and the Barrys in the world. I can't wait to get back."

"Amen. 'Course we could always just leave. We forfeit the rest of the money but..."

He shook his head. "It's not a lot but we need it, Grace. I don't want to sponge off my dad any more than we have to and it'll be another month before the session thing. I'm just going to have to do that thing we do."

She smiled. "As in?"

"Swallow it fast like a trailer park whore and hope the next one took a fucking bath."

Oh yeah, that thing, Grace thought. God, she was sick of this. She knew he was too, so there was no point in bringing it up and making things any worse.

Fran slid the sandwich in front of her, refilled their coffee cups and put the check down on the table, gliding silently away on her tennis shoes. Grace always thought waitresses and bartenders should go into the therapy business because they sure had enough customers that could use it. Fran was yet another woman who truly read her audience.

Grace handed Jack half the sandwich and he took it more eagerly than she thought. She took a bite of hers. It was just as good as the coffee. This place was an undiscovered treasure. The sandwich was gone before she knew it. She sat back, wiping her fingers on the paper napkin and watched Jack finish his. She felt better. Food could be a great cure-all sometimes. At least for a while.

"So Albuquerque?"

He nodded, his mouth full.

"It's a long haul. I'll drive for a while. We might have to find a campground or the usual later though. After that," she ticked off on her fingers, "Amarillo, Oklahoma City, Fort Smith, Memphis, and home. There's not much of this crap tour left. We can do it, cowboy."

Jack wiped his mouth and finished his coffee. "Cool. I'm going to throw some water on my face to stay awake enough to get back to the car." He slid out of the booth and Fran pointed to the right. She really did know her audience.

Grace waited, finishing her coffee and staring out the window at the dark desert sky. There were a couple of cars out there she hadn't noticed before. Probably Fran's and whoever the cook was in the back. She put down a twenty and sat the empty cup on the saucer. If she drove fast, they might get to Albuquerque by morning. Jack came back, looking a little better, drops of water dotting his Tyler Childers T-shirt, his hair damp.

"My turn. You good?"

He nodded. She followed the same route to the bathrooms, pushing open the door marked "Ladies". God, she really had to pee. Something about drinking coffee on the road was for her a direct pipeline from mouth to bladder. She should've known better, since they had a lot more hours on the road.

It was a two-staller and she went to the last one and closed the stall door, not sure why since there was nobody else there but old habits die hard. When she reached for the toilet paper roll, she glanced down and noticed a canvas strap on the floor, leading to a khaki backpack stuffed behind the toilet. For a second, tired as she was, Grace blinked and thought it was her own but with a longer look, it didn't have any band buttons pinned on the flap as she had on hers. Curious, she dragged it out towards her feet. It was fairly heavy. She flipped the flap over.

It was full of money, hundred-dollar bills, banded together. *Holy shit,* she thought. *Who the hell leaves something like this in a diner bathroom?* Was this a sick joke? She sat there, stunned, for a few seconds. She flushed the toilet and zipped up her pants, staring at the backpack like it was a coiled rattlesnake. She opened the stall door and went to the sink, washing the sandwich from her hands and stared into the mirror. Her reflection stared back at her, bright green eyes, just a little bloodshot and a face she'd found to be both a curse and a blessing. Her long brown braid was a mess of loose hairs, something she'd thought to redo but not now.

Instinctively, she looked behind her but the bathroom was empty, as were both the stalls, no different than when she'd come in. She stood there for a full minute, shock and disbelief warring with her common sense. This couldn't possibly be real. But it was.

Money like that could make all the difference to them. She and Jack could do whatever they wanted to do, play the music they created, start a real life together. They could walk away from this horrid tour, forgetting Barry and the Southern Mavericks. They could set up their own studio, put out the album, hell, put out a shitload of albums, hire a publicist and never have to worry about a thing in this world except making music.

The devil on her shoulder was deafened by the angel on the other who tried to sing louder. Money like that very likely came with a past, maybe a past accompanied by people who definitely would want it back, people that you wouldn't want looking for you. The devil drowned the angel out. On the other hand, anybody who came looking for it would have to know whom they were looking for, and there's nobody else here. Who would ever know?

She leaned both hands on the sides of the small sink, trying to think. It was a big world out there. Two people stopping here out of the blue for no specific reason might never cross anybody's radar screen. There was nothing to track them after they left this place.

Grace took a few deep breaths and looked around the small bathroom one more time. Nobody knew who they were and nobody was here to see what she did. If she didn't take it, the next person to come in here would. Grace pictured Fran the helpful waitress on the first bus to Cancun, wearing a bikini and sitting under a parasol on the beach, languidly downing margaritas while a pool boy hovered nearby. A hysterical giggle escaped her lips and she choked it back down.

Before she could think about it anymore, she hoisted the backpack and walked toward the dining area. Jack was standing by their table, chatting with Fran. Grace swallowed heavily and smiled.

"Ready?" he said.

"Sure am," Grace said. If her voice was little shaky, no one noticed. She waved her hand as they went out the front door. "Thanks for everything, Fran."

They got in the car, Grace quickly pitching the backpack on the floor behind the driver's seat without a word while Jack went around to the passenger side, sighed and reclined the seat. It was a good thing he was tired and unobservant. She was pretty sure he was half asleep before she pulled out of the parking lot, the coffee having little effect. She turned right on Interstate 40 and within seconds, the diner was a memory but the backpack was not.

She drove into the night, seeing only a few cars every now and then, her heart beating like a tom-tom and her imagination soaring from wonder to disaster. What she'd just done would change their lives forever. That was the one and only thing she knew for certain.

3

————

A *few days before*
Sinaloa, Mexico

Angel Vega flinched inwardly as Luis's hand stroked her thigh. She never let her distaste show, not after the first few times. She'd learned. She leaned back against the silk pillows, relaxing her legs as well as her mind.

"My little Angelita," he whispered in her ear. "I have raised a little wildcat, haven't I? I want to indulge you in this, *gatito,* but I think it is a mistake."

She raised her head but he pushed her back into the pillows, his hand gently covering her mouth. Sometimes that hand hadn't been as gentle on her mouth or anywhere else.

"No, no, no," he chuckled. "Never interrupt Luis when he is talking, my dear. Let us examine your history here. You have learned so much at my side, little one, and grown into the woman you are, even more enticing than the girl you were when you first arrived here. All because of me."

His fingers gripped her thigh, pressing harder and hurting now to make certain she knew she was his property while he made his point. Angel didn't make a sound or move a muscle.

He smiled, this monster she'd been a slave to for years. She wished for an angel of death to carry him away every day but the beneficent Madonna, if she even existed, which Angel was beginning to doubt, had never intervened nor listened to her prayers.

"So it is then, my little *querida*, you wanted to learn about my business, and be around guns. And fighting. I know you like that. Oho, maybe you wish to be like the Madonna Oscura, Escobar's female assassin." He laughed and made mock martial arts gestures in the air.

"Silly Angel. Now it is my entire life you wish to be a part of, no matter where it might take you? Luis likes that you want to become even closer in every way, but I have concerns about this. It is not who you are, foolish one. Even though I have allowed you to learn how to shoot a gun, for your own defense in case anything could happen that you would need to do so would occur when Luis was away, it was mostly an exercise and an amusement for you."

He sighed dramatically. "I have indulged you in most of these things because we have all seen what can happen when evil men do not agree with my business methods and having everyone capable of defense is simply good sense. I have even provided all the books you wanted, the English tutor, the French tutor, the music teacher, let you buy all your clothes and shoes and makeup and music and every other silly thing that young women think they need. I know it is boring out here at the ranch, with only the internet and movies, ordering things or having things brought to you, but it is the way to keep you safe. To keep us all safe."

He pulled his arm away and put his arms behind his head, gazing at her. Then, he sat up and opened the cupboard beneath the bedside table. He reached over and took a few minutes to light up a Cuban cigar. For him it was a ritual. For her, it was nothing but a disgusting smell that permeated her very bones. Only a few times had he burned her with the glowing end of the foul thing and she hoped today was not going to be one of those times.

"You amuse me, Angelita. So, to prove just how silly you are to want to engage in any aspects of my business, I am going to allow this. One time." He smiled at her. She held her breath for a moment, staring at the satin sheets.

"Then you will learn this is not a recreation for bored women but a serious business, not something you wish to be a part of and you will return to Luis satisfied. Once again you will play your guitar and order from Neiman-Marcus and make me happy with new ideas and greater enthusiasm. Never say Luis Reynaldo is a man who does not provide ample educational opportunities. Look how wonderfully you have learned English and French. Your guitar playing makes me happy. I am proud of you, my little Angel. You will find that the world I have provided for you is much better than what is out there, especially anything in Norte. Perhaps a day will come you can go to Paris with me and try out your new language skills. We will visit ateliers and perfumeries and I will choose the clothes I desire for you, and new scents for your skin that excite me. For now, I offer you this. You will return to Luis grateful once again for the learning opportunities I have given you."

Her face remained impassive. She didn't dare look at him. She had learned to never let her passion for anything show, because he would use it against her, sooner or later. He missed nothing. Still, her heart soared and all she focused on from his usual self-absorbed monologue was that he'd said she could go.

"Tomorrow, we are scheduled to do a transaction in Oklahoma City." He shrugged and took a sip of the tequila that was always on the nightstand.

"It's not a big one, this is true, but this is a market that has promise for us. It's the Albanians, those European peasant goatfuckers, so hungry and eager for a share. I've been thinking of doing business with the Europeans for a long time now, even those vodka-soaked Russians that think they are so special, with their girl slaves and nightclubs. We need to find new outlets besides the meth-addled Anglos that nobody can trust anymore and this is a good test for both of us. I hope the goat-fuckers are not as stupid as I think they are, but this is a first meeting and first meetings are always safe. I am sending Roberto and Chang. You will accompany them."

He pushed a button on his phone and Chang walked into the bedroom, closing the door behind him, stopping six feet from the bed, his posture stiff, hands clasped behind him. Angel didn't bother to pull the sheet over herself. Luis enjoyed having her on display nearly as much as he liked her discomfiture with it and Chang had seen her naked many times before. The beautiful Chinese man never leered or even really looked at her. It was as though he felt compassion for her, but Angel had never seen the slightest emotion pass the man's face, simply emptiness and a blind obedience to Luis's wishes.

Chang had been here for some time, looking for asylum after he'd apparently had a near-fatal indiscretion with a Hong Kong triad leader's wife. Luis had welcomed him with open arms, delighted that his reputation had provided an open door for such a distinguished and accomplished *sicario*. Chang had never disappointed even when Luis put him in suicidal situations but Chang always survived with aplomb, just to prove his merit. Luis did that to people. Angel had learned Luis's cruel whims well, along with much more in her years as his reluctant mistress.

"*Si, patron?*" Chang's sculpted face was impassive, his dark eyes blank.

"You will have a guest on your trip tomorrow," Luis said. "Angel wants to learn how we do business," he looked over at her, "or maybe just fulfill her desire to fly on an airplane and pretend she is a movie star. Who knows with women, ay?"

Chang's expression didn't change at all. He gave a small bow.

Luis sighed heavily, as though indulging a child with a new toy, finding it so tiresome he was waiting for the nanny to take the problem from his hands.

"I know you will take good care of her, as always, as though she was your own sister."

"Of course, sir." Chang didn't even glance at her.

Luis waved his hand in dismissal and Chang bowed again slightly in his Chinese way before leaving the room. Everyone knew Luis loved that about his favorite assassin. Homage and subservience were like sustenance to Luis and he relished those traits the way other men desired true love and affection. Those were his needs.

Angel had others and she suspected Chang did as well, for all the good it did either one of them.

Dark clouds roiled overhead and raindrops pelted the limousine's windows as they drove from the Oklahoma City airport to the warehouse where they were to meet the Albanians. Roberto and Chang both sat as impassively as they had for most of the Learjet's flight from Mexico, Roberto in his cheap black suit and Chang in his bespoke one, a major difference that amused Angel. Two AR-15s rested on the floor and she knew they both carried pistols as well. She was not armed herself, of course, since she was just there as an observer, according to Luis, and besides, this was a friendly deal, as far as any drug deal could be considered friendly.

She had spoken very little to either of the men on the flight, only to the flight attendant Marisol, a pretty Mexican girl who had eyed her with some trepidation. Angel knew Luis had likely fucked her, as he had all the maids and every other female that entered his orbit, and he flew often. She'd never cared in the least. It took the burden from her on those long days and nights when he was home on the ranch.

Oklahoma City was the first American city she'd ever seen, except on television and movies. It was very disappointing. Surely the rest of this much vaunted country had something better to offer than this grimy landscape. This place was ugly. Everything was gray: a lot of concrete, roads, buildings, billboards, strip malls and pickup trucks that whizzed past them throwing roostertails of water onto the limousine's windshield as they drove through the darkening night, the billboards and neon signs of the businesses they passed the only color. Trash littered the streets, wrappers, cups lined the curbs and empty plastic bags spun by the windshield like lost drunken birds, coming to land snagged on chain-link fences and steel poles, wound into grotesque shapes. People scurried by on the sidewalks, wearing coats turned up at the collar. A few carried umbrellas, but many were unprotected, simply enduring the misery of getting from one sheltered place to another.

They were not spending the night here, just doing a business transaction and going back to the plane, according to Luis. From what Angel had seen so far, she didn't mind that in the least. She wished their destination had been sunny and glamorous Los Angeles or somewhere she'd always wanted to go, but perhaps when Luis knew how well she behaved this time, he'd let her travel more often. She yearned for that with a longing that always took her by surprise but it shouldn't, not anymore. She was like a pet kept in a gilded cage and she hated her lack of freedom almost as much as the man who had taken it from her.

When they pulled into a warehouse, the doors sliding upwards, the utter silence was nearly as deafening as the rain that had been pounding on the roof of limousine. Two other vehicles, both Cadillac Escalades, were already there, pulled up facing them, and six men stood in front of them, four of them holding guns. They were all brawny gentlemen, their faces showing signs of Eastern European ancestry, their expressions grim.

She didn't know if this was usual or not, but Roberto and Chang didn't seem concerned, exiting the limo while Chang glanced over at her and put his hand out in a stop gesture. Roberto had taken one of the AR-15s but the other still lay on the floor. Chang apparently didn't think he'd need it.

She watched them walk up to the Albanians from where she sat snug in the limo's warm seat. She thought about pouring a drink from the bar on the side of the door. Luis may have been correct, this entire operation was quite boring. She wasn't sure what she'd been hoping for but whatever that was, Oklahoma City and this deal were definitely not interesting enough to be on that list.

The men conversed for a few moments while the driver of the limo unloaded the drugs from the trunk, contained in three aluminum cases, placing them in front of the vehicle. The Albanian men on the other side had pulled out three good-sized backpacks, placing them on the concrete floor alongside the cases.

Angel was reaching for the tequila and a glass when a girl, about fifteen, her bruised face very frightened, jumped out from one of the Escalades. She was carrying a backpack as well and heading straight towards the limo or maybe the open door behind it, Angel couldn't be sure. She looked like someone running for her life, as much of a captive as Angel always had been, without the pretty cage. If Angel couldn't get out of her own cage, maybe she could help this girl out of her situation. She opened the limo's door.

"Get in," Angel said. The girl looked at her and glanced back in fear as one of the men shouted.

"Now!" Angel hissed.

The girl scrambled into the limo, trembling and curling herself up on the seat. Angel picked up the AR-15. She wasn't really sure why but she didn't like the way the man had shouted. "Stay here."

She stepped out of the car, the door shielding most of her and especially the gun from view. No one seemed to notice.

Roberto was having a heated conversation with the leader, the man who had yelled at the girl. As she watched, Chang stepped closer to two of the men holding guns. He smiled and held up his hands in a gesture of peace. Everyone seemed to calm down, and the leader laughed at something Roberto said. Just then they all stared over at her and one of the men holding a gun made a remark that made them laugh further.

She hoped they weren't offering a trade and she put her finger on the trigger. She didn't have any experience with the mechanics of drug deals but she knew when there were angry discussions and when simple negotiations took this long, something wasn't right. The girl may have been just a distraction but when Angel glanced into the back seat, she was still sobbing quietly, curled into the seat, her eyes imploring.

Afterwards, Angel couldn't be sure exactly when it went completely wrong. Maybe it was always going to go wrong long before the warehouse.

One of the Albanians shot first, hitting Roberto in the leg which didn't stop him from mowing down two of his Albanian attackers, as bullets from both sides flew wildly throughout the warehouse, one hitting the limo driver who had gotten out of the car, gun ready, but collapsed face down on the cement floor at Angel's feet, blood pooling under him. The Albanians had very bad aim, but they weren't far away and they had a lot of guns.

"Get down!" she shrieked at the girl, who dutifully dove for the floor of the limo. Angel ducked down behind the door as bullets shattered the windshield. When she looked up, Chang's arms, hands and legs were a blur of movement, taking out two more of the Albanians. Angel sighted on another man with a gun and shot him in the head. Roberto took out the last standing Albanian, the man's automatic rifle clattering to the cement floor, but not before his last volley hit Roberto in the chest.

The acrid smell of cordite and blood filled the warehouse. She and Chang were the only people still standing. Angel kept the gun with her anyway as she knelt beside Roberto, the blood pumping out of his chest like a geyser. She put her hands on the wound, trying to stop the blood that just kept coming, spilling through her fingers.

"Just hold on, we'll get you out of here," she said. He stared up at her and shook his head. The blood continued to flow but his eyes were empty. Chang pulled her up, his hand firm on her arm.

"He's gone. We have to leave here. Now."

The limo was leaking red and green fluids into a puddle on the concrete, and the first Escalade's windshield was shattered as well. Chang went to the second Albanian Escalade and threw the backpacks into the backseat, even though one was covered in blood. He started back for the aluminum cases and Angel put her hand on his arm.

"No."

He threw her hand off impatiently. "What do you mean?"

"I mean, this is our chance, Chang." She stared into his eyes, and put her hands on his shoulders. "Fuck the drugs. We take this money and we leave here. Free of Luis, free of all this shit. You and I talked about having a different life once. This is our chance, one that might never come again. If we take it, neither of us will have to be slaves to that piece of shit Luis ever again." She always talked to him in English, as his Spanish wasn't very good. "*Comprende, tonto?*"

His nostrils flared. He stared at her with those empty eyes

and she thought for a minute he was going to kill her as easy as he had the Albanians. Maybe he understood Spanish very well. Then he nodded.

"But we take these." He picked up two of the aluminum cases. "Insurance."

She shrugged. "I don't care, let's just get out of here."

They set fire to the warehouse, the rest of the money and the drugs. In the end, they took along the girl, putting her into the backseat along with her backpack, which was carrying apparently everything she had or at least what she thought was important. Angel knew what it was like to be chattel and have nothing and how precious even small things could be.

Maybe, just maybe, they'd have some time before Luis, the Albanians or the DEA figured out the warehouse was short a couple of bodies and a lot of drugs and money. Or not.

4

It wasn't the yelling but the pounding on the water-streaked window beside her ear that woke Grace. Her eyes were bleary, trying to take in the empty Walmart parking lot, still dark except for the streetlights and the security lights on the building. It wasn't a view she'd have chosen but when her eyes began to close for the third time last night, she'd spotted the sign from the freeway and pulled in. Like many musicians and touring bands on a budget, they often spent the night at Walmarts all over the country. Unlike many retail establishments, Walmart didn't mind nomads and travelers and even let people use the bathrooms if they were still around at opening time.

The car smelled musty, between her and Jack, the sweaty clothes in the laundry bag and the remains of chip bags and cheeseburger wrappers they hadn't had time to deal with. Lightly falling raindrops streaked the windows and Grace jerked back when she finally turned her head. The yelling was coming from a mouth two inches from her face on the other side of the window. A girl, maybe nineteen or so, her long blonde hair wet from the rain, stood outside the car like a nightmare scarecrow, gesturing frantically.

She hesitated. They'd heard too many stories and had a few ones to tell of their own but the girl was alone, the rest of the lot deserted and she looked very frightened. Grace let the window down a few inches. The smell of rain on asphalt mingled with the spicy tang of mesquite poured into the stale air of the car.

"Please... help me." The girl glanced behind her as though a monster was about to leap on her. There was no one there. "He'll kill me." Her fingers clamped down on the edge of the window and she looked like she was going to shove the glass down with brute strength and that made Grace nervous. "Please."

Grace glanced over at Jack but he snored on. Shit. This ploy was a favorite that had gotten a lot of people robbed and even killed. The boyfriend usually hid behind the side of the store, behind the garbage bins or some bushes and ran out the minute a house or car door was thrown open.

She took a closer look at the girl. There was a large bruise on the side of her face and her lip was bleeding slightly. Usually they didn't go this far with the theatrics. She poked Jack.

"Hey, wake up. We got a problem."

He snorted, coughed and opened his eyes, staring blearily at her. "Whaa?"

Grace pointed at the girl. "Her."

Jack sat up and peered at the girl. "Oh man."

"Yeah. What do you think?"

"I think we get the fuck out of here, Grace. She'll find some other sucker."

"She looks harmless, Jack."

"They always do, Grace. We don't need this shit. I'm serious, start the car."

The girl's fingers were still on the window, her eyes pleading. Grace shook her head and began to peel the girl's fingertips from the window. After the first two, she let go and Grace put the window back up. She started the car and put on the windshield wipers. The rain was coming down a little harder now. She drove away but couldn't stop herself from looking back. The lot was still empty except for the girl, who had collapsed onto the pavement right where Grace had been parked, her head in her hands.

"I think she's for real, Jack."

"Maybe. Ain't we all, darlin'?" He wasn't having it.

She drove towards the street and then veered around the huge store building, through the alleyway where the trucks unloaded and around the back to where they'd been parked. The girl still sat huddled there in the rain, alone.

"What the hell are you doing, Grace?" Jack said, coming fully awake. "We don't have time for this."

"It's a kindness, Jack," Grace said. "Something we haven't seen lately. You know what they say, you do something good for somebody, it comes to you tenfold."

"Karma is bullshit."

Grace looked at him. "Worth a try."

She pulled up beside the forlorn heap on the pavement and rolled the window down. The girl looked up, tentative hope in her eyes.

"Get in," Grace said. "The back seat. Move stuff over and you'll just fit. You can forget a seatbelt, though."

She scrambled into the back seat behind Grace, shoving a guitar case and a small amp over to make room. Too late, Grace remembered the backpack on the floor. Oh well, she'd deal with that later. This girl looked too done in to bother to snoop and if she did, Grace could always dump her back out on the road to find another ride from another stranger.

Grace turned around. "Where you headed? The police station? Your mom's? The open road?"

The girl brushed the hair from her face, wiping her hands on her damp jeans. "Anywhere but here, wherever you're going. Thanks, thanks so much."

Grace shrugged. "The open road it is, then. Let me know if someplace appeals to you. We're headed to Albuquerque. What's your name?"

"Anya."

"I'm Grace and this is Jack. We'll get something to eat in a bit. Take a nap or whatever, okay?"

"Yes," Anya said. "Thank you for taking me with you. Most people would not have done this thing." She had a curious accent, one Grace hadn't heard before, Eastern European maybe. Questions could wait until later.

"I'm not most people," Grace said. "Lucky for you, Anya."

It was still dark, way too early for most restaurants or coffee shops to be open and Grace wanted to get as far away from the diner where she'd picked up that backpack as she could. Jack had drowsed off again. Grace glanced at Anya in the rearview mirror and the girl seemed exhausted, her eyes closed. Still, Grace was really tired and getting hungry despite the BLT at good old Fran's place, so when she saw a roadside café with an open sign, where a couple of pickup trucks sat in the parking lot, she pulled in.

They sat down in a booth overlooking the parking lot. Only two other booths were occupied, both by two men at each, earnestly talking. They looked Indian or Mexican, all of them wearing cowboy hats and weathered faces, as though they worked outside, maybe at a ranch herding cattle or sheep. There wasn't much else out here, so maybe ranches were the main employment. Grace had no idea. The waitress seemed to know the other patrons well, chatting and filling up their coffee cups. Dawn was breaking and they looked to be getting ready for their day.

When she came to their table, she smiled and took out her pad. "What can I getcha?"

"Two eggs, over easy, bacon and hash browns," Jack promptly responded, "and some of that great-smelling coffee." He gave her his best Jack smile and she openly melted. *Just like they all did*, thought Grace. *This guy.*

The waitress tore her eyes away from Jack and looked at Grace. "And for you, hon?"

"Same," Grace said, "with sourdough toast." She looked over at Anya. "Order whatever you want."

Anya hesitated and glanced at Grace. "I have no money," she whispered, looking down at the formica tabletop.

"Same for her," said Grace. "And two orange juices, please."

The waitress left, returning quickly to fill their coffee cups. Grace took a sip. It really was as good as it smelled. Another hidden treasure, this place too. Diners. You never really knew. What she did know is that it was time to find out what was going on with this girl. They didn't need the baggage and Albuquerque was as far as she was willing to drag her along.

"So Anya, tell me. Is there anyone you can call, or anyplace you can go?" Grace held up her cell phone.

Anya's eyes flickered rapidly. "My boyfriend stole my purse and my phone," she said. "I will try to remember the numbers." She smiled apologetically and gestured towards her swollen cheek.

"I know how that is," Grace said. "If I lost my phone, I'd be up the creek."

"See, that's the thing. I keep telling you to write stuff down for a backup, Grace," Jack said. "You don't seem to have a problem with that on our band stuff, just your personal stuff. Now you can see what a problem that can lead to?"

"Christ, you're such a Luddite," Grace said. "You'd be happier living in some cabin in the middle of nowhere, I swear to God."

He was still cranky this morning. They hadn't talked about Flagstaff yet, or more importantly, the backpack on the floor of the backseat. There hadn't been time, since he'd been too angry and tired and she too freaked out about the damn thing. Then Anya had shown up and there hadn't been a second to talk about anything. Anya was a definite complication. Still, they'd get there. Before she could answer, the girl nudged her.

"I must visit the bathroom," she said apologetically.

"Of course," Grace said, and stepped out of the booth, while Anya slid over and walked towards the bathrooms. Jack watched her walk away and frowned.

"Follow her," Jack said. "I'm telling you, Grace, I don't trust this girl at all. We should leave her here no matter what. We aren't her keepers and the longer we drag her around, the harder it'll be to get rid of her."

"Are you kidding?"

"No, I'm not. I'm serious, Grace. There's something off about her. I'd like to say I can smell it, but trust me on this. Go after her. Be quiet about it, too."

Grace sighed. Jack was always paranoid, especially when he was hungover. She got up and went to the alcove down the hallway, putting her ear to the door marked "Women". Before she opened the door, she could hear Anya talking to someone. That was odd, since there were no other women in the place except for the waitress, who'd been standing behind the counter when she left. That, and the fact that Anya said her boyfriend stole her cell phone. The conversation seemed heated. She pushed open the door.

Anya stood beside the sink, the water running, apparently to cover her voice, a cell phone in her hand, and jerked away when Grace entered the small space.

"I thought your boyfriend took your phone," Grace said, trying to sound casual. She wasn't prepared for the reaction.

"Go to hell," Anya hissed, shoving the phone into the

pocket of her jeans. She was no longer sweet and submissive. She didn't look like any sort of a victim anymore. "They will be here in twenty minutes and you will be sorry, you thieving whore."

"Whoa," Grace said, holding up both hands. "What the hell are you talking about?"

The girl's face contorted in rage. "You thought no one would know? The money you stole. They sent me this way to find whoever was there last night and I am now the lucky one, and not the one they will kill for losing the money. I saw it in your car, you dumb bitch. You will pay when they get here."

Holy shit, Grace thought. *Anya must've been the one who left the backpack in the diner bathroom for whatever reason, or at least she knew who did.* Grace's mind was whirling. She wished she'd never set foot in that damn bathroom or been tempted enough to pick up that damn backpack. She and Jack had to get out of here right now. Before she could turn around, Anya pulled a small knife from a belt on her waist.

"You are going nowhere, dumb American bitch. You belong to us now."

"The fuck," Grace said, backing up towards the door, hands out. Fast as a striking cobra, Anya lunged towards her, the shining knife in her hand. Grace's heart lurched and she froze for a second. Knives had always frightened her badly, the thought of being sliced open and the blood...

Self-preservation and adrenaline kicked in, dispelling the numbing terror and Grace knocked Anya's knife hand towards the ceiling and punched her in the face, not even sure how she'd managed it. The girl's eyes went wide as she slipped on the wet tile floor and her feet flew out from under her, her head striking the porcelain sink behind her, the knife falling from her hand and clattering onto the floor as she collapsed.

Blood pooled out from behind Anya's head as Grace looked on in horror. She felt like she'd just stepped into a Tarantino movie. She looked around but there was no one in the bathroom and apparently nobody had heard anything. She knelt and felt for a pulse on the girl's neck as Anya's eyelids fluttered and then stopped, the blue eyes open, staring at the nothingness of the ceiling tiles. Grace had never been good at this pulse thing but she was pretty sure the girl was dead. She pulled her fingers away like they were on fire and nearly sat down on the cold floor before self-preservation kicked in.

Oh shit, oh shit, oh shit, Grace thought. She dug the phone from the pocket of Anya's skintight jeans and picked up the knife, shoving both into her jacket pocket. She whirled around and put her hand out, bracing herself on the white tile wall. Her heart was hammering in her chest and she was having a hard time taking a deep breath. All she could think of was she and Jack needed to get the hell out of here. She slowed her breathing but her whole body was trembling. She walked out the bathroom door, slowing her steps as she approached the table where Jack sat sipping coffee in blissful ignorance. She grabbed his arm.

"We have to leave. Right now."

He looked up at her quizzically. "What the hell?"

"Trust me," Grace said. "No questions. Come on. I mean it." The waitress had gone into the kitchen and there wasn't a second to spare before she came back and they had to explain. Jack gulped down more coffee and stood up.

"You were right, there was something off about her. She's not coming with us."

"OK, OK." Jack put $30 on the table and she took his hand, practically pulling him out the door. The guys at the other tables glanced over, curious, but nobody said anything or called out for the waitress. People tended to mind their own business around here. No one seemed to notice that the party of three was now two.

Out in the parking lot, Jack took the wheel while she got into the passenger seat.

Jack pulled out onto the highway and floored it without Grace even asking. He'd always had a sixth sense. He looked over at her, eyebrows raised.

"It's kind of looking like there's some trouble here. Where's that damn girl and what do you need to tell me, Grace?"

"Forget the girl. She's history." She watched him flinch a little. "And yeah, we're in a heap of trouble, Jack. A big heap."

5

By the time Grace got to the part where she left Anya dead on the bathroom floor, Jack glanced over at her and shook his head, holding up his hand, which Grace had always found maddening and insulting and Jack knew that very well. "Don't say one more fucking word, Grace."

He took the next turnoff, some bullet-pocked sign that said "Miner's Lake, 14 miles". The road was gravel and after a mile or so, he pulled off into the desert and parked among the rocks, cactus and mesquite. Dust billowed past them for a few minutes while they sat there in silence, looking out at the arid desert landscape. A jackrabbit hopped past but there were no other signs of life.

Jack held out his hand. "First of all, give me her phone."

She handed the girl's cheap burner phone to him, which he promptly switched off. and took out the battery. Grace felt stupid. She should have thought of that herself.

"A smart person would just throw it out, but I've found you never know." He threw it in the glove box. *Well, he would know,* Grace thought. She knew Jack had been in juvie for something when he was fourteen and had more than a few police hassles since then, along with his brother, who was doing time for something she'd never asked about. They'd never really talked about his past in any depth, except he'd said music had been his salvation and when they met two years ago, Jack had been hers. Their joke had always been she'd saved him from a life of crime and he'd saved her from shoplifting and a life on her back because they were both so talented and pretty but it seemed they were the only ones who appreciated their own dark humor. Very funny then. Not so funny now.

He put the window down a few inches and lit a cigarette. "So, let me get this straight. You found a backpack full of money in that first diner bathroom in Arizona and just threw it in the car without even counting it," he gazed at her through a curl of smoke, "or telling me shit all about it."

"Well, yeah," Grace said. "I know I should've told you right away and maybe you would've made a better decision. But you were so tired and just didn't need any more hassle, what with the Barry stuff and all, I figured I'd get to it this morning. Then that girl showed up and there just wasn't a good time after that. Sorry, babe. I mean, I really am sorry. I know this is a big deal and you should've known from the start."

"It doesn't matter, ancient history at this point. I'm not sure I would've done anything different than what you did. Only now, we got a dead girl in another diner. We're leaving quite a trail, aren't we?" He threw his cigarette out the window.

"Christ, Jack, it's not like I meant to kill her," Grace said, her whole body trembling still even though the adrenaline had mostly worn off, but maybe that was why. "I'm going to have to live with that forever. She was just a kid."

"What I don't get is how she knew to find us at the Walmart." Jack chewed on his thumb callous and stared out the windshield. It was a nervous habit he had that drove her nuts. "She knew how to find us, like she was stalking us, and that's something we need to figure out."

"Hell, I don't know. My guess would be whoever left the damn thing came back to get it and talked to good old Fran. Maybe she told them what we were driving. I mean, there's only two ways to go from there, really, west or east and not too many people on the road in the middle of the night around here. She must've simply gotten lucky and trailed us."

"If she found us, how come her pals weren't with her?" He mused, staring out the windshield. "Something off there."

"How the fuck should I know, Jack?" She was yelling now and panic was running its little nasty fingers down her spine.

Jack sighed and pulled her over, holding her tightly against his shoulder. "It's OK, it's OK, Grace. I'm sorry. I'm not trying to be a dick. We're going to figure this out. Christ, what a mess." He sat back. "I think it's time we take a closer look at that backpack and see just how much money dear little Anya was willing to die for."

He opened the door and hefted the backpack into the front seat, grunting a little as he set it between them on the console. "Heavy fucker, I'll say that."

Jack threw open the big flap. "Holy shit." He sat back hard in the seat.

Just as she'd seen the night before, it was full of money. They silently began to count the banded bills, all of them hundreds. Finally the bag was empty, the banded stacks piling up on the floor.

"What've you got?" Jack said. "I've got $400,000." He shook his head in disbelief.

"Under that. I count $350,000 or thereabouts." Grace was stunned. She suspected there was a lot of money in there, but had no idea it was that much. "That's a lot of money, Jack. People die for a lot less than that."

Those piercing blue eyes turned to her. "Yes, and people get killed for a lot less, too. We're going to have to get really smart about this really fast or we're going to be two more of them."

"Oh Christ." The enormity of what she'd done finally caught up with her and hit her like a train wreck.

She opened up the car door, scrambled out and threw up on the gravelly sand, her head pounding. She'd put them on a road not to prosperity but to a violent death just like the girl in the diner. She wished she'd never seen that backpack last night. They had to find a way out of this mess. She shut the door and Jack handed her a fistful of tissues to wipe her mouth.

"What the hell are we going to do?"

Jack put his arm around her and pulled her close. "Hell, babe, I don't know. But we'll figure it out."

They clung together and for a few minutes, Grace breathed in the smell of him and felt the comfort they always gave each other. It wasn't enough this time. She pulled away and stared at him. For a second his eyes looked frantic and it scared her. Jack was never frantic. Then he shook his head as though he was clearing away cobwebs or maybe bad memories. "For starters, we get this money back in that bag and get the fuck out of here."

They put the money back in the bag except for one banded stack which Jack handed to her. "Put this in your bag, Grace. We're going to need it. I left my last thirty bucks cash back at that diner. We can't use an ATM or anything, or so the TV shows say. Which is OK, since we're running pretty low in that department anyway. I was hoping for a big payout in Albuquerque at the Launchpad but I don't think we're going to make that show. One good thing is, from the look of it, I don't think these bills are new, or tracked. Like they didn't come from a bank heist or an armored car or any of that. They looked used. Which is good in one way and bad in another." He grinned ruefully at her. "What the hell do I know? Everything I'm saying comes pretty much from a novel or a movie. But they do say people can track your cards and phones so it's cash and carry for us. Because somebody already tracked us so Anya could find us."

Grace stared at him. "How is it bad in another?"

Jack shrugged. "Have to assume it's money from another source, and the only ones I can think of off the top of my head are gambling, trafficking or drugs. They don't have new money, that's for sure. So..."

"Great. That's just great, Jack. So we have some cartel or whatever on our ass?"

"Maybe. Have to assume the worst, I suppose. Not too familiar with cartels myself. Not a big issue in Tennessee, far as I know anyway. Not my business."

Grace lifted the bag to put it in the backseat, opening the car door. The money didn't fit quite as neatly as it had, and for the first time Grace noticed a bulge on the backside, a zippered compartment. She sat the backpack down on the ground and pulled the zipper open.

"Oh shit," she said. A pistol was stored inside, along with a couple fistfuls of bullets.

"Jack, there's a fucking gun in here." She stared at it like it was a scorpion, waiting to sting her. There was no way she was touching that thing.

Jack came around the front of the car, bent over and picked up the gun. He slid the loaded cartridge out and shoved it back in like he'd done it a hundred times, and then filled his jacket pockets with the extra bullets, shoving the gun into the back of his waistband.

Grace stared at him open-mouthed and then snapped her jaw shut. "Old friend?"

Jack said nothing, only stared at her for a second and pulled her into him, his arms strong and comforting around her. It felt good and Grace's arms circled his waist, her head resting on his shoulder. She wanted to stay just like this but she knew they couldn't.

He kissed her temple and when she arched her neck, her mouth and it lasted long enough for the usual warm tingle to spread to the rest of her. This guy.

"We'll handle it, Grace. I love you and I'm not going to let anything happen to either one of us." He pulled back and smiled. "We're special, babe. We're Wilder and Grace and we got music to make. We'll get out of this. I mean, hell, now we sure have the money we need to make an album, do everything we've always wanted to do. I know why you took it, and just like I said, I would've done the same thing if I was in your shoes. The temptation here is just too great especially at just this moment and not like we don't deserve it no matter where it came from. Have to look on the bright side, you know? All we have to do is live long enough to spend it. We can do this, Grace."

They got back in the car, the cursed backpack in the back seat and Jack started the engine, turning back towards the highway. Just before they got there, sirens screamed through the clear desert air and three police cars, blue lights blazing along with an ambulance, whizzed by out on the road, going in the direction they'd come from.

"I guess they found her," Grace said tonelessly. "Although you wouldn't think it'd take half the local police force to contend with just one dead body." A feeling of dread settled in her bones.

"We can't afford to give a shit, Grace," Jack said. "And we are sure as somebody made little green apples not going to fucking Albuquerque. Anya heard us say that and she knows we're musicians. I don't know if she had time to tell anybody that, but we have to assume she did."

He turned left out onto the road and when the sign for Farmington came along, headed north.

6

A ngel watched him impatiently, flinging her long hair over her shoulder, a nervous habit. Chang finished pumping gas and hung up the nozzle as though it was contaminated, scrubbing his hands fastidiously on the sanitary wipes he always carried. Sometimes this guy was too much, with his bespoke suits and handmade Italian shoes. Even in the smallest Mexican village, Chang would find a hair stylist to trim his shoulder-length locks along with a manicurist, which was a miracle in itself.

The man was perfection, a beautiful god walking. Inside, he was one scary dude, Angel knew that well, which was the reason she'd known he was the perfect choice for her, especially for this. When you ripped off the cartel, and especially Luis Reynaldo, you needed scary and she could think of no better partner than Chang, Luis's unhappy and disillusioned favorite *sicario*. If he had a last name, in the two years she'd known him, she'd never heard it. Or maybe it was a first name. She never knew how it worked with Asians. Then again, she wasn't sure how a lot of things worked in the outside world but she was about to find out.

"You get any snacks while you were in there?" Angel said, starting the car, once he'd finished his ministrations and returned from the store with a sack. He settled into the passenger seat and she pulled out onto the road.

Chang held up two bottles of Smartwater and two apples. "Of course."

"Christ. No Doritos, no candy bars?"

"You need to take better care of yourself, Angel," Chang said. "That stuff is poison. I have some Niagen and Vitamin C in my pack, plenty extra for you. Have an apple."

"Maybe later," Angel said. There was no point in arguing with Chang, everyone knew that. You would lose and with something far more important than Doritos, you would be dead. Except for her, but this was no time to push his buttons because with this guy you could never tell and this was no time for an argument.

The phone rang and Angel snatched it up. "Talk."

"It's Anya. I am so thankful to hear your voice, Angel. I am in a diner called Eddie's on the 40, in New Mexico. I have found the people who took the bag. We have ordered breakfast and they are stupid, just some poor musicians. I will slow them down as much as I can for you." Then, Angel heard another voice, a woman's:

"I thought your boyfriend took your phone, Anya." There was a sound of a scuffle and the call ended.

Chang looked over. "We're less than half an hour away, Angel. Have an apple. You might need it."

"*Madre de dios.*" Angel pressed down on the accelerator. "Unless they have the brains of cockroaches they know now she's not whoever she says she is. Hopefully, they're hungry, slow and as stupid as she is. Although, from the sound of it, they aren't that slow. As far as this girl, we already know what she is. Trouble, and I apologize for ever being stupid enough to try and save her in the first place, let alone taking her with us."

~

LAST NIGHT, they'd been headed west through Arizona when Anya, who had been exceptionally quiet, had begun sobbing from the back seat.

"I'm sorry, I'm so sorry," the girl spluttered through the tears and runny nose. "We have to go back, I left it there because I was too scared to tell you. That you'd think I meant to steal from you. Please don't kill me, it was just a mistake. I picked up the wrong bag."

Angel pulled over to the side of the road. She turned around and grabbed Anya's hair, forcing her head onto the front console. "What the fuck you talking about, *puta?*"

Sobs escalated and Chang touched Angel's hand, shaking his head. She dropped the girl's hair and sat back, fuming.

"Just tell me, Anya," Chang said softly. "We will understand. We are not like the Albanians. there is nothing to fear. What did you do that makes you so frightened?"

His voice was like a soothing tonic and it calmed Anya down enough to tell him she'd picked up the wrong backpack when they stopped at the diner and then panicked when she'd seen the money instead of her own clothes and cosmetics. Frightened they'd think she was planning to steal it, she'd stuffed the wrong backpack behind a toilet and said nothing.

"Remember, I asked you to leave me, but you would not."

Angel remembered, all right. Anya had been tearful and so grateful that they had rescued her from the Albanians, but she didn't want to be a burden for them, she'd said. Angel had felt sorry for her and insisted the girl come with them to have a better life, rather than abandon her here in the middle of nowhere. Had they done that the little bitch would've been halfway to Mexico with the money, in Angel's opinion, so she wasn't really buying the victim routine because it didn't ring true.

It didn't matter anyway, since leaving Anya, a spectacularly loose end, could bring everyone down on them if the girl was so inclined. She was going along for the long haul and they'd decide what to do about her once they got to Los Angeles. Since they hadn't left her, now she was scared enough to tell the truth, that was all.

They'd gone back east as fast as Angel could drive. Her hands had clenched on the steering wheel, as though it was Anya's neck she really wanted to put her hands around. Once they found her, she was tempted to just shoot the girl in the head and leave her but it was Angel's fault they'd taken her with them in the first place, maybe even part of the reason the deal had gone so wrong. Besides, she'd been making an effort to control her temper. Killing her could wait.

The lights of the diner had loomed up and Angel pulled in. They'd sat down at a table just for show and Anya ran into the restroom and came out, shaking her head. The waitress, who'd said her name was Fran, had told them that no one had been there earlier except a young couple in an old red Explorer but she didn't see which way they went. Angel had watched Fran carefully. If the woman had stolen the money, she was the best liar Angel had ever seen, and she knew liars well. If the waitress had found that backpack, she'd be long gone from this place and not waiting around for someone to show up and ask about it.

No. Someone else had taken the money and the only possible candidates were the couple in the red Explorer.

Angel had pulled Anya aside. "Listen to me. If you want to live, you will find that red Explorer and that backpack. You will take the waitress's car, Chang will start it so she won't even know it's gone. You go east and look for them. They probably will stop and sleep, with any luck. Check all the rest areas and motels, even parking lots. When you see them, you call me."

Angel had punched her number into one of the burner

phones that Chang had picked up at the gas station and handed it to Anya. "Don't even think about running, Anya." She'd stared into the girl's eyes. "If you think the Albanians were bad, you have no idea what can happen to you from my hands," she'd nodded towards Chang, "or his. We will find you no matter where you go. Do not fuck this up."

Anya, properly frightened, had headed east towards Gallup, looking for a couple in a red Explorer at any of the places Angel had mentioned, while Angel and Chang had headed west, which Angel had thought was a much more likely destination. Covering both directions was the only move they had. If she and Chang found the money first, they'd just keep on going west.

They'd painstakingly checked every RV park, motel and parking area as they went with no luck. Finally Angel doubled back east down the 40. A nagging suspicion that they were headed the wrong way wouldn't leave her even though they hadn't heard from Anya. Angel finally had to pull over and get some sleep. Agitated and angry as she was, she still couldn't keep her eyes open. Maybe Anya would have better luck, but Angel didn't really give a damn what happened to the little bitch and secretly hoped she'd never hear from her again, money or not. She was glad to get rid of the girl and had been frankly surprised to have heard she'd had any success. They had bigger worries and wasting precious hours just gave Luis more time to find them, once he figured out they weren't as dead as the Albanians.

Now, driving as fast as they were, they crossed the New Mexico border and the Eddie's Diner sign appeared within twenty minutes. They parked around the side and Angel hopped out of the car with Chang following closely behind. There were only two tables occupied, both by men in Levi jackets and cowboy boots, finishing up their breakfast from the look of it, likely ranch workers as were so many she'd seen just like them in Mexico. Things were not so different on this side of the border, it seemed.

Angel looked around but there were no other corners or alcoves. Chang slid into a booth after carefully checking it for crumbs. Angel sat down across from him, the long fringe on her suede jacket's arms resting on the formica tabletop. It looked clean enough, besides they wouldn't be here long enough to get infected with anything, even if Chang didn't think so.

"Hey there! Good morning, where'd you two blow in from?" The waitress peered out the window and handed them the ubiquitous plastic-covered menus, covered with fingerprints and stains. Chang dropped his menu politely on the tabletop as though it was radioactive and Angel couldn't help smirking.

"Here and there," Angel smiled. "Lovely morning."

"Aren't you the most beautiful twosome I've ever seen around here?" the waitress's eyes were bright with excitement. "Oh my, that is some jacket, honey. I love it when you Hollywood people show up. This's twice in one morning now people like you've been in, beautiful couple if I do say so. You can't keep a secret around here, so it's not a secret any more. You can tell me. They makin' a movie, maybe a Kung Fu type Western?"

"Something like that," Angel said, her smile fading. "Coffee?"

"Sure, hon, sure."

She brought the coffee over in less than a minute, and Chang ignored it, pushing the cup and saucer gently away from him. He gave the waitress a dazzling smile and the waitress, an older woman in her fifties, seemed transfixed, not caring in the least about the snub on the coffee.

Angel sighed and took a couple of sips. It was hot but she needed it. The waitress seemed to come back to life. "So what can I get you?"

"You mentioned 'twice in one morning' before. We're

looking for some friends of ours, maybe that was them. When were they here?"

"You just missed them, hon. They left in a big hurry, not even taking the time to eat their breakfasts." She made a tsking sound. "Waste of food, you ask me."

"Hmm, that certainly is rude. I'm sorry, hope they at least tipped you well. Listen, do you have a bathroom?"

"Sure, right down there," she gestured to the right, past the counter. "Take your time."

"Be right back."

Chang shrugged and looked out the window.

She pushed open the bathroom door and the coppery smell of blood confirmed her suspicions. Their wayward Anya lay on the tiled floor in front of the sink. Angel stepped carefully, avoiding the blood that had spread nearly everywhere, mixing with the water on the floor from the overflowing sink. She knelt beside Anya, lifting her head. There was a faint pulse and Anya's eyes fluttered open.

"Angel. Thank god."

"*Si, mija*. What can you tell me?"

Anya's eyelids closed and whatever life force had been keeping her alive this long dissipated.

Useless. Angel pulled her hands away and the girl's head dropped to the floor with a thunk. She stood up and washed her hands, yanking paper towels out of the dispenser. No women must have come into this place this morning, but then Anya hadn't been there long.

She could almost hear Luis's voice in her head. This is what happened when you let sentimentality overrule your common sense. She should've known better than to let her emotions make bad decisions. She'd felt sorry for the girl who'd found herself in the same trouble she'd been in for years and that was a mistake. She couldn't afford any mistakes now. She jerked open the door and strode angrily back to the table, sitting down.

"Anya's in the bathroom dead, Chang. We need answers and we're sure not getting them from her. Do your job. You owe me for not noticing that little whore carried a backpack into that restaurant in the first place and never brought it back out. I don't care that she needed to fix her makeup or whatever. You're supposed to be the professional here."

As soon as the words were out of her mouth, she knew it was ridiculous to blame Chang for something she should've seen herself, especially the fact that the girl had come in with a backpack and left without one. Yes, she was tired and her nerves were jangly at best, but it was just as much her fault as his. After all, she'd been the one to let the girl come with them in the first place. That had been a mistake and it embarrassed her.

Chang stood up and bowed slightly. Angel wanted to smack him but she knew better, besides, he always did that shit. "She was a distraction. I am filled with shame that I allowed this problem to occur, Angel."

"So redeem yourself, *sicario*."

He took off his suit jacket, folding it precisely and placing it on the seat of the booth. Then he took off his cufflinks and stowed them carefully in his pants pocket. He rolled up his sleeves, three perfect folds. Angel strode behind him and shot the deadbolt on the glass doors and turned the sign to "Closed".

Two of the cowboys had paid their bill and left while Angel was in the bathroom, never knowing this was their lucky day. He handed her the Glock and Angel sat down at the counter, the gun in one hand and with the other, opened the glass door of the pastry box. She ate a chocolate donut, while she watched Chang do his work. He was amazingly proficient at it and certainly didn't require any assistance from her. A good thing, since she wasn't in the mood. Her job had always been a little different.

Within five minutes, the other two cowboys, the night waitress, the cook and the day waitress who'd just arrived, were face down on the diner floor, their hands zip-tied behind them.

A puddle of urine was spreading below them on the floor. Angel couldn't tell exactly who it was coming from but it didn't matter anyway. *What kind of people went about their business and never bothered to check and find a dying girl in their bathroom*, she thought. Maybe the same kind of people that had put her in this position in the first place, a little voice in her head answered, which she quickly dismissed. She needed no reminders. That life was behind her. At least she hoped it was.

"So, my friends," Chang said, "you are telling me you remember nothing about the people that were here with this dead girl we find in your bathroom? Nothing at all? No chitchat you overheard?"

"Please," the night waitress burbled through the snot and tears on her face. "They didn't talk to me about anything about eggs. I forgot about the girl they came in with. I didn't even notice she didn't leave with them. I'm sorry."

Chang broke her arm and she screamed. "Are you sure?"

The screaming stopped after a few seconds and sobbing replaced it. "They were talking about meeting somebody named Barry and some mavericks, that's all I remember." Her eyes rolled up into her head and Angel sighed. People were so soft. A little pain and they collapsed. They didn't know how hard life could be. They would get no more information from this woman. Angel got up off the stool, the gun in her hand.

She kicked one of the cowboys. "You, overhear anything, remember anything, *amigo?*"

Stoic, this one. He spit at her. "Go fuck yourself, cunt."

"That's not nice," Angel said and stabbed him with a bread knife she'd found on the counter. It wasn't easy but she'd had a lot of practice, thanks to Luis letting her train with his men, a whim he enjoyed. His friend shouted over the other's cries.

"Stop!" He said, turning his head from where Chang had positioned him face down on the floor. "The woman asked me how far it was to Albuquerque. That's all I know."

"Ah, you see?" Angel stooped down beside him. "Wasn't that easy? Now, what did she look like?"

"Pretty, really pretty, kinda like you," the man said, his breath coming in panicked gasps, "long dark hair, big green eyes. Her boyfriend was near as pretty as she was. We laughed about it."

"Gets lonely out there with nothing but sheep, eh?" Angel said. "Anything else, *muchacho*?" *And my eyes are brown, you asshole,* she thought.

The cook, a hefty gentleman, couldn't take it anymore. "We don't know anything else. I never even saw them, and neither did Wendy, she just got here. This is senseless. If it's these people you're after, go get them. You're wasting time here. Just leave, we won't say anything. I swear."

Angel stood up and looked at Chang, making a circular motion with her hand. Time to wind up the show. He nodded and took the gun from her. She picked up Chang's coat and put it over her arm, coming to stand beside him.

"We are going to leave you now. Unfortunately for you, you saw us and the next people to ask you about anyone may not be as nice as we have been. Having a very bad memory about what we look like might save your lives. We have colleagues who will return to visit all of you if we hear you have described us to the police. Remember that, because we will leave you alive as a kindness but it might not matter in the end. *Vaya con Dios*."

Chang frowned. "We should not leave any loose ends."

She'd always admired his efficiency. She truly felt a little bad about these people and knew they couldn't afford witnesses, not here or anywhere. Worse things could happen to people besides a simple death and she knew that better than anyone. Still, she couldn't do it. She shook her head and unlocked the door.

Chang sighed, lowered his gun, and opened the door for her. "This is a mistake. We can't afford to be foolish."

Angel stared at him. "Perhaps, but they did nothing to warrant having their lives end this morning. They aren't Albanians, Chang, or anybody evil. Just ordinary people who have been touched by the madness that you and I have lived with for too long. We can afford to be merciful."

This time, he climbed into the driver's seat and started the car. She followed silently and got into the passenger seat.

"So Albuquerque then?" she said, as he pulled out onto the highway. "I've always liked music. We have learned they're good-looking musicians, and said something about mavericks and a guy named Barry. Maybe we can enjoy some entertainment on our quest to find our nameless thieving friends."

7

———

Jack stopped in Farmington and got out to pump gas while Grace went inside to pay, using one of the stolen hundred-dollar bills. She was a little nervous about it, never having seen a hundred-dollar bill in her life, but the clerk didn't blink an eye. Jack had insisted they use no cards and there was hardly any money in the bank anyway. She paid for the gas and got two coffees with extra sugar and cream. She breathed a sigh of relief, leaving the coffees on the counter while she took the usual key on its foot-long plastic board and headed for the bathroom.

It was the typical filthy toilet-paper littered space, the floor looking as though it hadn't seen soap and water since the summer of love. She perched over the dirty toilet, the first relief she'd felt in some hours, thighs trembling. She really needed to start working out. She zipped up her jeans and rinsed her hands under the faucet, staring into the cracked mirror. There were no paper towels because there were never any paper towels in these places, so she wiped her hands on her jeans.

The same bloodshot green eyes stared back at her. She didn't look like a murderess, just a very tired woman who could use some sleep. She croaked out a laugh and stopped herself before she let it go any further and got hysterical. Instead, she wove her long brown hair into a neater braid. All neat and sparkly now. The all-American girl next door.

She went back to the counter and handed the bored young clerk the key and picked up the coffees. "Thanks."

He didn't even notice her new and improved look, staring at the TV screen behind him. Grace looked up as well and stopped cold.

"Death and chaos at local restaurant!" A man in a gray suit with carefully arranged blondish hair sat behind a desk while across the bottom of the screen a banner headline screamed "Death in a Diner" in yellow letters.

"Early this morning, police were alerted to something residents of New Mexico rarely see! Thank goodness for that! Six local residents were assaulted, and an unidentified woman was found dead at a local restaurant, called Eddie's Diner, west of Gallup. According to the McKinley County Sheriff's office, investigations are ongoing for this horrifying crime and tell us the FBI is on the way. Could it be more drug-induced violence? Just a random psychopath? News update here at KOAT at six. Remember, when we know, YOU know!"

The clerk turned around. "Man, that sucks. Glad whoever did that ain't around here." He looked out the window. "Course, it ain't all that far away, now is it? I'd better be on the lookout."

Grace nodded. "Yes, that'd be a good idea. There's a lot of crazy people out there these days. You never know, am I right?"

"You said it, lady." He turned back to the TV. "You take care, now."

Jack was waiting in the car. She handed him one of the coffees and shut the door. "Holy shit, Jack. Get the hell out of here."

He headed north out of the gas station. "What the hell, Grace?"

"All those people back at that diner were messed with by somebody and they found Anya's body." She sat in the passenger seat, the coffee ignored in her hand. "All because of me." Her voice had risen nearly to a shriek.

"Stop it. Right now."

She made a choking sound and Jack glanced over at her and then back at the road. "It's done. You didn't mean for any of it to happen. You made a mistake but it's not one you can take back, Grace. Whoever left this money, now we know for sure somebody wants it back. All we can do is stay as far away from them as we can and stay alive."

"There's no other options, is there?"

"No. We'll make it work." He took her hand and gripped it tight. "We have to."

After a minute, he grinned at her. "Buck up, babe. At least we got money. We're rich now."

Grace swallowed her hysterical giggle. "That's for damn sure. Drive on, Mr. Wilder. I've always wanted to see the real West."

"My pleasure, ma'am," Jack said. "Durango, here we come."

Durango was, well, sort of cute, Grace thought, but still victim to the usual strip malls and tire shops as you drove in. Downtown was sort of what you saw in movies with a main street and storefronts. Not big enough to hide in, for sure. Maybe big enough to get something to eat and figure out where to go next.

Jack pulled into a slanted parking slot in front of a restaurant and they went inside. It would be a nice change from leaving before they had a chance to take a bite, if things went well. She still had the change from the gas station in her pocket.

"Cheeseburgers are the food of the gods, aren't they," Jack

said, taking another huge bite. She couldn't disagree. She hadn't thought she'd be able to eat anything but found she was starving. These were good cheeseburgers. Even the fries were great, hand cut and sprinkled with sea salt. They both ate like they'd never had food before and by the time the homemade apple pie arrived, Grace wasn't sure she'd be able to eat it. After one tentative bite, though, she managed it and all the food seemed to fill that empty place inside her. Almost.

"Guess we know how the West was won," Jack said, leaning back on the leatherette seat. "All this time, it was the damn food."

She smiled back at him. "Of course, remember chuckwagons? We haven't had much to eat in the last couple days, unless you count Taco Bell burritos at noon yesterday and half a sandwich last night. We seem to have a habit of leaving restaurants at the wrong time."

"Colorado so far ranks high in at least one department," Jack said. "People seem friendly, too."

"Where do we go from here?"

Jack flipped open the map she'd picked up in Farmington, his pale hair a curtain falling over the folds of paper like he was reading a treasure map to the Holy Grail which right now maybe it was. GPS on the phone was all well and good but they needed a bigger picture and easy to see elevations. "Grand Junction, about six hours north of here. I don't want to hit Denver. We'd have to go into the mountains and there may be a lot of snow in the high country if we go over the Rockies. I think a smaller city is OK, but bigger than this if we want to get rid of the car. It seems like the best bet, Grace. We don't know if there's anybody following us, but we can't afford to think they aren't, after that news report. We don't know if they know who we are, or what we look like, but with our lives at stake, we can't afford not to be paranoid."

She couldn't disagree with that. They wouldn't be going

back to Nashville anytime soon until they were through trailing trouble after them and bringing it to people they cared about. Until they were, as the saying went, home free. That was starting to look like it might take some time.

They walked down the street, holding hands like it was any normal day and they were just normal people. She nearly giggled at that thought. They'd never exactly been normal people anyway, neither of them growing up with white picket fences, or being suburban ranch house kids.

Still, it was nice to be out of the car and not panicked but Grace knew it was just a delusion and brief respite before they got back in and everything went crazy once more. People smiled and nodded as they went along, passing the usual tourist shops, a bookstore and a bank. Seemed a nice little town. They strolled along and turned back when the street turned more residential, making their way back to the Explorer.

"You want me to drive for a while?" Grace said.

"Sure," Jack said and flipped her the keys.

They pulled into Grand Junction late afternoon as the sun was getting low. Another cute Western town, about twice the size or more of Durango. *Cute must be a requirement in this state,* Grace thought sourly. She was tired and she got surly when she was tired. Jack had been dozing for the last two hours and she was about done in. She pulled over to the side of the road past most of the business district and nudged him awake.

"We're here. I'm for getting a motel," she said. "You think the car can wait until morning?"

Jack blinked and rubbed his face. "Actually, no, I don't. We need to dump the Explorer. We have to assume whoever lost that money knows two things about us, what kind of car we're driving and probably some inkling of where we're going, since we talked to people and may have been overheard in our own conversations. Hopefully, they think it's Albuquerque but we can't count on that. An old red Explorer isn't the most unusual car on the road, but I bet it's the only one that pulled into either of those two diners in a while and somebody might remember that. It has to go."

Jack looked around. Car dealerships were on this stretch, and where there was new, there was used.

"Most used car lots are open later into the evening. People get tired and are in a hurry to wrap things up without too many questions. Let's look around for one that looks like they need the business and won't be too picky."

Grace stopped at a stoplight and decided to head towards the fast food-car lot corridor. Being on tour, she'd learned most towns were laid out exactly the same. She glanced at Jack.

"Now that you mention Albuquerque, we need to call Barry, Jack. Whoever's after us might be looking for anybody we could be with. The Mavericks aren't my favorite people in the world, but they don't deserve that shit coming down without some kind of a warning and we don't need any more dead people on our ticket."

"Christ, I should've done that before. Barry's probably having a cow." Jack dug out his cell phone and hit Barry's number, glancing at Grace as it rang. She pulled over.

"Hey man. Uh-huh, yeah, I know... So, here's the thing, we had some car trouble on the road and we can't make it tonight." He paused and put the phone on speaker, rolling his eyes at Grace.

"What the fuck Jack? You're telling me now? I can't find a steel player or another singer at this point. I thought you two were more reliable than this.

"By the way, this place is great. We're going to get a big crowd tonight, just so you know, you fucking losers."

Grace sighed and made a thumbs down with her fist.

"Man, I am so sorry," Jack said. "I really am, Barry. There's another thing. Along with the car trouble, we ran into some people that aren't so nice. Long story, no time to go into it now, but wanted you to know. They may be headed your way, asking about us."

"What?"

"I said, we ran into –"

"Yeah, yeah, I heard you," Barry said. "Why would anybody be asking about you?"

Jack stared over at her, shaking his head. "They're just assholes that we had a little run-in with on the road, the car trouble and all. No big deal, just thought I'd give you a heads up in case anybody comes looking for us and takes it out on you. You know the kind of freaks you meet on the road once in a while. Probably nothing to it, but you know, watch your back."

"You mean, watch yours, don't you Jack? What kind of bull-shit are you trying to sell me? I'm not buying it. I'm telling you right now, when we get home to Nashville, I hope you and Miss thinks she's a star aren't looking for any more road gigs because I'm not keeping your fuckup here a secret, pal. You two think you're so damn special and we're all tired of your prima donna act anyway. Don't bother to come back. Don't bother to come crawling to me for backup work either. I wouldn't have you two back up my granddad on his one-holer."

"Sorry you feel that way," Jack said. "Take care, Barry." He hung up, not waiting for Barry's next comment.

"Well, you tried. Hope they don't have any trouble," Grace said. Fact was, they were pretty fucking special. Jack was one of the best lap steel players and singers around and Grace had a voice that ranged from a throaty alto to a pure bell-like soprano with ease. They could be the next Civil Wars. The main reason she'd picked up that goddamn backpack last night in the first place was never having to put up with any more mediocre minor leaguers like Barry. Hopefully it didn't get them killed instead of famous.

"Fucking Barry." Jack leaned back in the seat. "Keep heading down this street. The car dealer signs are just lighting up. I'll sleep a lot better without any pursuit dogs having an Explorer on their radar. Might as well have a target on the back window."

Grace couldn't disagree with that, but she wouldn't be doing a lot of sound sleeping anyway. She wasn't a fan of Barry or any of the guys in the band but she was worried. The people after them could be looking for a touring band and there weren't all that many out there playing in Albuquerque tonight. If they found the Mavericks, maybe they'd find out about her and Jack and that wasn't beyond the realm of probability. Whoever these people were, they seemed to have a bird dog nose for ferreting out things buried in the everyday workings of the world. Every time she thought about Eddie's Diner and their hurried exit, a chill went down her spine. They must've been only minutes behind them.

"Maybe we should get on a plane and just go to Canada or something, Jack," she said. What about that?"

"You know, that occurred to me too," Jack said. "Couple of things though. We don't have passports. Even going into Canada, that could be an issue. Second, we walk into an airport and pay cash for one-way tickets to anywhere and Homeland Security sends up an alert immediately. Not to mention, carrying backpacks full of cash through security which would be an even bigger mess if not downright impossible. We could buy a big suitcase and put the money in it, and check the bag. They only check one out of a hundred, if that, but I don't want to take the chance."

He was right, of course. She felt stupid for even bringing it up. It looked like it was the road for them. Even trains had people that would remember them and there was all their gear, which would never work. Of course, they'd have to abandon that gear and every other piece of their life. Her stomach started to churn.

"If we go by private plane, anybody we hire to fly us anywhere is sure as hell going to remember a couple that looks like us with music gear even if we ditch that, and paying with a lot of cash. We could pay him off, but if these people looking for us are as good as we have to think they are, they have money to burn to bribe him and the pilot will be on the hit list too, once they get the information out of him. We don't want anybody else on our conscience."

"For god's sake, they're not magical or clairvoyant. Come on, Jack. This isn't the CIA or somebody after us or we'd be either dead or in jail already with the tech they have."

"Listen to me, Grace. I think they're much worse." He gripped her arm, hard. "If it was any kind of law enforcement, they'd have had us long before now. They might not have the tech, but they have something else."

Frightened, she stared at him. She'd never seen Jack this intense. "What's that?"

"Need and revenge. And we have to assume absolutely no morals or scruples whatsoever. That's what. I've seen it before and trust me when I say we have only one goal right now. Getting the hell away from these people and disappearing before they find out who we are or anything more about us. That they know anything, and how much, is making me nuts. The bitch of it is, we don't know, but we have to think they do, plan our actions accordingly and run like hell."

He loosened his grip on her arm and put his hands on his head. "Sorry, babe, sorry. I don't mean to be an asshole, but I'm just starting to realize how fucked up this is and how smart we're going to have to be to get out of this alive. I want to protect you and get out of this mess with both of us in one piece. But I'm not sure I'm that smart." He looked up at her. "But I have to try to be, and so do you. I've seen some shit, but this way beyond that. It's the not knowing that's driving me crazy right now."

Grace swallowed, the bile rising in her throat. "I got it, Jack. Believe me, I got it. I love you, and we're going to walk out of this in one piece, I swear to you."

8

———————

Angel cruised the downtown Albuquerque area slowly, looking for possible music venues. Chang gave her a running commentary on each of the bars and restaurant venues they passed while checking back and forth to the Albuquerque Weekly tabloid but so far none sounded right. They headed further out of the downtown area.

"No touring bands, just local stuff...only folk singers. Punk...only big name bands and none are playing tonight... wait, maybe this one."

She pulled over to the curb, the back end of the stolen Escalade sticking out but she didn't care. She looked at the nightclub. It wasn't any place she'd ever thought a music venue would look like, but what did she know?

"Looks pretty quiet." Just one neon sign for the Launchpad was lit, a tacky purple spaceship pointed into the setting sun, but there was no activity, no lines or box office open. The marquee said 'Tonight! Southern Mavericks from Nashville! Doors open at 8.'

"Well, that means nothing happens before nine, at least," Chang said. "Let's keep going."

"No, I have a good feeling. I think this is the one, and there's that mavericks thing. Let's go get something to eat. There's nothing around here. We'll come back."

Chang shrugged and put his phone away.

She pulled back out onto Central, ignoring the horns from the drivers she blocked. "I heard there's some good Mexican food here. Should be, since my ancestors were here way before any of the Anglos. We're going back to the Old Town. I heard about a place that I've always wanted to see."

The ancient cottonwood tree that the restaurant had been built around reached through the grated ceiling in the middle of the courtyard and fascinated Angel. They'd gotten a table close to it, as she'd requested. La Placita had been here forever, situated on the Plaza and across from the original Governor's Palace. Angel loved it from the minute they stepped inside. The food was good but it was the place and its place in time that she really loved, and even Chang found the sea bass he'd ordered palatable enough for him. Angel licked the last of the honey from the sopapillas from her fingertips and smiled at Chang's frown of distaste, only doing it to irritate him anyway. Prissy Chinese bastard.

"Ready?" She threw a hundred-dollar bill down on the snowy tablecloth, not waiting for the check. She felt better than she had in a while. She was very tired, yes, but they were on the right track. This whole disaster could end tonight on a satisfied stomach full of enchiladas and no more worry. Their prey could be at the Launchpad and then she and Chang could get on their way. She swallowed the second to last of the little blue pills Luis had given her that perked her up. Oh well, it wouldn't be long now.

"I don't like this going further south towards the border," Chang said. "It's not safe for us. Every mile is closer to Luis or people he has on his payroll."

Angel resisted the urge to swat him just as Luis had done to her when she'd said something that irritated him. She was going to have to work on that, especially with this man, who would clearly not react well.

"No kidding, Chang. You think I like it? Just for the record, *amigo*, there is no place safe for us until we get to Los Angeles until we get to my *tio* Pablo and his connections. Maybe not even then. I haven't seen the man since I was ten."

He sighed. "Just giving you my thoughts, Angel. Do not be angry with me. This lost money has put us off track. It is not good."

She couldn't argue with that. Stealing money from the cartel wasn't an option that would ever be safe. She knew that well but given the rare opportunity in Oklahoma City, she had to take it.

She couldn't have returned to one more night in the bed of Luis Reynaldo. She'd fantasized and then logically tried to plan an escape for years to no avail. The debacle in Oklahoma City and discovering that Chang could be an ally had finally made it possible. She knew it was her own fears eating at her and she was taking it out on him. They got back in the car and headed for the club. The pills kept her awake but didn't do much for her mood.

"Forgive me, Chang." She pressed down on the gas. "We'll make it right, my friend."

The neon lights on the front of the Launchpad had been amplified and there were no parking spots close by, every spot taken, even up and down the block. She ended up parking two blocks away in front of a used furniture store. They locked the car, of course, but she was nervous about leaving it on the street here, even if the two other bags of money and the drugs were in a hidden compartment under the back seat. Clever Albanians. Even so, she'd heard things about Albuquerque and none of them were conducive to trusting people on the street or anywhere else. Street crime here was high, and it made her laugh to have to worry about that when people of the sort Luis had on his payroll were out there, each one of them leaving bloodier strands in the same tapestry on the veneer of civilization that most people lived with unknowingly.

There was a long line to get in the door, and she endured a hand stamp from a fat bearded guy who leered at her as he held her wrist. Angel ignored him, eager to check out her fellow patrons in the first music club she'd ever visited. It was somewhat disappointing.

Lots of boots and jeans, even midriff tops displaying too much unattractive white flesh despite the cold weather, seemed to be the favorites. If this had been Los Angeles or New York, from what Angel had seen on TV, most of these people would have been made to wait or even been turned away from the looks of a lot of them, but if fashion was any guide, this place was definitely not that.

By the time they got inside, it was a madhouse. People were jammed together, most of them standing, as there were few tables, and those were of the standup variety and already claimed, people putting down their pitchers and glasses of beer as a stamp of ownership. Everyone had a drink in their hands from the bar at the back which was doing a brisk business and a blue haze of smoke, from marijuana and cigarettes both, even if supposedly illegal inside, wafted overhead lazily in the colored lights from the stage and the neon signs at the bar.

The space was bigger than it had looked from the street, maybe big enough to hold 300 or 400 people. Angel and Chang wound their way through the crowd to the merchandise tables at the far side, mostly empty of customers this early, manned by two people who weren't doing much business selling T-shirts or CDs yet, and near to the offstage area with its door marked 'private', where the band was likely hanging out.

Angel fingered the t-shirts laid out and looked at the CD and vinyl offerings. Most were for a band called the Southern Mavericks, tonight's headliner, which she'd never heard of but then she hadn't heard of hardly any popular bands. She'd been handed to Luis Reynaldo by her father when she was fourteen and Mexican and some classical music had been all she'd heard for years, with the dubious exception of Taylor Swift, who Luis thought was a goddess but Angel hadn't been as impressed. Angel had learned to play the guitar, a Gibson Luis had given her on her sixteenth birthday, and it had been her salvation, making up songs and singing them to herself. She picked up another CD, from somebody called Wilder and Grace, a striking couple on the cover.

"Are they here tonight too?" she asked the guy behind the table. "They look interesting."

"Probably won't make it tonight," the bearded guy behind the table said. "Maybe next time. You'd like 'em though. They're really good."

"Hmm. Too bad," Angel said. "Why not?"

He shrugged. "Some kind of road accident or something, they tell me."

"I'll give it a try anyway," she said and handed the guy ten dollars. She slipped the CD into Chang's outer suit pocket and he grimaced. He hated having anything in his pockets that might skew his designer perfection.

She glanced over at the stage door and the security guy caught her gaze. He winked and shook his head. This was going to be a long night. She moved away, Chang at her side.

"Go get us a couple of beers," she said to Chang.

"They won't have anything worth drinking."

"Of course they won't but we don't have to drink the shit," she said. "We just need to hold the cups and blend in." She wasn't exactly sure how she came to be the one giving orders, but for some reason, he didn't seem to have a problem with it, simply nodding his head. Angel eyed his Armani suit as he walked away and smiled ruefully. Blend? Never happen with the Asian Mr. Gucci, but the beer would help.

Just as Chang came back with their beers, the stage door opened and closed quickly behind a tall young blonde woman with a guitar who made her way to the stage, her gold-fringed shirt shimmering with each step. After a minute, the lights came up and she peered out at the crowd. More people were still coming in and it was getting very full. The woman took the mic in her hand.

"Hey there, Albuquerque!"

Whistles, foot stamps and yells greeted this announcement. "I'm Tracey Lynn from right here in New Mexico, and I'm going to give you a few new songs to warm y'all up for...the Southern Mavericks!"

At that, the crowd roared. *Hell yes*, Angel thought. *Let's get this show on the road.*

Tracey Lynn sang her little heart out. She wasn't bad, but Angel thought even Taylor Swift didn't need to worry about the competition with this one, and after thirty minutes, she mercifully left. Anticipation was building now and people were lining up at the bar to get their drinks before the main event.

The stage spotlights went out and she saw the dark outlines of people filing out of the back room, heading up to the elevated wooden platform. There was some fiddling around and then the lights came back on. The crowd roared and clapped as a tall man with a beard and curly hair stood in front of the mic, a guitar dangling from its strap. He was dressed pure fancy cowboy, similar to Tracy Lynn's fringed shirt, and so were the rest of the band but the crowd seemed to love it.

"Albuquerque! How you doin'?" He pulled up the guitar. "I'm Barry Jenkins, and we are the Southern Mavericks!"

Everyone yelled, stamped their feet, whistled and the band

launched into its first song. When they were about three songs in, Angel found herself tapping her foot. They were all right, good musicians but not memorable, but as usual she didn't have much to compare them with. She noticed there was no girl in the band and none of the guys could be classified as pretty. The name Barry and something about mavericks was all they had to go on but that was enough at this point. It was too coincidental. Chang was as still as a statue and she nudged him now and then to try to get him to at least feel the beat for all the good it did.

Another hour passed. Her feet hurt and her ears were ringing before the Mavericks played the last song, thanked the crowd and left. Gone like a magic act once the spotlights went out and the house lights went on, leaving the audience blinking and half blind. There was no other act and certainly nobody pretty. The T-shirt guy had been right, the duo called Wilder and Grace had not shown up. The house lights came up and the crowd surged for the street doors while Angel headed for the stage door. The same security guard, now accompanied by another one, shook his head. People were milling around the merch table, so it was clear the band hadn't left yet, especially not without their merchandise sales money.

"Come on," she said to Chang and they followed the rest of the crowd out the front door, down the street and into the nearest alley. They ended up at the back door of the club in a parking area where some of the band members were loading the music gear into an ancient looking RV. So much for security guards. Barry Jenkins sat on a milk crate smoking a cigarette. Chang hung back and watched as Angel sauntered up to Jenkins.

"Hi." Angel said. "Great show, man."

He glanced at her and his eyes lit up. "Hello yourself. Glad you liked it, honey."

"Oh, I sure did," she said. "Say, I'm a freelancer, doing a piece for Rolling Stone on you guys and I was hoping you could spare me a few minutes. I'd sure like to chat."

"Weelll now, I think I could do that. You want to come sit in the bus, have a beer and we can get to know each other better?"

Angel eyed the RV and shook her head. "We could, but how about we have a little more privacy? I'm staying at a friend's place just down the street."

Barry looked her up and down and didn't have to think it over for long. "Hey guys, I'll be back in a while. You take it easy and have a couple beers, OK?"

One of them waved and grinned and Barry gave him a thumbs-up gesture that Angel thought was a bit premature but she said nothing.

He followed her out to the street and finally noticed Chang, about six paces behind them. "Who the hell is that?"

"That's John, my photographer. Ready for your close up, Barry?"

She could feel him hesitate so she put her arm through his. "Handsome guy like you makes for great photos. All kinds of them, you know?"

They stopped at the Escalade and Angel clicked the locks.

"I thought you said we're going to your friend's place," Barry said, a little suspicious now. He looked around but the street was dark and empty. Angel opened the back door.

"Just get in the car, Barry," Angel said. "Let's do this the easy way."

Now Barry balked. "What the fuck? What is this, a kidnapping? I'm not even that famous. My agent might be impressed but trust me, he won't be shelling out any money."

Chang stepped next to him, his size and stance all he needed to be intimidating. "The car, Barry."

Barry swallowed and climbed in reluctantly. Chang sat next

to him, close enough that Barry was uncomfortable. Angel got into the front passenger seat.

"We're not going to hurt you," Angel said, her voice soothing. "We just need to ask you some questions."

"Yeah? You could've done that back at the club so forgive me if I don't believe you."

"No, Barry, we couldn't. This is confidential business. Now, where did your band play last night?"

"Flagstaff."

Angel nodded. "Do you have a girl in the band? A pretty one?"

Barry was sweating, fear coming off him in pungent waves. Chang sniffed in distaste.

"No, our band doesn't have a girl. The only girl we ever perform with on this tour is in a side act, sucking along on our tit. Wilder and Grace. Think they're something special, those two." Barry muttered. "Besides, they're not with us anymore and I don't know where they went. They took off last night, her and Jack."

"Ah." Angel sat back. "Where did they go?"

"I have no idea," Barry said. "He called me a few hours ago and said they had some car trouble or something..." his voice trailed off and his eyes darted from her to Chang. Suspicion was beginning to dawn. "I fired him right there over the phone, both of them."

"I'm not sure I believe you, Barry," Angel said softly. "Give me your phone."

He fished it out of his jeans pocket and handed it to her.

"Thanks." She shoved the phone into her pocket. She reached below the seat and retrieved a knife, glittering in the shadows. Barry made a sound like a dog about to upchuck his dinner.

"I swear to god that's the truth, girl, you'll see it on the phone," he stammered. "They have their own car, they don't travel with us in the bus. Her name's Grace Whitney, and her boyfriend Jack Wilder is our lap steel player. They're from Nashville, just like us. They're kind of standoffish, you know? They don't hang with us much." He was babbling now and Chang smirked a little.

"Sssh for a second Barry," Angel said, turning the knife around and around in her hand, a habit she'd had for a while. "Just take a breath. What do you think?" She addressed this last to Chang, who shrugged.

"Details. Descriptions. Car."

"Sure, sure. Anything you need," Barry said, visibly sweating now. "She's hot, dark hair, built, you know, and he's quite the draw for the ladies, blonde, blue eyes. One of the reasons we hired them. Good PR for the fans. They call themselves Wilder & Grace and I let them sell this EP they made, and their dumb t-shirts. They drive this old Explorer, red."

"Anything else?"

"No, I can't think of anything. I swear I don't know where they are or I'd tell you, I really would. They think they're too good to ride in the RV with us, like we'd contaminate them or something. They never said and I didn't ask 'cause that kind of attitude pisses me off. They're real prima donnas, those two. I mean whatever they did, they're no friends of mine, not really, you know, so –"

"Sssh," Angel said again and reached back and put the tip of the knife to Barry's throat. He swallowed so hard the tip bit in a little and a thin trickle of blood ran down onto his shirt. "Oh, Christ, please..."

"I believe you, Barry. Sure there's nothing else you can tell me?"

The stench of urine filled the car. Chang stiffened.

"No," Angel said and made a lowering motion with her hand before turning around. "Barry, here's the deal. I'm in a good mood tonight even though you just pissed in my car. Normally I'd be upset about that, but you've been helpful.

"Here's what's going to happen now. You're going to get out of the car and go back to your friends. You're not going to say one word about any of this, not about us, not about Grace and Jack. Tell them some gang kids tried to mug you, or whatever you want. I know your name, your band, and I will find you and I will kill you and everyone in that RV if you ever breathe a word of this conversation to anyone, ever. Understood?"

Barry nodded, his eyes wide. "Yes, yes I understand. I'd never say anything, I swear. Thank you." He was close to babbling now.

"*De nada*," Angel said. She didn't like it but there really hadn't ever been a choice and she'd known that the second she'd seen Barry up close. She looked at Chang and nodded.

The viper-like strike of Chang's fingertips crushed Barry's windpipe before he could take a breath and he never got another one. They left the body on the sidewalk. Chang got into the driver's seat and drove calmly away down the empty street.

"This was a man who did not care about his friends," he said. "He was not trustworthy."

"*Verdad*. He would have talked to anybody and not just his friends but would've called the police the minute we were out of sight," Angel said. "I don't like having to do this and this man was innocent of anything to do with us, except for not being a very good singer. But, he was a definite dangerous loose end. Now he can't identify us and I don't think anybody back there took much notice of anything except he left with a girl. It was pretty dark behind the club."

She leaned the seat back. She hadn't realized how very tired she was, even with the pill but there was no time to stop and rest. Now they knew who they were after. Unfortunately, they'd had to go the wrong direction to get that information and they had fallen behind. Wilder and Grace had definitely not gone south. There wasn't any time for stopping to sleep through a night.

"Still, we are leaving a trail that someone like Luis may mark. We have no time to waste. We must head north. Wake me up when we get to Farmington."

9

———

"You're gonna be real happy with this beauty, my friends. She's a peach."

Darryl, or so his name badge read, patted the front fender of the white Honda Odyssey in the same manner as he'd earlier patted his belly that threatened to engulf the Denver Broncos belt buckle. "Hold all your camping gear and then some."

"I'm sure the kids will love it," Grace gushed, holding onto Jack's arm. "Don't you think so, honey? Just what we need."

"Hell, yes, there's nothing little Joe Bob and Annie love more than catching a string of catfish at the river camp, ain't that right, honey?" Jack put in.

Darryl laughed heartily for no reason except that Grace figured he was probably overjoyed at screwing them out of at least a thousand dollars, rather than the thought of their non-existent children camping in the woods.

"Well, then, let's wrap this up, kids. I like doing business with good family people like you. Why I'm in this business, to make people happy with my cars."

They followed him into the prefab office, obviously on its

second incarnation from a trailer park. The place smelled like an ashtray, the floors filthier than any bar she'd seen and the windows were covered in smoke film and fingerprints. All Grace hoped at this point was that the damn car ran well and carried them far away from Grand Junction and anybody that might be looking for a couple driving a red Explorer.

She was too restless to stay sitting in there while Darryl fooled around with his papers and forms. She went outside to wait in the Explorer while Jack stayed inside the sales office of Gold Mine Used Cars sitting precariously on the edge of his cracked orange plastic chair. For another five hundred bucks, Darryl had agreed to hand over the title and a bill of sale with no questions asked and notarized on the spot with no ID by the gum-chewing office girl who looked up from scrolling on her cell phone long enough to bat her false eyelashes at Jack. Cash, they'd quickly discovered, was king in Grand Junction and, Grace suspected they were going to find out, pretty much everywhere.

If this was a movie, crooks on the run would at least tie up Darryl and his assistant and threaten them with their lives, Grace thought, *before they had a chance to blab to anyone who came around*. But this wasn't a movie, and they weren't crooks, just people who'd taken a foolish risk. Grace was pretty sure, even dumb as he looked, Darryl hadn't bought a word of their nonsense by the end. Luckily, he didn't look like a guy who cared.

Jack finally came out, jiggling the Honda keys in his hand and she rolled down the window. "Now what?"

"Darryl knows a salvage yard to get rid of the Explorer." He held up his phone. "Trouble is, they don't open until morning."

"Well then, we're spending the night here, looks like. About time we had some sleep anyway," she said. "You take the Honda and follow me."

She drove down the road, eyeing the motel choices. None

looked like the Ritz, but that wasn't what she was after. She wanted any motel big enough to have parking in the back, behind the building. Holding onto the Explorer for a night was a chance she was willing to take right now, because they needed sleep more than anything if they were going to have clear enough heads to get away from the people who were likely coming after them.

She signaled and pulled into the sprawling Mountain Rest Motel, undismayed by 'WiFi, Magic F*ngers and D*nuts' sign and parked in front of the office. Jack idled in the nearby parking spot while she registered, requesting a back room, away from road noise. They parked both the cars and hauled in the guitars, the cooler, their one suitcase and the backpack. There were only a few lighted windows in the place, and only four other cars, which was good. The back parking lot was not visible from the road.

"Christ. That feels good." Jack was sprawled on top of the bed. "I was going to argue but you're right, Grace. We need to sleep and figure things out. I feel like we've been on a roller coaster that goes on forever."

Grace handed him the ice bucket. "That's because we have been. I'll make dinner, but we'll need drinks."

Jack headed out the door to the ice machine while she unpacked the cooler. Cheese, salami, a few sad grapes and apples were floating in the lukewarm water. She supplemented some of that with the Italian bread, avocados and tomatoes she'd picked up in Flagstaff, along with the 1776 Pepper whiskey they both favored, unwrapping the two glasses from the bureau.

She spread out their meager charcuterie board, slicing up the cheese and salami with her Swiss army knife, and using the butcher paper as a platter, it set on the little table in front of the window, sinking into one of the upholstered chairs beside it. It was the usual roadside motel, the stale room freshener trying to disguise the smoke-filled cheap carpets and drapes. She wasn't expecting anything different. Unless you had at least $100 a night to spend on better than crap, life on the road was bleak which was why they usually slept in the back of the car. As far as luxurious went, she'd never seen it except in spy movies, in either a hotel or a place to live. Still, it was a bed, a shower, soap, and right now, a refuge they sorely needed.

They made quick work of the food, and started on the whiskey.

"I'm so damn wired and tired I'm probably not making the most lucid case here," Jack said, well into his second whiskey. "But bear with me, Grace." He sagged in his chair but his eyes were clear. "You, which means we, took that money. Yes, it can change our lives. It already has but I'm hoping for a lot more than running on nerves once we're safe. So, no more to say on that. Done deal.

"That's one. Two, whoever had it wants it back and is willing to kill for it. Case in point, the diner. Good thing we heard about that. These aren't nice people, which we assumed."

He finished his whiskey. "Three, that means we can't give it back with a 'sorry' without probably ending up dead. Which leads me to four: we run, and we run smart enough they never find us."

He poured more whiskey. "We have no connection to them or anyone, it was a random thing, but they may have found an in. We can't be sure and we have to assume they will find out something about us. People with that kind of money have connections and they aren't afraid to spend more to get more. Your thoughts?"

"I agree with every word you said. And, I'm not saying sorry anymore, Jack. I took that money because it could be a future for us, one we've wanted and deserved for a long time." She took a healthy drink herself.

"I'm not looking for justification, just stating a fact when I say the music business is different now. People can say it's luck or 'you're so talented' but there's hundreds of musicians kicking around Nashville, Los Angeles, Seattle that are extremely talented and 'luck' is a fickle thing that you can wait your whole life to find, like a leprechaun or a winning lottery ticket.

"The only thing that was going to get us where we wanted to be was money and enough of it to say fuck all of them. This tour taught me that. That's all I was thinking when I saw the money in that bathroom. And now, a girl has died for it, which for some weird reason makes it even more important to me."

She grimaced. "It has to mean something now. It was like I was meant to find it so it could make a difference for us. We can do something good with it instead of just using it to pull some bullshit heist or pay for another drug deal that only makes people more miserable."

Jack sat up, putting his glass on the table. "Agreed one hundred percent. It was weird timing, but I was ready for it, too. One more night playing with Barry and those assholes and I swear to God, Grace, I think I would've killed one of them."

He stood up and held out his arms. "It's you and me, babe, just like it's always been. We can do this, or at least try our best. Unlike what Townes said, I ain't waitin' around to die any time soon."

They made love desperately and wonderfully for the first time in days on a soft mattress for a change, despite their worries, and slept well for the first time in a long while. They were still breathing and in good health when Grace opened her eyes. It was dark, just a faint light coming through the slit in the drapes and she shoved them further aside to reveal a shadowy pre-dawn. Perfect. She turned back to the room and saw Jack's phone on the nightstand, showing one message.

She prodded him awake and handed him the phone.

"Barry texted."

He pushed the hair out of his eyes and propped himself up

on an elbow, opening up his messages. He stared at the screen and dropped the phone as though it had bitten him.

"What?" Grace said.

"Read it."

Grace picked up the phone. The message was obviously not from Barry.

"We'll see you soon, Wilder and Grace. Run, run, fast as you can."

She looked over at him but Jack was already pulling on his jeans.

"Doesn't look good for Barry, and Christ knows I'm sorry about that," he said. "All I know is we need to get the hell out of here and I hope that new car moves fast."

They emptied out the Explorer and packed the Honda with room to spare in record time, even for them, having learned to do this constantly on the road.

"Goddamn," Jack said, sliding the panel door shut on the Honda. Despite the phone message, with a little sleep he looked better than he had in the last few days. "We should have gotten one of these soccer mom vans long ago. We could even sleep in this thing without banging our toes on the door. What a difference a day makes, eh Grace? Looks like we're in the money now. Next thing you know we'll buy a house in the suburbs and have kids to go with the car."

"Very funny, Jack," Grace said. "Which way is the wrecking yard?" She'd downed three aspirins and was a tiny bit hungover. The sleep and sex had been great but it wasn't enough to dispel the feeling there was a black tornado coming upon them now, like retribution for enjoying themselves. Which of course there was, if that message meant anything.

"Follow me," Jack said, setting the car's GPS and starting up the Honda.

Grace followed him out of the motel in the Explorer, the trusty old car going to its crushed metal death. *Better you than me, pal*, Grace thought, patting the dashboard. *You've been a good horse.* She wasn't sure why she was getting sad over the demise of the old Explorer but it had served them well for a long time. Still, it was stupid and more than that, indicative of her mind-set, which she figured had better change to a much more cynical one if she wanted to survive longer than the goddamn car. Stupid to worry about a car when Barry and who knew else had run into their pursuers and could likely not be in any better shape than the Explorer would soon be.

It only took a few minutes at the salvage yard, as they were the first customers of the day. The guy that owned it came out of the trailer pulling on his suspenders, his feet bare. She suspected he lived in the place. Jack got out of the Honda and went to talk with him. It didn't take long, and he got back into the driver's seat. He pulled out his phone and took out the battery and the sim card, and crushed them and the entire phone beneath his boot heel, kicking the remains under the nearest wrecked car.

She sat down in the passenger seat of the Odyssey and looked at Jack. "So where we going?"

"To safety, I hope," he said and drove out of the wrecking yard. The guy still stood beside the Explorer, still counting the money Jack had paid him to insure the car was completely destroyed, and not saved for parts.

"You sure he's going to trash it?"

Jack sighed. "Christ, Grace, there's no guarantees in life but I sure as hell paid him enough, so there's no point in worrying. Unless you want to stick around while he crushes it, we're getting the fuck out of here. I don't think he starts that thing up more than once a day and he didn't seem to think this was the right time. Probably needs his morning jack-off and we got him up early."

North out of Durango, it was pretty country, she'd give it that. The Honda had a CD player and much better speakers than the Explorer, which was admittedly the lowest bar, and they listened to music as they drove along. Neither one of them wanted to talk about the text or Barry. There was little point, since they were powerless to do anything about it. Barry was the last link to them but he didn't know anything more about her and Jack except that they'd been on tour with him, or maybe that they lived in Nashville, or at least nearby.

She noticed Jack had taken to wearing the gun in his waistband, familiarly, like he'd done it before, but had stowed it in the glove box since he got back in the car. Grace shifted in the seat, guilt a warm mantle around her shoulders, sinking into her bones like poison. She felt helpless as well, but there was something else building. A wave of deep burning anger directed at people she didn't even know, or maybe the world she'd lived in that had led her to take that money. It was hard to know. What wasn't hard to know was that she'd do whatever she had to do to protect Jack as well as herself from the consequences of her impetuous action.

10

———————

There was a lot Grace didn't know about Jack, before they'd come together, and she'd never cared about anything except she loved him and that was all-consuming. She knew his father, a kind and generous man who'd been hugely supportive of their music, and although they never talked about anyone else in his family, she knew he had a brother, from occasional things Barnett had said. She hadn't pried, because her own family history wasn't one she was proud of.

Grace had grown up in a trailer park near Gallatin, Tennessee, and never knew her father. Her pretty mother was a waitress at a nearby roadhouse and supplemented her income with the men she sometimes brought home after the bar closed. As mothers went, Hazel wasn't going to win any awards when it came to affection or responsible parenting. Grace learned early on to not make a sound from her tiny bedroom, and after having her face smushed into her Cheerios when she was in first grade, never to ask any questions about her mother's visitors.

Hazel Whitney didn't want to have a kid to take care of, and

Grace learned not to expect anything from anyone but herself. She'd done well in school, because it was her only refuge and even at a young age, her only hope for a life beyond that trailer. Her solace came from books and music, a lot of which she created herself on a guitar that one of Hazel's longer-term boyfriends, some of whom stayed for a time, had left behind one morning and never returned to retrieve.

Hazel had handed it to her with a laugh. "Here, kid, get a hobby. That guy won't be back. I'd pawn it but it don't look like it's worth much. Keep you out of my hair."

Music became her salvation, since the first time she'd played an actual chord on that battered guitar. Soon she began to make up songs and the music to go with the words in her head, which sometimes came spilling out from a place inside her that needed to emerge into the world, the only way she knew to express how she felt. She never played her music for anyone else, but that didn't matter. Creating it was enough.

Grace never really had any friends. There weren't any other kids in the trailer park, and Hazel didn't bother to spend anything but the bare minimum on Grace's clothes and little else connected to a daughter she only considered a burden. It wasn't until she was in fourth grade Grace discovered that most kids didn't do their back-to-school shopping at Goodwill, as her classmates unkindly pointed out. She learned to block out their snide comments and not pay attention to the girls that mocked her, even though it hurt but by the time she entered high school, it wasn't the girls that were the problem. It was the boys.

Shabby clothes couldn't hide the fact Grace was beautiful, even more so than her mother, any more than they could disguise her body, but she didn't know it. Because she was poor and was shunned by the popular girls, the high school jocks figured their attention would be gratefully welcomed and weren't happy when their ham-handed efforts at seduction were soundly rebuffed. Grace began leaving school early for the walk home to avoid them, but one afternoon her luck ran out when Pete Maxwell, the captain of the football team who'd been harassing her for weeks, and three of his pals accosted her just before the entrance to the trailer park, pulling up in Pete's pickup.

Before she could run, he hopped out and stuck his arm in front of her, halting her flight to safety.

"Hey, Grace," Pete said, grabbing her arm. "We've been waiting for you. Maybe you won't be so mean to us, out here where there's nobody to see us, you know?"

He pushed her back up against a pine tree, shoving his knee between her legs. "You been hurting my feelings for a long while now, girl, and it's time we put a stop to that attitude of yours."

"Let me go." She kept her face blank, trying to show no sign of the fear she felt.

"Well, no. See, you're going to have to make up for all that disrespect you been putting out, Grace. I know you want to be nice. Time's up, sugar."

He bent down to kiss her but before his lips touched hers, his head snapped back and he dropped her arms, staggering backward.

Hank Enfield, Hazel's current boyfriend, held Pete's hair in one hand and a raised fist in the other. Hank was a big man, well over six feet and 250 pounds, and Pete Maxwell looked like a Ken doll beside him. His friends backed away, eyeing the scene, the smirks on their acne-pocked faces quickly fading.

"Looks like we got us a situation," Hank drawled, dragging Pete a few feet further. "I think we could call this a case of an unwelcome suitor. You know what they used to do to randy boys like that around here?"

Pete swallowed, wincing as Hank jerked his head a little. "What?"

"Shoot 'em and bury 'em in the woods. Leastways, that's what my daddy told me."

Hank dropped Pete on the ground. His friends had already backed up and were turning to run. Pete's face was red as he scrambled to his feet.

"Get your cracker ass on out of here," Hank said, "but remember this. I ever hear about you messing with Grace again, it won't go so easy as this. You hear me, boy?"

Hazel's boyfriends had been a mixed bag over the years, but Hank was one of the good ones and had always been kind to Grace. He'd slip her a little money for lunches and whatever and had never once looked at her the way the boys at high school did. He'd watched Hazel with her and knew there was no future for Grace with Hazel or this place.

"For some damn reason, I love your mama," Hank said. "She's a hard woman and a lousy mother, but somehow we click and I know she needs me, or she will. You are a different story, Grace. You're smart and destined for a better than this. You got a talent that'll wither away you stay here. Those boys or some like them, will try again, no matter they're scared off for now, and I can't always be around."

That evening, after Hazel went to work, Hank taught Grace how to punch, how to balance on her feet and a few other tricks. They practiced all that for a few days before Hank, a long-haul trucker, had to get back on the road. A week later, he drove her into town just before midnight to catch the last bus to Nashville. Hank's sister had assured him that Grace could stay at her place and she'd help get her a job in the restaurant where she worked. Hank pushed a thin envelope of cash into her hand and hugged her.

"You're going to be fine, kid. I'll handle Hazel." Grace hugged him, clutched her backpack, got on the bus and propped her guitar up in the empty seat beside her. She never looked back. She'd never seen Hazel again, but Hank's kindness had changed her life.

Nashville wasn't easy, but Janine, Hank's sister, was a good soul and had been true to her word and given her a start. She'd kept singing and writing music and between tips and restaurant jobs, she'd made out. She slept on a sofa bed in Janine's den and tried hard to help out around the house. For the first time, she found a true friend who cared about her. Occasionally Hank stopped in when he was on the road. He'd finally left Hazel but he always made it a point to check on Grace and she loved them both.

She'd met Jack at the Bluebird one night. Getting a job there was a coup, everyone in Nashville knew that and Grace knew how lucky she was. Twice she'd been lucky enough to fill in when an act didn't show up but unlike the movies, nobody was impressed enough to offer her a star-studded career, not that she'd been expecting that. She was always on the lookout for singing gigs, solo or working with a band, and she'd wrangled quite a few.

One night, Jack showed up, playing lap steel for Adrian Reilly, the hottest new singer in Nashville. She watched their set. He was good, really good, and after the show, she brought beers to their table. The minute she and Jack laid eyes on each other it was like that stupid scene in the Godfather, the lightning bolt thing, and they'd been together ever since.

They had some kind of magic when they were together, and wasn't just their relationship. From the first time they'd sung together, his voice low and raspy and hers soaring and falling in tandem, they finished the song and stared at each other in shock. This was another kind of magic and one they were almost afraid to let out of the box.

She didn't regret a minute of their last two years together, except for the frustration and disappointment they'd both experienced trying to make a career for themselves in the music business. Yes, they were good, even that elusive very good, but that magic they had together never seemed to click out there in mythical music land, where so many others were wandering as well. Still, they knew they had something special and they weren't going to give up. She looked over at Jack, his fingers beating on the steering wheel in time to the music, concentrating on the curving road.

"So, you want to tell me how come you're so familiar with that gun?"

He smiled lazily, his signature Jack thing. "Yeah, I knew we were going there. The Wilder family sordid history. I was hoping to slip all that by you before the wedding, cause then you'd be stuck with it and my lovin' arms would make you forget. But since we are where we are, darlin'," he sighed and reached over to run his hand down her cheek, "here's the Wilder family saga. I mean, hey, time you knew the worst anyway, and I hate secrets."

She knew there was something in his past, because of the way Jack would always avoid talking about it and how once in a while, she'd walk into a room when he and Barnett were talking, and the conversation would stop. She'd never asked and never wanted to dig further because whatever it was, it wouldn't change how she felt. She sat back in the seat and turned the music down and Jack went on.

Jack grew up on a hog farm in rural Sumner County, north of Nashville and Gallatin. Barnett Wilder had been a musician in his younger days but times were hard and so was the music business, then just as it was now. When Barnett went back to the farm he'd fled from at sixteen, he welcomed the old life, got married and raised a family, but he'd taught his children how to appreciate and play music as well. While he was happy to be back to his roots, Barnett had spent too much time in cities to completely re-adapt to life on the farm and knew improvements had to be made for the good of the land as well as productivity. Still, money was always tight, no different than it'd always been, even if wealth was a relative thing in Barnett's view.

Jack and his two brothers grew up wearing patched clothes and ran barefoot most of the year, but they were relatively happy and ignorant of their status in life until the year Barnett had the accident that took off his right leg from the knee down. Even with the boys to help, they ended up selling off most of the hogs and even some of the timber land to get by and things got desperate. When Jack's mother Emily died of cancer when Jack was twelve, Barnett blamed himself for not having the kind of money that might've made a difference for her. Rather than turn bitter, the gentle Barnett decided getting even and making money was a better way to reset the scales of justice to a more equitable position.

The Wilders had always had a still that made great whiskey and helped put food on the table, but newer opportunities presented themselves in the form of methamphetamine and oxycontin and Barnett industriously took to distribution of that product like, well, as Jack inelegantly put it, a pig to slop. He eventually enlisted the assistance of his three sons, even Jack, the youngest then fourteen. They started running product over half of northern Tennessee and southern Kentucky in three old pickup trucks, their slatted bottoms and sides covered in pig shit and usually a stoat or two that discouraged any law from looking closer.

Things went well for a time as Barnett was a careful man. They got a new stove, a new roof, new clothes and shoes and books for Jack and his brothers, as Barnett was a man who knew the value of education. Barnett stashed most of his cash, never flaunting it like some. This was a business rife with competition and rivalries and to lord it over anyone or call attention to yourself was a guarantee of a comeuppance, which could be deadly. There were always some who had no respect for the boundaries or traditions of others.

Like many families in the South, the Wilders' feud with the Gaynors was well known, and had been active for generations, since before the Civil War. Shootouts and fights, usually over women or territory, had been the occasional set-to for two hundred years and some animosities never die. Now it took on a new dimension.

Unfortunately, the Gaynors had discovered the lucrative meth business not long after Barnett Wilder did, and sooner or later, old hatreds coupled with business competitiveness led naturally to violence. One night, the Wilders' home place burned to the ground while the brothers were out on runs and they arrived home in a smoke-filled dawn to find nothing but charred timbers and a father fighting for his life in the county hospital. Jack's older brothers Tim and Warren drove to the Gaynors' compound to settle the score because they knew exactly who the culprits were.

Against his brothers' orders to stay at home, Jack hid in the bed of the truck and when Warren was shot dead, he picked up his beloved brother's shotgun and side by side, he and his brother Tim killed the four Gaynor brothers who had taken so much from them.

When they arrived back at the hospital, the sheriff's men arrested them both, but Tim swore Jack had not been with him at the Gaynors. Tim was convicted, despite his plea of self-defense, and sent to Riverbend prison in Nashville. Despite Tim's protests, Jack was sentenced to a year in juvenile detention in Gallatin. When he got out, he went to live with Barnett, who had sold what was left of the old farm and bought a house in Nashville. Jack finished high school and did two years at Vanderbilt, but most of the time he and Barnett made music and that became his life, worth more to him than finishing college for a future in engineering which he didn't want. It was music that sang to him.

"And there you have it," Jack said. "Or most of it, anyway. I know Barnett will blame himself forever for getting into that dirty business but at that time..."

He lit a cigarette and rolled the window down halfway. "We all hated it but we made the excuses that justified it. Doesn't matter anymore. It's over and done. Atonement is a thankless bitch, Grace."

Well then. She thought back to the time she'd spent with Barnett. He was a gentle man, soft-spoken but sometimes had such a sad look in his eyes, especially when playing some of the melancholy tunes he wrote, and she'd always felt there was a story there but had never pried. It made sense now, as did a lot of things.

Barnett made guitars now, beautiful things that he took the utmost care with, selling for four thousand dollars and often much more on a custom job, depending on the buyer's specifications, and his reputation was stellar. His workshop behind the house was a refuge for him, and for Jack and her as well. Just walking into the place that smelled of fresh-cut wood, the tang of glue, the floors littered with sawdust, was like entering a temple to the divinity of music and the instruments that brought it to life. Now she understood Barnett and even Jack much more than she ever had before.

"When does Tim get out?"

"Not for a long time," Jack said. "There's a parole hearing in October and he's got a chance, so the lawyer says. My dad's pretty excited, but trying not to be. We've been disappointed before."

Grace was silent for a few miles. "Jesus, what a mess I've put us in, just when your family might be reunited. Barnett gets one son back and loses another. We might be out here in the void for who knows how long?"

"Can't think that way, Grace," Jack said. "We'll figure this out. I've been in worse spots."

She strangled a laugh. "After hearing that, I'll say you have. Still, you have to admit this one's a doozy, right out of left field."

He shrugged, staring out at the distant mountains. "Doesn't matter. We do what we have to do. I learned that the Coke hard way and now you know how."

"Where we headed? You have some destination in mind, or we just running?"

"Oh, I got one. You're going to love it. For now, Salt Lake City. You get to be a good Mormon lady for as long as it takes us to get through that sanctimonious shithole. You know, the sweet gentle sort that doesn't have a pack of stolen money." He grinned. "Some of the restaurants even have coffee. Likely run by atheists who stay for some mad reason."

"What the hell we going there for? What about Wyoming?"

"Just passing through on the way through to points west and north, my lady. Not enough people in Wyoming to get lost among, trying to blend in with those that are some suspicious of outsiders, which most of them are, just like Southerners. People are pretty much the same everywhere. Don't worry, we won't be staying."

He looked over at her and laughed. "The look on your face, though. That was priceless."

"You'll pay for this, Wilder. 'Laugh while you can, monkey-boy'," Grace said and she couldn't help but smile, even though it belied the tragic history she'd just learned.

They stopped at a roadside restaurant near a town called Price and walked around a bit to get the kinks out before going inside. A man was filling up the newspaper box and Grace took one of the papers before they went inside. They ordered burgers and Cokes from a friendly waitress that Grace had fully expected to be wearing an ankle-length cotton dress once she noticed the two long-bearded gentlemen in overalls at the counter, but the woman had on old jeans and boots. She had a pot of coffee going and had no problem with the Cokes. Grace chided herself to not be prejudiced about rumors and to try and take everything as it came.

Jack went to the bathroom. Grace opened up the paper and on the front page was a follow-up article about the diner on Interstate 40. No real news there, except that local officials suspected the dead girl found in the bathroom was of Eastern European origin which led to more speculation on cartel involvement, since one of the assailants was thought to be a Hispanic woman. That was interesting. She flipped the paper over and gasped softly.

Barry Jenkins's picture was beside the story about his murder sometime before midnight last night in Albuquerque. His throat had been crushed and he'd been found on the sidewalk of a downtown street near the club where his band had played the night before. Authorities were investigating any possible connection to the more northern fracas but at this point no conclusions had been drawn except that New Mexico seemed to be having a minor crime wave.

Jack got back from the bathroom as the waitress deposited their food on the table. Grace had lost her appetite but Jack took a big bite and chewed happily. She waited until he swallowed before pushing the paper across the table.

He put down his burger, eyes scanning the print. "Fuck." He stared over Grace's head at nothing for a few seconds and then directed his gaze back to her.

"I tried to warn him. Barry never listened to me, or anybody else. I never liked the guy but he sure as hell didn't deserve this."

"We should have known, given the text. I feel terrible about this, Jack. It's my fault, you can't deny that. These people, whoever they are, are ruthless and evil." She resisted the urge to look over her shoulder or out the window. Inside, nothing had changed. The two bearded men sat placidly in their seats and no one had come in.

They sat there in silence, their food languishing on their plates long enough the waitress ambled over. "Everything OK here? The cheeseburgers not what you wanted?"

Jack forced a smile. "No, no, it's fine. We just got some bad news from back home."

"Oh honey, I'm sorry. You want me to wrap those up for you?"

"You know, that'd be great."

She was very efficient and even put the fries in aluminum foil so they'd hold a little heat and they left, getting back into the Odyssey. Even then, they sat there for a moment longer, Grace in the driver's seat now.

"There was this band I used to listen to back in high school," Jack said, "and I can't get their name out of my head right now. 'You will know us by the trail of our dead' or something suitably artsy and hip."

At the stricken look on her face, he put his arms around her. "Sorry, Grace, sorry."

"It's OK, Jack." She started the car. "We head to Salt Lake, and then to wherever you got in mind we can hide until this is over. These people may have learned something from Barry, but they have no idea where we are, even if by now they know who we are and we need to keep it that way. Hope you like trout fishing and elk hunting and all that western mountain man shit, because baby, if you don't now, you'd better learn. We have to disappear and God knows for how long."

11

Angel stirred, the sleep-inducing thrum of the car's engine missing. It was still dark. She smelled gasoline and glimpsed Chang through the back window, putting the nozzle back into the fuel dispenser. He went back into the small market and returned, wordlessly handing her a cold Coke. He started the car and pulled away from the gas pumps, parking off to the side of the building, near a couple of picnic tables.

The cold liquid felt great on her throat and she drank half of it straight down, and burped. Chang didn't bat an eye, which was nice.

"Where are we?"

"Farmington, as you said. There's nothing here."

"Ah." She drank some more soda. "Where did you go, my little rabbits? The wolf is coming for you."

He glanced over at her, his face expressionless as usual in the luminescent glow from the dashboard lights. "The wolf has to know where to go if it's going to catch anybody."

That was indeed a problem. She studied the road map she'd picked up yesterday. Big country, the USA. She'd have to think as they would. From here, they could be anywhere. She discounted west first off. That's where they'd come from and she didn't think they'd go back. Certainly not south to Albuquerque. If they didn't know about their friend Barry yet, they soon would.

East? They were from there, after all, from what she'd read about them. Nashville, like the Mavericks. Which was exactly why they wouldn't go that way, even if it meant heading for home, or especially so. She had a sense they weren't that stupid. That left north. She scanned the map again. Colorado. They'd have to start somewhere. She picked up the CD she'd bought at the show in Albuquerque and opened the case. Yes. There they were. Wilder and Grace, and photos of both of them. The waitress had been right. Very pretty and easy to notice.

"Wait here," she said and went into the station. The bored clerk behind the counter smiled at her.

"Well, hello," he said. "What can I get for you, senorita?"

She held out the CD liner, ignoring the racial slur. "Ever see one of these people before?"

He glanced over and shrugged. "Not that I know of."

Angel put her hand around his neck and smiled. "Take a closer look, *por favor*? Like maybe yesterday?"

He leaned in. "Yeah, maybe her." He put his finger on Grace's photo. "Yeah, definitely. She seemed in a hurry but I'm pretty sure that was her. Never saw him but she was with a guy who was pumping the gas."

"What kind of car?"

"How the fuck should I know? I see a hundred cars every day."

Angel pressed down on his neck. "Think, *muchacho*. Was it a truck, a car, something else? Blue, white, red? You saw the car, just put it together with the guy pumping gas and her."

"Hey lady, you're hurting me," he whined. "Let go, OK?"

Angel dropped her hand although she didn't want to. She

wanted to go get Chang and put this jerk's face into the counter. "Sorry. It's just that this is important, to me you know?" She pulled out a $50 bill. "Maybe this will help your memory."

He looked at the money, blinking rapidly. "Let me think." He closed his eyes. "OK, yeah, I think it was some kind of SUV, red but old, needed a paint job. Definitely an SUV." He opened his eyes. "That work for you?"

"Yes," Angel said. "It does. Which way did they go? You remember that?"

The clerk shook his head, rubbing his neck. "No, can't say as I do, but most people coming through here are headed for Denver or Grand Junction, through Durango."

"North, then?"

"Well, yeah." He stared at her, eyes still defiant, money or no.

She left the money on the counter anyway and got back in the car.

"They were here."

Chang nodded. "Now where did they go?"

She pulled out the map again, musing to herself. "If I wanted to hide, would I go to a big city or would I go where I could find a hidey-hole with less prying eyes?"

Chang started the car and waited patiently.

"Go north, Durango. I'll think about where after that."

They stopped for breakfast in Durango on the main street. Angel looked around like it was a place from another planet and she had to say that for her, it nearly was, like the cowboy movies she'd seen on TV. They had breakfast at a cutesy restaurant, where she ordered huevos rancheros and they weren't half bad. Chang had tea, two poached eggs and sliced avocados, and sniffed with disdain when she told him bacon was delicious and licked her lips.

She showed the pictures of Grace and Jack to the waitress who shook her head with finality and even showed them to two of the other waitresses but they shook their heads. It was a long shot, she knew that, but still, she was beginning to worry she'd made a bad decision, although it would've been a lucky break to hit the same restaurant. Chang had nothing to say although he seemed unperturbed.

They walked down the street and at every restaurant and shop, Angel stopped and showed the pictures to the staff, with no luck. Now she was almost certain she'd messed up. Jack and Grace were probably halfway to Kansas City by now. She was angry at herself for being so sure. They walked back to the car and in front of them, a man was putting up a chalkboard with a lunch menu in front of a western-themed restaurant. Angel stopped him before he went back inside.

"Hi," she smiled. "Are you only open for lunch?"

He nodded. "That's right, and dinner. We open in five minutes if you're hungry."

"Oh, I am. Could I ask you a favor?"

"Sure."

"You ever seen either of these people?" She showed him the photos. "It's important that I find my sister."

He shook his head. "Nope, but you could ask Wendy, she's the one works the front. She's right there." He gestured towards the woman setting out silverware and napkins on the tables inside. Angel walked through the open doorway.

"Hi, your boss said I could ask you something," she said, holding out the CD liner. "I'm looking for my sister, we had a death in the family and she's on vacation with her boyfriend. Have you ever seen either one of them, maybe yesterday?"

Wendy studied the photos for a second. "Oh sure, I remember them, such a cute couple."

Relief flooded through her and Angel felt like she could finally take a deep breath. "Great, thanks so much. Any idea where they might be headed?"

Wendy cocked her head. "Now that I think about it, he was

looking at a road map and I think he said Grand Junction." She shrugged. "Can't tell you that's where they went, but I do remember hearing that. Good luck to you, honey." She went back to setting out napkins and Angel headed back to the sidewalk and Chang.

"Got them. Let's go."

"You know," Chang said from the passenger seat as he sipped his Arizona tea, "this is how the Americans say, 'needle in a haystack' or something like that. What it means is --"

"I know what the fuck it means, Chang," Angel snapped. "We're going to Grand Junction. I've got their scent now and we're less than a day behind. The wolf is coming." She pressed down on the accelerator. "Run fast, little rabbits."

12

————

Luis Reynaldo detested the United States. A bleak but greedy country controlled by banks and Wall Street, peopled and run by men in designer suits and their overdressed bejeweled and botoxxed women who thought the world was theirs for the taking, making it easy to prey upon those less fortunate and lord it over them every day, especially those whose only desire was to be like their fraudulent empty idols, the herd of semi-humanity that existed on cable TV, the Kardashians, Rodeo Drive, QVC shopping and the vacuity of influencers and social media. The hypocrisy of their words versus their actions used to amuse Luis, but for years now, his loathing had far overcome any amusement these hollow people could give him, coupled with his fury at their continued disdain for people of his own nationality.

That sort of thinking was exactly why he had enjoyed making millions by giving those vacuous people the very solace they craved in their emptiness once they realized how much their pointless lifestyles needed a boost they could find in no other way. It didn't change their delusional thinking in the slightest but only expanded a never-ending and guaranteed profit cycle for Luis and men like him all over the world. They filled an endless dark hole of need that only drugs could satisfy, because genuine self-awareness or compassion for others never would.

Early spring in Oklahoma City represented the worst of the American landscape, reinforcing Luis's views. Too early for flowers or budding trees, the city was full of the detritus of winter: dirty streets and cars, plastic bags blowing everywhere, discarded food wrappers, broken bottles and who knew what else in the gutters. The dank smell of despair and desperation overshadowed the pathetic neon signs and screaming bill-boards touting a life none of the people on these streets would ever have.

The limousine slowed as it came near their destination, the burnt remains of the warehouse where everything had gone wrong. A chain-link fence, sagging but sporting a chain, padlock and yellow crime scene tape denied them further access. Luis had the reports from his informants in the Okla-homa City police, but he wanted to see everything for himself. He was a man who noticed details and this incident had little reportage of those, but they were there, if a man knew how to look closely.

Normally he would never venture near the scene of the rare debacle that involved his business, as he was a very careful man. Still, he wanted answers he might never get otherwise, especially when it came to the deaths of his best *sicario* Chang, and more importantly, his poor beloved Angel. He could not bear the thought of never again seeing her beautiful face, seeing her lying on his bed, or hearing her bell-like voice singing the songs she had written on her guitar.

He whipped out a white linen handkerchief to dab his eyes, and then proceeded on to his forehead and cheeks. *Dios mio*, it was an inferno in this car. Perhaps he should not have eaten all those enchiladas on the plane. Angel was always telling him to lose weight and holy Mary, just see what had become of him in a few days without her?

"What do you want to do, *jefe*?" Mario, Luis's number two, sat across from him, cradling a gun in his arms. Mario was always prepared, Luis knew, and that is why he trusted him with his life. Two more of his men sat on the banquette to the side, and another in front with the driver.

"What do you think?" Luis said. "I want to go in there. Find a way. That's your job."

He thought of calling his man at police headquarters but he didn't want to waste time. They were here, no one else was, and bolt cutters were standard equipment with his crews. Mario issued instructions to the men and within minutes, Luis stepped out of the car and accompanied by his men, walked into what was left of the warehouse.

Luis had already known the Albanians were not trust-worthy partners, but he hadn't been prepared to have them fuck him over on the very first deal. He was hoping they would be more sensible than that, unlike the Russians. Blowing up the first deal just wasn't done in this business. That was sacrosanct. Everyone knew you waited for at least one more deal, bigger than the first one, before you made a move like that and Luis had planned to get them first if they displayed any tendencies he distrusted, like he always did. He truly hated it when things went out of order.

The police report had mentioned bodies, seven or eight recovered from the ashes so far, along with a limousine and an Escalade. Evidence recovered was a case full of cocaine, and at least one duffel bag from the looks of the clasps, and that had been full of charred paper. Plus, a lot of guns and a lot of bullets. They were working on that.

They walked through the warehouse. The burnt-out vehicles were still there, but the bodies were at the morgue, of course. His man had told Luis it was too early to determine yet if there had been a woman's corpse among them, maybe in a day or two more. He wandered around the space himself, stepping carefully through the debris, and looking carefully at the remains of the Escalade and the limousine, pacing carefully through the rest of the warehouse. It didn't look as though any of the filthy goat-fucking Albanians had made it out of here, either. At the back were the remains of another sliding garage door. Luis observed everything carefully, looking around the expanse, taking his time. He turned abruptly on his heel and headed outside to the limo. Mario and the rest of the men followed hurriedly.

"You find something, *patron*?"

Luis ignored him. "Get in the car. We have work to do. Back to the hotel."

The car purred along and Luis poured himself a shot of tequila from the bar beside him. He tossed it back and poured another.

There had been another car there, maybe an Escalade, since those Albanian sons of disease-ridden whores loved to use them as carriers with custom compartments. They thought of themselves as designers, much to the amusement of the entire world. The burned one didn't have any and never had. The Albanians wouldn't have had just one car, not how they operated. Somebody had left that warehouse in the other car. Somebody that had a lot of his money and a lot of his cocaine.

Life was a crooked road sometimes, no matter how much you paved it to go on the course you set, or along the lanes you constructed so nothing could veer in the wrong direction, Luis thought. That was important. It was people that fucked you. Always the people. He hoped it was not people that he loved that had done this, but only the ones that no one would miss. Mourning his Angel would be easier if she had left this world in the inferno of that warehouse, instead of having to kill her himself. He had to be sure, now that he knew someone had left that place of death.

He poured another tequila and gazed out at the ugly city. He would no longer do business in Oklahoma City. It was off his list from now on, along with any Eastern Europeans. Albanians, Armenians, Czechs, Bosnians, and those tattooed vodka-addled fucking Russians. They'd moved in everywhere in the United States and the stupid Americans didn't care, all they worried about was a bunch of poor brown people trying to cross the border so they could mow lawns and work in restaurants. What they truly needed to be concerned with was the Europeans who were well versed in brutality in ways American law enforcement were only beginning to discover. He hated this country and this city was like a talisman for the worst of it. Tomorrow would bring his answers.

13

"You ever been here before?"

"Couple of times," Jack said. "On a tour, a fill-in with Willie at the State Room. You wouldn't think so, to hear about the place and the Mormon church and all, but this is a fairly lively music scene. At Kilbey Court, they got a little of everything, even a lot of acoustic and punk bands. The kids here are like kids everywhere else and they come out in droves, sucking down Molly and banging the night away, so the song goes. Only difference is on Sundays they go to church with mom and dad and feel all cleansed by Jesus until the next Friday night."

Grace smiled. "Guess the kids need some outlet what with no smoking, drinking, coffee, or sex, music gives them that."

Jack snorted. "Take sex off that list. Mom and Dad might be able to control the first three for a while but they can't ever stop that one. They tend to get married young," he wiggled his eyebrows, leering. Grace burst out laughing.

"My point is, the kids I've seen here are pretty much like kids everywhere else, trust me. Who knows, maybe all that church and family stuff isn't so bad. I'm not one to judge, that's for sure."

Grace took the turnoff towards downtown Salt Lake City. "Well, that gives me some hope for the future."

They drove through the city, mainly because Grace wanted to see it. *Who knew when they'd be through here again, never if she could help it,* she thought, *or if they'd even see next week, so fuck it.*

The famous temple sat right there, replete with its golden angel on top, alongside the usual buildings, stores and restaurants, just like every other downtown. She drove past and got back on the freeway. Never been much of a tourist anyway.

"Jack."

"What?" He was buried in the map again.

"Where are we going? We need to stop running and figure out a plan."

"That's what I'm doing, Grace. Pull into the next minimart. We need some burner phones. Still need to communicate. Probably paranoia, but it's just one more thing, you know? I don't know what the hell I'm doing, but we can't be too careful. I mean, I doubt it's the NSA after us, but some people have a lot of tech skills I sure as hell don't. Then, we'll find a place to spend the night. It's going to be a long day tomorrow."

God, she hated it when he did that keep it to himself crap but he was a processor, one of those people who didn't want to lay out his ideas or plans or even songs before he'd a chance to refine them, sometimes too much. She never felt threatened by it, but right now it was particularly annoying. Just to have authority, she kept driving for a long while until Jack finally said to pull into the next gas station with a minimart.

He jumped out of the car and went inside while she pumped gas. He came back with his sack of phones, whistling like he didn't have a care in the world. That was another thing about Jack. He only whistled when he was agitated or excited about something, so she knew he hadn't been just map-gazing.

"There's a place about five miles up, according to the store clerk. Cabins, and a good restaurant," Jack said. "His brother owns the place, he says. The Ashley Forest Resort."

"Sounds pricey." She knew she sounded pissy but she couldn't help it. "Maybe your new pal is setting you up."

"I doubt it, on both counts. Come on, Grace," Jack shot back. "Besides, we're rich, or so a little bird told me."

The place was nice, but not resort-nice, in spite of the sign. The Log Cabin restaurant sat to the side of the office building, smoke curling out of the chimney and it reminded Grace of that label on the fake maple syrup bottle. Jack came back out with a key in his hand and she drove around to a lane that forked. She veered right, passing log cabins set among the pine trees and pulled at Number 14. Home again, home again, said Grace to herself. How sweet. She'd bet it even had chintz ruffled curtains. God, she was getting pissy.

It was kind of comforting in a way. Indeed, there were ruffled curtains, and it was decorated in cheesy forest cabin, with even a tiny kitchenette. A stone fireplace took up one wall, with a queen-sized bed on another, and under the big window sat a couple of upholstered chairs with a table on which sat a basket of muffins and some fruit. She liked it. It was the nicest place she'd ever stayed in by far.

Jack brought in their stuff and sat it down, along with the few groceries from the supermarket they'd stopped at just outside of the city. He busied himself putting stuff in the fridge and on the counter and then walked over and pulled her into a hug.

"Sorry. I'm doing that thing I do but I've been doing a lot of thinking."

That was all it took for Grace burst into tears. She'd wanted to fight, her usual response to crisis but as always, when anyone was kind, she dissolved into a puddle.

"Christ, Jack, this whole thing is so fucked," she sobbed. "How are we going to get out of this?"

He held her tight until the tears subsided. Somehow they ended up on the bed with the moose embroidered on the comforter and Grace's eyes didn't open again until she heard Jack cracking twigs of kindling into the fireplace where brightening flames met his efforts in dispelling the dim light of evening.

"Hey princess," he smiled. "Feeling better?"

She was naked, her clothes a pile on the floor, as was he, the firelight flickering off his bare skin where he crouched in front of the grate. "Some." She grinned. "I could use some dinner, though. Isn't that the usual enticement even if we do it backward?"

They finally made it to the Log Cabin restaurant before they closed, ordering ribeye steaks, supplemented by some good whiskey. The place was mostly empty, which was fine with them but the waitress was nice and they left her a large tip. They walked back down the road to their cabin, feeling satisfied and just a little more normal, holding hands.

"I have a plan, Grace."

"Hope so, because I don't have shit unless it involves living in a bear cave for the rest of our lives."

Jack laughed softly. "I think I can do better than that."

The air smelled of pine and mesquite and as they stepped onto the porch of Number 14. Grace stopped Jack and kissed him, not wanting to go inside. It was peaceful here and peace had been in short supply. Utah had some good things. She was optimistic for the first time in two days.

When she reached for the door handle, the door was slightly ajar and they both jerked back like they'd been stung. They peered through the crack. There was a man inside, rifling through their bags, and one bag in particular.

"What the hell, Jack?" she whispered. They huddled in the shadows on the porch.

"Stay out here. I got this."

Jack edged around the open door. There were no lights except the glow from the fireplace but there was no doubt about what the guy was doing. He was big, dark-haired and bearded, wearing a plaid flannel shirt. He'd found even more than he was looking for, and had the backpack in one hand and Grace's guitar case in the other as he headed towards the door.

"Hey man," Jack said.

The bearded man turned, surprise and panic on his face, and took a couple of steps sideways, eyeing his chances to make the door.

Jack didn't hesitate. "Stop. Right there. It's not worth going to jail for."

The bearded man dropped the guitar and the backpack and punched Jack in the face before Jack could react, barreling past him through the open door. He only took one step before Grace whacked him in the face with a chunk of firewood from the stack on the porch. He went down, blood pouring from his broken nose. They dragged him inside and shut the door.

"Nice hit." Jack massaged his jaw. "Dumb bastard cold-cocked me. Haven't had that happen since junior high."

"Thanks. Yeah, I was thinking baseball. Saw that in some movie and always wanted to do it. Besides, neither one of us can afford to punch people, break a finger or two and still play guitar, even though this was one of those times a punch would've been profoundly satisfying."

The guy was coming around, glaring at them and blubbering nonsense through the blood and snot running down his chin. Jack kicked him in the ribs before Grace had the chance.

"So, Ronny," Jack said, perching on one of the chairs, the Glock he'd taken to carrying in his waistband now in his hand, "this your side gig here? Directing people to the cabins and then ripping them off while they have dinner?"

"Fug you, ashoe," said the guy. "You ashalted me."

"Indeed I did." Jack looked over at Grace. "Forgive me, darlin', for not introducing you before. This charming specimen of western thuggery is the helpful clerk from the gas station down the road. Meet Ronny, or so he told me." Jack dug his toe into the man's side again. "Is that your real name?"

"Yesh, fugger."

"And articulate too," Jack said. "Doesn't say much for the friendly tourist industry in Utah, though. You been a busy boy, Ronny. I wonder how many unsuspecting tourists you've robbed over the years. Quite a cottage, or I should say, cabin industry you got going here. I think it's time you found another hobby, dude."

Ronny gave an inarticulate growl.

Grace was growing impatient. It'd been a long day. "What do you want to do with this idiot?"

Jack shrugged. "Not sure. Kill him and dump him in the woods? Actually, that'd be easiest because we sure do need to get some sleep." He winked at her.

"That's one. Or, we can tie him up and take him with us for a while. Dump him somewhere else. You're right, we do need some sleep. We don't have time to bury bodies tonight."

Jack grinned. "I like the tie him up option, Bonnie Parker. I'm fresh out of digging energy tonight. Gaffer tape's in the equipment box."

"Fuggers!"

In the end, they had to put him in the back of the Odyssey, since he continued to moan through the hole they'd put in the gaffer tape when they left him on the floor in front of the fire. He was trussed up like a Thanksgiving turkey but putting tape on his mouth was dicey, since his nose was broken and Grace was afraid he'd suffocate even though Jack was not. He'd get enough air through the hole, Jack said. People were resilient. Still, nobody could sleep through that whiney shit. They threw the moose quilt over him. Nobody would hear him past the quilt and the car itself. Besides, it would save time in the morning.

"Sleep tight, Ronny," Jack said, shutting the cargo door. "You're one lucky bastard you're not sleeping in a shallow grave instead of that nice comfy car."

Jack's face was a mess, a huge bruise on the side of his cheek and a black eye beginning to swell. Grace found some ice in the tiny fridge and put it into one of the plastic bags from the supermarket. It didn't help a lot. Jack was silent, clearly furious. They fell into bed, and Grace started to giggle, a little at first, then uncontrollably.

"Oh man, the look on that dumb shit's face when you said 'kill him and dump him in the woods' was priceless."

Jack hugged her tighter. "Don't get hysterical on me, Grace. Now, we do have to get rid of the asshole somehow. We sure as hell can't call the cops, since he clearly looked in that goddamn backpack and knows we have a lot of money on us and we can't let him spill that. The stupid shit was probably just going for the usual, luggage, purses, whatever and in this case, music gear since we don't have tinted windows on that soccer mom special, and he might've spotted that. The money was a bonus he had no idea about but he sure as hell does now."

She looked at him and his eyes were cold, staring at the ceiling.

"Besides, gunshots are loud and we aren't the only people staying here."

She didn't know if he was kidding or not. Now that she knew more about his past, she couldn't help but wonder a little. She took a few deep breaths. "I know, but we can't kill him. That's not who we are, Jack. People have died already but not because we pulled the trigger."

He kissed the side of her neck. "People don't always know who they are, Grace, until they come face to face with choices. Stop worrying. We'll get rid of our excess baggage and he won't be robbing anybody else for a while if he's scared enough. Maybe he'll give up his life of crime. My granny would call us reformers that have given Ronny a chance at God's grace. She'd say Ronny will be redeemed in Jesus's love. He's a fortunate guy, didn't even have to do a penance. Well, except for the tape and his uncomfortable night in the car, maybe not what Jesus had in mind. Go to sleep, Grace, and quit worrying. Now we've got a somewhat busier day tomorrow than I'd planned."

14

———————

Luis did not sleep well, even after half a bottle of El Mayor tequila, his favorite. He always had a case or two stocked on the plane. He woke early, obsessed with his love for Angel, staring out at the grey skies. He didn't sleep soundly anymore without Angel nestled beside him.

"Mario," he shouted. The bedroom door opened immediately.

"I am here, *patron.*"

"Order some breakfast, perhaps these *norteamericano* barbarians have some decent food, but we can't hope for that. Do your best."

"*Si, patron.*"

Luis sat up, his stomach churning. Even the steak he'd eaten last night was subpar, disappointing given that they were in the middle of the country that prided itself on its Angus beef. He lurched into the bathroom.

Half an hour later, dressed in a black Armani suit rather than his preferred white, worn in deference to the foul American weather, he stood in front of the full-length mirror. The expert tailoring of the suit disguised a great deal of the bulk of his belly. His hair was still mostly black, but silver threads wound their way through the waves, and in his close-trimmed beard as well. He'd thought lately of shaving it off, but Angel said she liked it. He wasn't sure. He suspected that sometimes she flattered him for no reason, but he always forgave that, because he liked it, just as liked everything Angel did. Just thinking about her gave him pause and he leaned on the counter, breathing slowly while his anxiety subsided.

He knew he looked good for his age, close to forty-five now, downright ancient and God-given lucky for someone in his position and profession, but not unexpected, especially to him. To survive and prosper in this business, you had to be smart and ruthless, and he'd learned those lessons very early and he'd learned them well. He had started as a *sicario* himself back in the early days and he'd risen to the top because he was willing to do whatever he had to. That would never change.

He opened the door to the sitting room just as the room service waiter was leaving. Silver domes topped the plates on two carts and Mario was setting silverware down on the table-cloth beside the window, not that there was much to see except gray skies and an ugly city. Luis sat down as Mario took the lid from one of the plates, sitting it down in front of him.

"What the fuck is this?" He poked the colorful salsa-topped omelet gingerly with his fork. It was not even fluffy.

"*Lo siento, patron,*" Mario said. "It is what they call a Mexican omelet. It was the best I could do from their menu here."

Luis sighed heavily. "Never mind, my friend. I will manage." He took a sip of the coffee and perhaps it was the slight hang-over stoking his need, but it wasn't bad. You had to make do when on the road. He ate half the miserable omelet, foregoing the potatoes and toast. Americans thought potatoes made up for any sins in their dishes, like the Irish.

His one trip to Dublin he'd practically starved for three

days. Black pudding, what the fuck was that. Their cuisine was appalling, the only thing worse was the English and their boiled everything. The only thing the Irish did well was being poor, even though they had great poets and butter. Perhaps that was why. Luis knew great achievements came from suffering. Maybe he'd look into doing business with the IRA. They always needed money and they were more trustworthy than those cursed Albanians, that was certain. Wordlessly, he finished the pot of coffee while the other four sat around the coffee table at the end of the room.

"Call our man."

Mario took out his phone. "I tried earlier, but the coroner's office didn't answer." He put the phone to his ear. Someone did this time and Mario nodded as the man talked, finally putting the phone down.

"He says he wants us to come down there."

Luis nodded. "Something's not right. You see? I know these things. This is why I couldn't sleep."

The limousine pulled up outside of the main Oklahoma City precinct that also housed the coroner's office and morgue. Mario and Luis entered and were quickly escorted to the coroner's office in the basement by Detective Alan Schmidt, a tall middle-aged blonde man who had been on Luis's payroll for fifteen years, just as so many across the country were.

The white-tiled walls may have been clean and antiseptic, but the chemical tang in the air did nothing to hide the smell of death. It was decidedly unpleasant but Luis didn't care. Some things had to be endured to get what you wanted. He was not a squeamish man.

"Sorry to have to get you down here, sir, but this is not exactly what we were expecting," he said, holding open the door to the coroner's office. "I thought you'd want to get this firsthand, so to speak." Schmidt gestured to two metal chairs beside the desk. "Have a seat, I'll be right back."

In contrast to the white-tiled stainless-steel sterility of the rooms they'd passed, the head coroner's office looked like a dusty gray trash bin, amplified by the cracker crumbs and empty coffee cartons on the desk. Mario sat down in one of the chairs but Luis remained standing. The overhead fluorescent lights flickered which in Luis's opinion, was a blessing since a brighter look at this hovel wasn't something he wanted to see more clearly. Schmidt came back with another man in a white coat who held out his hand.

"I'm Dr. Zuckerman, Mr. Reynaldo. Nice to meet you." Luis nodded and ignored the proffered hand. Zuckerman, an older man with thinning hair and cloudy glasses in need of a good wiping, didn't seem to care and officiously sat down behind his desk and opened the file folder he'd carried in with him, riffling through the few papers it contained.

"Well, let's get down to it. According to our reports, we have identified eight bodies. There are no more. All men."

Luis stared at him. "That can't be correct. There was a woman there. That we know."

The coroner glanced over at Schmidt and licked his lips. Maybe he was nervous, after all. "If there was, she didn't die there, in that fire or by any other means, so far as we can tell."

Luis said nothing and after two minutes, the silence in the room became oppressive. He glanced over at Mario whose face was impassive.

"What about can you determine someone's race from bodies so damaged? I have heard this is possible," Luis said.

Zuckerman cleared his throat. "Yes, it is possible, but difficult. Frankly, in an instance like this, very difficult."

Luis nodded at Mario who took an envelope from his coat pocket and set it down on the desk.

"Perhaps this could make your task easier. You see, Dr. Zuckerman, from what information I have, there are some discrepancies. One of those bodies should have been a woman,

God rest her soul, or so we believe, and the other may be Asian, Chinese specifically. If none of the eight bodies you have is Asian or female, definitively, that information would be very valuable to me."

"I see," Zuckerman said, his eyes flicking to Schmidt. He picked up the envelope and peered inside. "I'll do my best to have that information for you by this afternoon. If that will suit."

Luis nodded. "The earlier the better." Luis rose from the chair and Schmidt opened the door. "Thank you."

Ensconced back in the limousine, Luis leaned back against the seat cushion. "Call some of our friends and find the best Mexican restaurant in town. At least we won't go hungry while we wait for some answers. Then, the airport. The plane is more comfortable than that infernal cheap hotel." Luis would never forget that excuse for an omelet. For him, it only said no respect not to mention poor culinary skill.

By three o'clock, Luis had his answers. Definitely no female and no one of Asian descent. Luis poured another tequila while the pilot finished his pre-flight. He drank slowly while he made call after call, finally putting the phone down as the Gulfstream headed west chasing the dying sun. They wouldn't be hard to find, not with hundreds of people in many towns looking for them.

Mario brought him another bottle of tequila. Luis stopped him before he sat back down in his seat.

"*Gracias,* Mario. You always anticipate my needs and I am grateful. I am a man of sorrow today, a man bereft. You know that. Betrayal is the worst thing people can do to one another. Do you agree?"

Mario's face was solemn. "I do, *patron*. There is no mercy for those that care nothing for those that have given them everything."

"We will not be going back to Mexico until this is over," Luis said, and finished his tequila. "I will personally tend to this... aberration. Very personally." He stared at Mario. "Do you understand?"

"I do." Mario said. He opened the new bottle of El Mayor.

. "I am always with you, *jefe*."

15

———————

Chang drove slowly down the main highway through Grand Junction. Angel peered through the windshield, her head swiveling back and forth from one side of the street to the other. She wasn't entirely sure what she was looking for, but her senses were on high alert for anyone that looked like their prey, or a red Explorer.

She was not certain she'd been as observant as another cruise along the street could bring. She knew Chang was right, it was a needle in a haystack, but she felt like a bloodhound on the trail and her nose even twitched a little. She was tired, and she may have missed something. She'd taken the last of her pills an hour ago and it was making her more alert, just now kicking in. She smiled to herself when they reached the end of the business district, the highway out of town looming ahead.

"Turn around, please. Let's give it another run."

Chang shrugged, and she couldn't see him rolling his eyes, because he was too sly to ever do that, but the skepticism was coming off him in a vaporous cloud she could sense. He dutifully executed a U-turn and the neon lights of car dealerships and hamburger chains were beginning to light up as they drove back down the business corridor.

A quarter mile down they stopped at a streetlight.

"You know, Angel," he said, "we might do better to just go on with what we've got. It's enough to disappear and more. Chasing down these people gives Luis a chance to find us before we get to them. Getting away from him should be our first priority."

Angel's hand closed on his arm like a vise just as the light changed. "Pull over, *cabron*."

He didn't hesitate, she'd give him that. "Listen to me, Chang. I know Luis will soon be on the hunt, maybe he already is, who can tell? We have to assume he is. That only makes it more important for us, because we can't afford to lose a single dollar of this money. I don't know about you but I've had to work too hard for it."

She released her hand. Chang sat like a stone statue, staring out at the street but Angel wasn't finished and she didn't care.

"You want to start a new life? Clearly you do, or you wouldn't be with me right now. So do I, and that's why we're tracking these thieves down. That's my money, and yours too, for having to put up with that man for years. You, killing people for him, and me, opening my body every time he demands it, pretending I care for him when he sickens me every time I get in that bed. For that, and so much more, listening to him preen himself on his prowess and how handsome he looks, hiding that belly beneath his bespoke suits, or telling you," she smacked her fist on Chang's arm and he never flinched, staring into her eyes without a blink, "to kill his rivals or to torture some poor bastard for having the guts to stand up to him. That, my friend, takes all the money we can get and each and every *centavo* is one we deserve.

"To leave that life behind forever, to go where he can never find either of us must be our goal and we may need everything we can get to make that happen. I will never let someone take that away. We will find them. We took an opportunity like it was a gift from God, and I don't want to lose any of that or have it go to those who stole it and don't deserve it as much as we do. To me, this is sacred."

Chang took his hands off the wheel, put them in his lap and turned towards her. "Angel. I understand. Luis stole my pride and my dignity, just as he has yours. That is why I am here beside you. I chose to let him do so and have found it, well, troublesome to leave his employ and have been foolishly complacent until now. You did not have that choice and I have watched your pain for some time. If I did not care, I would have left you in that warehouse or anywhere along this journey we are traveling. You know what I'm saying is true."

She was shaking, her breath coming in short bursts. She put her head between her knees but that only made it worse. She felt Chang's hands on her, lifting her up.

"Breathe. I will count. One, two, three four in, one two three four out, from the gut."

He held her and she followed his commands. After a couple of minutes, she felt better.

She fell back onto the headrest. *Full-blown panic attack, you stupid woman*, she thought. She looked over at Chang, his dark eyes staring back at her.

"Thank you."

He shrugged. "I am here for you, Angel."

She knew that. He'd said it before but she hadn't believed it until now.

"Chang. I'm sorry." She twisted her neck and felt the bones crack and rearrange. "It's just that –"

He put two fingers gently to her lips, the first time he'd ever really touched her. "I know."

He put the car in gear and pulled out onto the road. "You need to keep a keen watch, Angel. I trust your instincts."

She breathed deeply and returned to staring out the window like a hawk searching for a rabbit.

"Stop."

Chang pulled over quickly, just past a car lot with a neon sign that read "Gold Mine Used Cars". In the front row was a red Explorer, its sun-faded hood boasting a sign that promised a "Smokin' Hot Deal, Today Only!!" Angel glanced over at Chang, taking off her seat belt in anticipation before he turned off the car. He gave her a rare grin and followed behind her.

"Hey there, folks." The paunchy man strode purposefully towards them before they were within ten feet of the shabby office, and held out his hand. "Darryl Ackerman. What can I do ya for this fine evening?"

Angel ignored his hand, as did Chang. "We're interested in that Explorer out front, the 'smokin' hot deal' car. It's just what we're looking for. Perhaps we should go into the office and discuss this?"

His smile only faded a little once he'd gotten a closer look at them, she had to give him points for that. They didn't look like people who'd want an old Explorer, but then who really would?

"Well, sure," he said. "But don't you want to take a closer look at the car? You just got here."

"Not right now," Chang said. Darryl looked at him and swallowed audibly. "All righty, then, folks. Follow me."

The office was empty, even the front desk, Angel noticed. The place smelled like cigarettes and cat pee as they went into the second room, partitioned off with a dirty plexiglass panel. They sat in the plastic chairs Darryl directed them to and he brought out a folder from his desk drawer.

"We just got this little beauty in yesterday. Best deal in Colorado."

"Darryl." Angel put her hands on the desk and leaned over to him. "Tell us where you got that car."

A long minute passed while sweat popped out on Darryl's

forehead. He didn't make eye contact with either her or Chang, glancing around the room as though looking for help but there was no one else there. "Well, it was a funny thing," he said finally. "This couple sort of traded it in."

"Really? Tell me the truth."

"Ah, well, OK, OK, you got me. Cards on the table time." Darryl looked down at the desk but there were no answers there and he raised his head.

"I know I'm busted. You're investigators from the state board, and I know you're onto me with this one. Not sure how you got on this so fast but you guys are good, I'll say that. Proud of how efficient the state of Colorado is, have to say."

He gave them a weak smile which quickly faded as he looked at their immobile faces.

"Just so you know, I'm sorry, but maybe we can come to some arrangement here, even though I been fined for this shit, sorry, this stuff before."

Angel exchanged glances with Chang, trying not to laugh. This man was a very poor excuse for a criminal. They kept their faces blank and said nothing, which only seemed to make Darryl more agitated.

Darryl took a swig from the Coke on his desk which smelled heavily laced with bourbon. "Christ. OK, here's the thing, full disclosure. I got the car back from the salvage yard. If you report me, this time I'll lose my license. How about $1000 bucks for each of you, everyone goes their merry way and the car just disappears?"

Angel sat back down while Chang leaned forward. "All things are possible, Darryl. Start from the beginning, please."

Darryl coughed, wiped his forehead and lit a cigarette. Chang frowned and Darryl hastily stubbed it out. "Sorry, sorry."

"Anyway, this couple came in and bought a car from me, for cash, too, which you sure don't see every day but who am I to argue, right? Weird thing is, they didn't want a trade-in on that Explorer they came in with. Then they asked me about a salvage yard."

He gestured towards them. "Well, you guys know all about how it works. I have a deal with this guy at the salvage yard and when he gets cars are still worth some money, he sells me back the cars people don't want instead of trashing them like they thought." His eyes darted around the office again like he was searching for Jesus before landing back on Chang who was most definitely not in the savior business.

"I mean, I think of it like a service, in truth. Ecological and responsible, you know? No point in just trashing a car, right? Nobody gets hurt and me and Don make a few bucks. So, that's the deal. No harm, no foul. Well, except for you guys and the state of Colorado." He gave a forced chuckle. "Which we can work around. So, we good?"

"Just a few more details," Angel said. "Do you have the title for this car?"

"Of course." Somewhat aggrieved, Darryl opened the folder and thrust a piece of paper at her. "I do a legitimate sale."

"I'm sure you do," she said, taking the title. "Grace Whitney, 1121 Brown Avenue, Nashville, Tennessee. That the owner, then?"

"Oh hell yes, pretty girl, and her friend, too. Sold them a Honda Odyssey van. I knew it was a good car for them, since they had all that music gear. And those kids they wanted to take camping."

Angel nodded. "What color?"

"What?"

"What color was the Honda?"

"Oh. White, as I recall. They have nothing to do with this." Darryl looked at her quizzically. "What difference does that make?"

"Everything." Angel said and looked at Chang.

Chang leaned over the desk and flipped the switch on the neon lights outside and the lot darkened, leaving just the desk lamp as illumination. Darryl's eyes grew wide and he began to stand up, but Chang's hand was already in motion and he killed Darryl with the simple stroke with which he'd dispatched Barry, the three fingers of his left hand the same size, blunted from years of training with the triads.

"Loose end, then, Chang?" Angel wasn't quite ready for it this time even though poor Darryl was no upstanding citizen. But especially after Barry, she was experiencing an emotion she'd had little time for in her life. It was compassion, and she knew it was dangerous for them both. She tried to tamp it down.

"Yes, Angel."

"I know your obsession with details, Chang. I'm thinking, though, we may be leaving more of a trail than not. Your methods are quite distinctive. No more unless it's life and death, by that I mean ours. This man was no threat."

His eyes flashed. She knew he was angry. Chang couldn't help who he was. She also knew he was angry because he knew she was right. He'd been a pawn as much as she had, and killing to solve problems was all he knew, shutting down anything that could interfere with his survival.

"You want to do anything with the Explorer?" he said.

"No, nobody knows about it except us. It doesn't matter anymore." She put the title back in the folder that Darryl had placed on the desk and then put it back into the drawer.

It was full dark when they left the office. They got back in the Escalade and drove away, Gold Mine Used Cars dark and quiet for the night, all sales final.

"Where?" Chang said, eyes on the road.

"North. You all right to drive tonight? Wake me up when you're tired or we get to Salt Lake City. They aren't that far away. I can feel it." She closed her eyes, knowing he would be fine.

Chang was like gold. Beautiful, slippery, smooth and extremely dangerous, but at least for now, her gold. It would be nice if he had a conscience or a little more self-control. Ah well, you couldn't have everything. She had freedom and she was going to keep it no matter what she had to do or who she had to do it with.

16

———————

Water poured off the eaves of the cabin, waking Grace to the dawn light, what little there was of it. The rain was seemingly relentless, pounding on the roof like the low thrum of a bass drum. At another time and place, she'd have loved that sound. Today, it just got in the way of everything they had to do, not the least of their tasks that guy in the trunk.

Grace tiptoed into the kitchenette and made coffee from the premade packets Ashely Forest Resort supplied, standing at the counter and waiting. She'd bought cream from the market, detesting the powdered packets, and poured it into a cup, staring at the coffeepot. *For Christ's sake, finish,* she thought. She glanced over at the alcove and the bed where Jack snored, oblivious. Just as well. Being alone with your first cup of coffee of the day was a blessing, one she'd learned to cherish.

She stared at the backpack on the floor. Goddamn thing had brought nothing but trouble. On the other hand, it brought possibility, too. She shook her head. She needed coffee or maybe something far beyond that. No, she told herself. You're never going back to that shit. Those days were over. A little voice in her head seemed to disagree. *If there's ever been a time, this is it, girl. It's easier with me along for the ride and it might be quite a good ride.*

A gurgling noise like a dying frog announced the completion of the brew cycle. Grace poured a cup and sat down on the couch, staring out at the rain. It was truly awful coffee, but at least it was hot and felt great on her throat. She wondered how their friend was doing in the trunk. That guy was a complication they hadn't needed.

Jack stirred, coughed and flung the blankets to the floor.

"There's coffee."

She heard the bathroom door slam. He'd never been good company in the morning. It would be at least thirty minutes before he was back in human form. She smiled. More Grace time. She even made toast.

JACK OPENED the tailgate door and threw their bags in. Ronny was still wrapped snugly in the moose quilt, and to Grace's relief, his eyes flew open.

"Hey man," Jack said. "How you doing?"

Ronny blinked frantically. Jack ripped the gaffer tape from his mouth and Ronny opened it to yell, but Jack shook his head and instead Ronny just took a big breath.

"You want, I can put it back on," he said, "but you shut it, I'll leave it off. We clear?"

Ronny nodded, his eyes flicking left and right, clearly panicked and knowing he had no options left.

"Good choice."

Jack drove as they headed north. He hadn't had much more to say to her than he had Ronny, and Grace was worried. The rain poured down on the windshield, the wipers barely keeping up with the sheets of rain. The sky was even darker the further north as they went. This was one nasty storm.

This whole thing had changed him. Her, too, of course, but she didn't like his silent introspective thing. Jack had always had those moments since she'd known him, but this was something far different than anything they'd ever been through. Although, from what he'd said about his family, maybe he'd been in a similar situation before. He'd never talked about such a particular instance, but there may well have been one, for all she knew.

She shook her head. The Wilders were good people and this was no time for introspective ancient history, especially now that she knew more of it. This was a time for smart decisions and no stupid moves. So far, they had no indication anyone was following them except of course, for the phone text, but Grace was apprehensive. She couldn't help checking behind them when they were on the road or even in a restaurant. A feeling like a small icy snake kept crawling up her spine, unfurling when she least expected it. It didn't feel good, that was for sure, and her stomach wasn't cooperating. Last night's dinner wasn't sitting very well anymore and she didn't think Jack's was either.

It was still early and they hadn't seen many other cars on the road. A few miles down the road, a wooden sign pointed towards a state picnic recreation area on the Pioneer River and Jack swung the Honda onto the gravelly dirt road, mud and water flying under the wheels. Grace glanced over but his face was set, reflecting nothing beyond the rivulets of water on the windshield and she didn't say a word. They came to signs, one pointing towards the boat launch and the other to the camping area. Jack turned onto the road for the camping area and drove a little way. There was no evidence of anyone camped there and there were no other cars anywhere, just forlorn picnic tables.

The place was devoid of humanity. Jack turned off the Honda and looked at her.

"This is where our unwelcome guest leaves us."

He unbuckled his seat belt. Grace put her hand on his arm. "Are you sure about this? We don't want this guy to die of exposure or something. He's a thief, yeah, but he doesn't deserve that."

Jack shrugged. "You get what you sign up for, Grace. There's risk in everything. We sure as hell are living proof of that."

He leaned over and kissed her. "Stop worrying. It's not that cold anyway. Somebody will find him by noon and he'll be eating chicken soup at his girlfriend's house in no time. Ronny can tell any sad story he wants, but he sure as fuck won't be telling anybody the truth. He's just as guilty as we are. If he wasn't scared enough before, he sure is now."

They got out of the car, the earthy smell and the scent of pine forest welcome in spite of the rain pouring down. Jack opened the tailgate and Ronny's eyes flicked open. Jack took Ronny's head and shoulders and Grace maneuvered his legs and feet as best she could, dumping him on the leaf-covered ground. The gaffer's tape was holding fast in most areas, but Grace could tell the rain and humidity was letting it soften here and there. It made her feel a little better. He'd probably be able to get out of this in a half hour or so, and his mouth was uncovered.

"You fuggin asholes," Ronny pronounced after he hit the ground. "You gonna leave me out here?"

"Pretty much," Jack said. "You got your ass into this, pal. Could be worse. Could be a bullet in your brain. Ain't my problem. You chose a high-risk vocation that hurts other people. That it came back on you means you need a new calling. We're doing you a favor here, giving you some meditation time."

"Help!"

Jack laughed. "Nobody's here. Don't rile up the bears,

Ronny. That's the only thing I'd worry about, I was you. Although there's worse things, like me and some of my friends, should you ever breathe a word about just how you got in this predicament in the first place. We know just where to find you."

Ronny's eyes went wide.

"Pick up his feet, Grace," Jack said. "We can't leave him out here on the road where somebody can run over him."

That was certainly true. Dutifully, she did as he asked and with Jack in the lead, they dragged him over to the backside of a picnic table overlooking a small ravine leading to the river below. Grace was panting. The guy was heavy as shit. Just as they were going to drop him there, Jack tripped over the railroad ties some park architect had thought was a great landscaping idea and fell sideways into the ravine, dragging Ronny's taped-up body with him, the rain turning the hill into a mudslide ramp. Grace gave an involuntary yelp and dropped Ronny's feet as she felt Ronny's weight slide beyond her grasp, grabbing onto the railroad tie to stop her forward momentum so she avoided going down with the two of them. She scrabbled back, digging her heels into the mud, the rain streaming down her face as she struggled to her feet, her breathing ragged with exertion and fear.

"Jack?"

Silence.

She looked over her shoulder. The place was deserted. "Jack? Are you OK?"

Still no answer. She peered down the hill. It was raining so hard at the moment she couldn't tell how far they'd fallen, or see anything below. The only thing worse than running for your life was running alone if the man you loved died because of your mistake. She yelled Jack's name again and again.

It seemed like hours but was only a few minutes before he appeared below her, plastered with brown mud like some movie monster, the rain running in streams over his hair, face, and clothes. She reached out a hand to grasp his as he reached out at the summit of the hill, pulling as hard as she could while he struggled for footholds from below. He fell belly first onto the ground, gasping for breath.

"Jesus, are you OK? Where's Ronny?"

Jack leaned over and put his hands on his knees. "Down there, about twenty feet or so. He's fine, don't worry. Fucking hill." He took a few more deep breaths.

"Let's get out of here." He pushed himself up.

"Wait a minute," Grace said. "Is he really OK? Seriously, Jack."

He grabbed her shoulders. "Christ, Grace, I'm not a murderer. Last time I looked, he's fine. Face up and all. See for yourself, you're so damn worried, over to the left. Hold onto me. Be careful you don't slip."

She peered over the edge, blinking past the rain, leaves and dirt on her face while he held her hand. Jack was right. Ronny was laying twenty feet down the hill, his white face visible even through the rain, face up as reported. He glimpsed her face just as she saw his, and he started yelling loudly. "You fuggers. Help!"

She turned back to Jack. "Well. Seems to be alive and kicking, well yelling anyway. I'm sure somebody'll find him before long. They sure can't help but hear him. He's got quite a set of lungs on him. Still, this weather worries me. Maybe we should drag him back up here."

Jack wiped the mud from his face and turned his head upwards into the rain to finish the job. He flung out his arms and even though he was soaking wet, the mud began to run off his clothes.

"Grace? Remember that day when I gave a shit?"

"Yeah..."

Intensely bright blue eyes stared at her through the wet

hair plastered on his pale face. "Well, this ain't that fucking day."

Grace knew when to pick her battles. Ronny had made his choices and so did they. They got back in the car and headed north. More collateral damage but at least this time, he wasn't dead.

THEY COULDN'T HAVE KNOWN the rain would come down in torrential amounts, likely a record that year for northern Utah. They couldn't have known that the river would rise substantially, or the hillsides would erode and slide effortlessly down into the torrent below. They couldn't have known that the unstable earth would carry Ronny further down into said river, before anyone chose to drive into the Pioneer River recreation area, or that he would drown in that river for his unfortunate choices and be discovered two hours later. They couldn't have known a great many things about that rainy morning.

17

———————

Angel woke to the sound of the windshield wipers, barely keeping up with the torrential rain hitting the glass. Chang was concentrating on the highway in front of him. It was more or less countryside, trees lining the road, here and there an occasional house. Light struggled through the black clouds, fighting a mostly losing battle with the gloom.

"Hey, I thought I told you to wake me up. This doesn't look like any kind of city."

He glanced over. "Yes, that is true, but this time I knew they were not in that place, that Salt Lake City."

She snorted. "How is that, Mr. Bruja? You having visions?"

He shook his head. "No, Angel. But that place is not a good place for anyone running. As you say, we don't blend in. I don't think the couple we are after do either. It is a place for these righteous Mormon people whose god would not like people like us, and some angry young gangs that answer to no one, except perhaps people that work for Luis."

Angel laughed. "Oh, you think so? How the fuck would you know? Maybe they blend in, unlike you. Not that you don't have some wholesome values, I'm sure. I mean, you're here with me, aren't you?"

Chang's face was impassive as always and he kept his eyes on the road. "All these things are known facts, Angel. I make it my business to learn things about wherever I may be. Also, Luis has eyes and ears everywhere, you know that. Even in a place that purports to be godly, maybe even especially so, there are people that are hungry for what he has to give them. That means people loyal to Luis will be looking for us. There is no point in making it easy for him."

He took a quick glance at her. "It is my opinion that you need coffee. It seems to help your disposition, especially in the mornings."

She snorted. He was such a know-it-all. She felt like smacking him but that wasn't a great idea, given Chang's skills, and especially in the rain, even though the Escalade said it had stabilizers, whatever the hell that was. She'd learned to drive on the ranch in Luis's Mercedes and had learned nothing about cars except how to turn them on, steer, accelerate and brake. This car had many things she'd never seen before. Also, he wasn't wrong. She sat back in the seat, sighing heavily, but he paid no attention. They did need to make some plans, so Chang was right, once again. Coffee would go a long way to making her more coherent.

"Where exactly are we, then?"

"Heading north, just past some place called Bountiful," he said, putting on the turn signal and slowing as he turned into a minimart with gas pumps. Unfortunately, there were two police cars there already, blue lights lighting up the grey day, impossible to see from the road since they were parked on the far side of the store itself.

"I don't like this," Angel said, narrowing her eyes at the vehicles. "We should get out of here."

"Neither do I, but to turn around now would invite suspicion. Besides, we haven't done anything. At least not anything they could possibly connect to us." Chang turned off the car. "It's too late now. Besides, we both need the restroom and some sustenance. I'm sure they have the usual sugary things you like so much to go with your coffee, and I'd like some tea, so come with me."

Angel stepped out of the car and reluctantly followed him in. Three uniformed police men were talking to the clerk and hardly gave them a glance as they walked by. Other than that, it was the usual sort of place they'd seen before. Coolers lined two walls, filled with beer and soda, while the aisles were full of chips, candy, donuts, peanuts, the usual unappetizing junk road snacks. A grill of a sort was on the back wall, advertising pizza slices, hot dogs and what they called a 'full breakfast' with a picture of scrambled eggs, toast and bacon that looked somewhat appetizing in the photos but the rancid smell coming from the warming box told a different story. What was different from most roadside stations was the large array of travel and road items. *You could outfit yourself and your vehicle in one stop,* Angel thought, *especially if you liked camo and American flags.* They headed for the restrooms at the back.

When they came out, the policemen were still talking to the clerk at the checkout desk. Chang filled their tea and coffee cups at the self-serve counter while Angel slowly perused the aisles, listening to the men's conversation. Two of the cops were white, older and heavyset with a younger trim black officer rounding out the trio. He was talking in a friendly non-threatening tone to the clerk, who looked nervous as a trapped raccoon. Angel felt kind of sorry for him.

"So, let me get this straight. John, the last time you saw Ronny was yesterday afternoon? Was he supposed to work today?"

"Yeah," said the young guy, clearly nervous. "I knew something was wrong when he never showed to open, 'cause he usually does. I mean, he's usually pretty reliable, unless you know, he had a big night out or something," he glanced over at the other man. "I mean, that can happen to anybody, you know?" He picked nervously at one of many pimples dotting his chin, eyes darting from one cop to another.

One of the cops, the heavyset older man, snorted and crossed his arms, leaning on the counter. "Sure, sure, John. So, tell me more about Ronny and anybody else you might remember from yesterday. Say, customers that were odd or different, anything like that. Did he get in a confrontation with anybody? Anyone out of the ordinary or weird come in, start some trouble?"

The other older officer was fooling with the video camera and finally set to what he was looking for, inserting a tape and checking the controls. Angel wandered into another aisle, seemingly fascinated with the unappetizing choices of pork rinds or trail mix. Chang had taken a sudden interest in the large assortment of mud flaps, most of which had silhouettes of naked girls or macho sayings. He kept shaking his head and then held up one with a silhouette of a fat guy that said 'Murica' and raised his eyebrows.

"Blending?" he whispered and Angel choked back a laugh. Chang smirked and moved on to an assortment of ball caps. She sidled up the aisle closer to the conversation at the counter.

The clerk coughed. "No, no, nothing like that. I mean, shit, dude, Ronny was a nice guy." He stopped and swallowed, looking like he was going to be sick. "Sorry, man. I can't believe this." The kid's face was paper white. "How did Ronny end up in the river? Isn't that what you said?"

The officer put his hand on the clerk's shoulder. "It's OK, man, take your time. I know this is a shock. You're doing fine."

The clerk blew his nose and tried for a smile, failing. "It's just that he helped people out. He was a really helpful guy, Ronny, and always nice to me. He'd even recommend his brother's place down the road, if people were looking for a place to spend the night. I heard him do that a couple of times yesterday."

"Oh, really?" the cop said. "You mean the Ashley Forest joint? That place has had a lot of robberies in the last few months." He looked over at the two other cops who nodded and seemed quite interested in the line of inquiry. "Ronny ever mention anything about that?"

The clerk flushed. "Uh, no, dude, not really. I mean, Ronny had his quirks...but I don't think..." He looked like he wanted to be anywhere other than here. Angel could certainly sympathize with that.

"No worries, kid. We'll get back to that. So who came in yesterday that he sent to his brother's place, if you remember?"

"In fact, now that I think about it, there was this one guy, who was really nice and all, and he bought a few burner phones, which we thought was a little odd. Pretty sure he mentioned Ashley Forest to him."

One of the other policemen held up a hand, interrupting the narrative. The video was running on the small screen above the counter and all their attention went to that, including Angel's. Chang came up beside her and she shook her head, gesturing back to the aisle full of snacks. He nodded and picked up a package of multi-colored candy, studying the contents like a devoted student of chemical additives.

"That the guy?" the heavyset cop said, pointing at the screen. He looked over at his two companions who seemed intent on the screen, too.

"Yeah," said the clerk. The older man paused the video. "Good-looking guy with long hair, that's him."

Angel looked up at the screen, and grainy as it was, especially from ten feet away, she recognized Jack Wilder. She looked around but Chang had disappeared. Then she saw him a couple of aisles over. She picked up a box of donuts and some bags of chips and headed toward him.

"Let's get out of here, that's Jack Wilder on the video. They were here."

Chang seemed unperturbed, his hands full. She looked down. He held black t-shirts and two ball caps, along with a pair of large white-framed sunglasses.

"What the fuck?" she hissed.

He smiled serenely and nudged her towards the counter. "Camouflage."

They put their purchases on the counter, edging around the policemen.

"Hi," Angel smiled, glancing at all of them. "Sorry to disturb you all, but can we pay for these things? Sounds like you have a problem here, so we'll be just as quick as we can. Don't want to stand in the way of law and order."

"Of course," said one of the older cops, and they made room for them, the conversation temporarily halted. While the clerk rang up their purchases, Angel smiled again at the men beside her. Even though she'd been on the road for days, she knew the power she'd always held. They were curious, yes, but even more, they were fascinated, which was her goal, to deflect attention away from Chang.

"My goodness," she said, "we've got a long way to go until Seattle. I hope rain all the time isn't in my future." She pushed back her hair over her shoulder and opened her jacket a bit, pushing her chest out. "I sure wouldn't like that. Have any of you ever been there?"

While the clerk put their purchases in a bag, Chang took the warm cups in hand, listening to the policemen happily assuring her that Seattle was nice and didn't rain all the time, from what they'd heard, and not to worry at all, wishing them a safe trip. He was essentially invisible beside the dazzle that was Angel.

"Thank you so much, gentlemen," she sang out as they turned to leave. "I hope everything turns out all right here, there's so many criminals out there. We law-abiding citizens are counting on you to keep us all safe."

"Thank you, ma'am," they chorused. "You travel safe now." She knew Chang wasn't thrilled but she also knew it worked and they'd gotten away perfectly safe.

They got back in the car while the discussion inside carried on, with a couple of wistful glances as their car pulled away. Angel turned out onto the highway, going north.

"Jesus God. Could we get luckier? They were here yesterday," she said, gripping Chang's arm in one hand while steering with the other." She picked up the coffee cup and took a sip. It wasn't bad, considering the source. Then again, at this point she'd drink damn near anything even resembling coffee, she was so jacked up to be on the right trail. She shoved two of the small powdered donuts into her mouth.

Chang smiled, calmly sipping his tea. "I believe we need to pay a visit to the Ashley Forest place before the police do. I don't know what happened to Ronny, but I have a feeling our friends just might."

Angel looked over at him appraisingly. "How did you know not to stop in Salt Lake? Or, to keep going north?"

Chang shrugged, his eyes resting on her. "As I said before, just a feeling. There is no place interesting to go from there that doesn't lead to a major city, Angel. I think our friends Jack and Grace know to stay away from them, some sort of animal instinct perhaps. They are headed to the wilderness, or at least as close as they can get to it."

"Go on. Why?"

"Because they are frightened, Angel. They are seeking a

haven, like wounded animals, knowing they may be followed. They don't know this for certain, of course, but they somehow sense it. They may have seen the news reports or heard from their musician friends about poor Barry."

"Yes, I see that." Angel's head was clearing, between the coffee and stale donuts. "I'm not certain I wouldn't do the same, you know?"

Chang gazed at her. "We are doing the same. It would not have been my first choice, but by following their feckless trail, perhaps we are staying away from anyone who might pursue us as well."

"You mean Luis?"

"Of course I mean Luis," Chang said, somewhat impatiently for him, Angel noticed. "You must realize by now he will know that we are not among the dead. He pays off many in the police in America. So it is not just his informants and employees that have eyes out for us. There are many in law enforcement on his payroll. I am sure he wants to find us and punish us. He is a bad man, but not a stupid one, Angel."

A shiver ran down her spine, in concert with the rain on the glass in front of her. She knew that, of course, but she'd been so consumed with chasing the couple who'd stolen their money she hadn't been thinking about anything else, especially the real threat that could be behind them on the unconventional trail they'd been traveling.

The sign had a green pine tree and an arrow that said 'Ashley Forest Resort, one mile.' She slowed a little and turned into the next right, the sign now proclaiming that they had arrived, and parked the Escalade in front of the log cabin with the office sign over the door, incongruously in neon, jarring against the pastoral landscape and name.

"You want to go in, or shall I?" Angel said. Her coffee was still warm and she hoped he'd say yes.

Chang wasn't fooled in the least and turned up his suit jacket collar. "I'll be right back."

He was back in the car within five minutes, brushing the water from his hair, as fastidious as a cat shaking raindrops from its paws.

"They were here last night. They used the name Mr. and Mrs. Green, but it was them. They registered their car as a Ford pickup and nobody corrected it. I hope no one knows different because those cops back at the gas station seemed pretty interested. We don't need a contest." He used Kleenex to wipe his face and hands and picked up his cup of tea.

Angel shifted impatiently. "And?"

"Fifty dollars goes a long way. They left early, before the maids or maintenance people came on shift so no one saw them leave. Dead end. However, the television is replaying the local news.

"Apparently, the notorious Ronny we have heard of back in the minimart was found in a picnic area a few miles up the road, taped up like a New Year's goose. He drowned when the river rose this morning." He took a sip of tea, his dark eyes meeting hers. "His brother was quite distraught, according to the desk clerk, who was only too happy to talk about it."

"I am quite sure he was. I think good old Ronny made some bad choices on who to rob last night," Angel said. "Asshole brother was likely in on the scam. Jack Wilder may be a little more dangerous than we thought."

She started the car. "Our friends didn't strike me as homicidal maniacs, but they now have something of great value to protect. Then again, none of us starts out that way, do we, Chang?"

Chang didn't smile and his eyes were like black pools when he stared at her. "No, my Angel, we don't."

He drained his tea, put his head back on the headrest and closed his eyes.

She drove north, as fast as she dared with the rain. They weren't that far behind now. It was like following a vague promise that came in and out of focus but she felt they were headed in the right direction, the same sort of instinct Chang had felt. They'd been very lucky so far, she knew that well.

Maybe Chang was right. They were all just animals looking for a haven. For them, there was a big bad wolf on their trail just as surely as she and Chang were the wolves that would take down Jack and Grace. She was starting to feel like she knew them, almost like they were friends in some odd conjunction. In a way it was comforting and in another way, a way she didn't want to think about very long, it made her sad.

She'd made the mistake of listening to their CD on the car player while she drove. They were good, maybe great. He could play a guitar like a god, and then there was Grace. She had a voice as pure as a depthless well, an ethereal angel. Angel found herself going back and listening to them over and over. She smiled ruefully. How ironic she might be the one to silence those skills, when she valued them so highly.

She sighed and sipped more coffee. You never knew where life was going to take you. A week ago, she'd been in Luis's compound, resigned to her hated pampered life, knowing that as she aged, so did her value to him diminish with each passing year. Luis set great stock on value, and when he saw none, he rid himself of anything that he deemed worthless. He liked fresh and young, and she was no longer the fourteen-year-old he'd first taken to his bed.

Jack Wilder and Grace Whitney had value, at least to her. Unfortunately, they were also thieves who had stolen something she desperately needed. Their value was diminished because of that, just as hers was destined to be for Luis.

She wished she'd never listened to their music. It made things difficult, when she knew there was only one path she had to go down.

God, she wished it would quit raining. She wasn't a good driver and it never rained much near the compound in Sinaloa, the only roads she'd ever driven on. She wanted to go fast, faster than Jack and Grace could go. To catch up to them quickly and end this, but she knew that was foolish. They couldn't afford to make stupid mistakes.

18

———————

Mario Valenzuela had never learned to enjoy Las Vegas. Still, when the sun broke over the horizon and lit up his room in the Octavius suite at Caesar's Palace like a slice of heavenly light through the floor-to-ceiling windows, he lay back in bed and felt grateful. The town below may have been a draw and a haven to many that Mario considered the worst of humanity, but from up here it was glorious. He opened the sliding door to the balcony and gave thanks to God for the beautiful morning, taking deep breaths of the rarefied air from the top floor. Even though his profession required him to turn a blind eye to his personal beliefs, Mario was a deeply moral man, one often in conflict, even though he worked for Luis.

It was quiet in the three-bedroom suite. Clearly, Luis had not yet awakened and started issuing orders. Mario had quietly made sure of that the evening before when he'd ordered up a healthy supply of El Mayor tequila.

He'd been Luis's second in command for three years now since his predecessor's demise and followed his *jefe's* commands no matter how much he silently disagreed with them. There was only one way to survive and prosper in this business, and blind obedience was the first rule. The second was to be alert and wait for an opportunity to advance, as Mario knew well. This day, as every day, it was only the first rule that mattered. *Today,* he thought as he stepped back inside, *as every other day, was not likely to be the second.* Luis was determined to find Angel and Chang and punish them in ways that made even Mario's stomach churn as he'd listened to Luis's angry and drunken rants all the way to Las Vegas from Oklahoma City and through the long evening that followed.

They'd landed in Las Vegas because Luis liked Las Vegas, and because the few threads they were beginning to weave together had pointed west, so it was a good central command post. That Angel and Chang would be found Mario had little doubt. Even so, he would have no choice but to be at Luis's side for what was to come, stomach or no.

He headed to the well-appointed bathroom. The shower was delightful, six heads directing water to his body, as he liberally poured the fragrant herbal soap on his hands and head and let the water wash it away along with his frustration, thankful that Luis only liked to stay in the best places. He stepped out, toweling off, and looked at himself in the mirror. Dark eyes stared back from a chiseled face, his curly hair falling forward, and his body pleased him as well, the muscles a strong vee towards his slim waist. He smiled at his reflection, pleased with what he saw. *A little Benicio del Toro today,* he thought, *with a touch of Banderas.* He laughed at his own comparisons, but there it was. There was no need to shave, it gave him a touch of grit that he liked. He put on his usual black suit with a white shirt, and as always, the bolo tie with its large oval turquoise set in silver that Evangelina had given him on their first Christmas together.

As he was tying his shoes, he heard Luis bellowing through the door.

"What the fuck, *cabrones?* A man needs his coffee."

What the fuck indeed. Mario sighed and stood up. He wasn't supposed to be a *maldito* housekeeper along with everything else he had to do to keep Luis happy. Tomas and Jose should've handled it. Too bad they hadn't had brains enough to order room service before the man woke up. Christ, he wished he was back home having breakfast with Evangelina and the children but it wouldn't be long now.

Once called, the room service carts rolled in with great efficiency, the silver domes glittering in the morning sun, the servers adeptly throwing tablecloths over the tables and placing the table settings for four. They poured the juice and coffee and waited for a minute to ensure all was to their liking. Mario stuffed bills into their hands and shooed them out the door. They didn't need to take any wrath from Luis, who always found something not to his liking.

Luis emerged from his room, tying his bathrobe belt. "Ah, I see it is time for breakfast. I would like some coffee first." He poured a cup from the silver pot on the table, glaring at Tomas and Jose. "Finally."

He sipped the coffee, staring alternately at the view outside and at the three men who stood waiting in the room.

"If we are still here tomorrow, I want coffee delivered first, *comprende?* Then, the food. This is the way civilized people arrange things. You do not wake up and stuff food in your mouths, but wake up slowly with the coffee, then see how your body agrees with the day."

He finished his coffee and poured another, the steam rising from his cup. "Sit."

They all did and after Luis raised the lid on his plate, only then did they venture to do the same.

No one was disappointed. Perfect *huevos rancheros*, topped with *pico de gallo* and garnished with sliced avocados awaited them. Platters of sliced strawberries, kiwis, mangoes, tangerines and bananas were nearby, along with brioche toasts and English muffins, slathered in butter with little pots of several kinds of jam available on others. The waiters had poured fresh squeezed orange and papaya juice into the crystal goblets on the table before they'd departed.

Luis surveyed the repast and picked up his fork. "It will do. Much better than yesterday."

Mario ate sparingly as was his usual, watching Luis. The man ate like the peasant he was, scraping the last bit of egg yolk from his plate with a brioche, wiping it clean. He'd seen it many times and had never gotten used to it. After breakfast, Luis sat back in his chair and surveyed the three men in front of him.

"Soon we will know where they are. Soon we will have them in our hands. Soon they will know what it is to fuck with me. And you," he gestured towards them, "will be the men who will bring their retribution down on their heads, while I shall personally direct you."

He lurched away from the table, tugging on his bathrobe belt, and headed back towards his bedroom, waving away any followers, not that anyone had offered assistance. "Monitor the phones and channels."

No one gave a sigh of relief, at least the two idiots were too smart for that, Mario noticed. Tomas speared a slice of mango and chewed it thoughtfully, while Jose poured the last of the coffee and stared out the window. Mario stood up and surveyed the Las Vegas skyline as it melted into the desert that surrounded it. It was going to be a long day. While Luis's network of distributors and informants covered the country like an invisible poisonous spiderweb, it was no guarantee they would spot Angel or Chang soon. On the other hand, those two were pretty memorable, unless they'd gotten smart enough to disguise themselves well, or taken paths away from anywhere Luis's people could possibly spot them. That, given America's healthy appetite for their wares, was pretty much nowhere. It was simply a matter of time before they surfaced somewhere inquisitive eyes would find them. Keeping Luis amused and relatively happy in the meantime was going to be a job no one would want, but Mario knew that was precisely his task.

That said, once they were found, the nightmare would begin and that was a chore that would also fall to him while Luis supervised, a chore no sane man would ever want.

19

———

They crossed the border into Idaho, not a place Grace figured she'd ever see. At least the rain had stopped as that hadn't helped to lighten her black mood. She glanced over at Jack, serenely driving the Honda along at a steady 70 mph and turning onto interstate 84, occasionally singing along to a Mary Gauthier CD. Since they'd dumped Ronny at the rest stop, he hadn't had much to say and she hadn't wanted to talk about their predicament for a while anyway. But she knew they had to. Jack hadn't been the same the last day or two, which she took full responsibility for, but still, she didn't like him clamming up on her, like he was going to solve their problem and take care of it all by himself. They didn't work that way and never had. They were a team, never more important than now.

"Jack."

"Yeah," he said, glancing over at her.

"Where the hell are we going?"

"Away, darlin', as away as we can get." He smiled and looked back at the road. "Trust me."

He'd been on one of the burner phones, talking earnestly to

someone three times that she knew of, once this morning and twice on the road when they'd stopped for gas, some of the conversations long, and hadn't shared any of that with her. She had always trusted him, but she was finding it increasingly hard to do so. He wasn't the same gentle Jack she thought she knew, the man who looked out for kids on the road, or took an interest in stray dogs, or gave all his spare change to the home-less guys they'd run into outside the Orchid Lounge. While he'd still probably do those things, because that was Jack, he was different somehow. He was harder now, like somebody who'd run you down if you stood in his way, and she wasn't quite sure how to deal with it.

He turned off at the Twin Falls exit and cruised into the small town. They went down the main drag and Jack turned and went a block behind, parking in an empty lot beyond the main street stores and turning off the car. He sat back and looked at her.

"So?" Grace said, trying not to sound as irritated as she was.

Jack reached over and pulled her gently towards him, kissing her. "So, Grace. Here's the thing."

She jerked back. "What thing is that? Godamnit Jack, I'm feeling like I'm wandering in some dark haze here. What the hell is going on? Who've you been talking to?"

He managed to look contrite. "Barnett. I told him everything."

At the shocked look on her face, he stopped. He took off his seat belt and turned to her. "He's cool. We can trust him, you know that. Listen to me, Grace. We have to find a way to stash or hide this money, at least most of it. You know that as well as I do. I'm not ashamed to admit we're in way over our heads. We needed some advice. So, I called Barnett."

He sighed. "He's an old hand at this game. He's been hiding money for years and he told me what to do. He says there's this thing called 'monero', it's a cryptocurrency, and he set me up with an account, I don't know, they call it a wallet or something. Anyway, you give them cash and they convert it to digital currency that only you can access. You can go to these exchange guys, they're all over the place, like in pawn shops and money exchanges and they just do it. Yeah, they take a fee but it's worth it. We don't have to be dragging all this cash around. After Ronny, I'm just as paranoid about getting robbed as I am about anybody that's following us. This deal Barnett told me about is totally secret and secure."

Grace stared at him, her mind whirling. She'd never heard of digital or cryptocurrency, aside from an occasional Bitcoin thing on the news. She knew the computer and internet but most Tech had never been her thing.

"And this is good how?"

Jack stared at her. "Are you kidding me? We're running around with a backpack full of what has to be illegal cash through these redneck counties and if we even get stopped for a tail light out and they get a whim to search the car, not to mention who might be after us looking for the money, we're fucked. You think some sheriff like Bull Hogg or whoever wouldn't take the money and we'd just be two fugitives who happened to get shot escaping?"

He ran his hands through his hair. "Christ, Grace, think about it. It's the best way. This is an untraceable network, there's no trail, nothing. Not even a safe deposit box which you have to be around to access, or some train or bus station locker, which is stupid. We've both seen too many movies for that one. It's the new age, babe. And, I trust my dad. He's been doing this for years and he knows his shit, you know?"

Grace was silent. He wasn't wrong, not about any of it. While she didn't know anything about cryptocurrency, she did know his dad. If Barnett was advising him, Jack had a trust-worthy mentor. That he had been in the illicit whiskey and drug business, she didn't care about in the least. Maybe he still was, for all she knew. Barnett was a good man and he would take care of his son as well as her, because he loved them, that she did know.

Jack took her hand, those blue eyes boring into hers. "Barnett says to tell you he loves you and that he'll do anything he can to help us. I'm sorry I've been so squirrelly the last day or so, and I didn't talk to you about this." He looked down. "I don't know, Grace, there was a lot of shit going on, with the money and being on the run, and then that idiot Ronny. I was starting to lose it, maybe some delayed PTSD shit.

"I felt like we needed some help, so I called my dad when you were asleep because I didn't know where to turn to get us out of this mess. I didn't want you to think I blamed you or anything like that. Because I don't. After I thought about it for about five seconds, I knew I'd have done the same damn thing you did in that diner bathroom that night."

He stopped talking and took a deep breath. "In fact, this could be the best thing that ever happened to us. We can use this money in a smart way like nobody else could. We deserve it, Grace." He grabbed her shoulders. "Nobody makes music like we do, we just need a chance to prove it and make them hear us. Could be this is our best shot. These people have no idea where we are, far as I know. So we just lie low for a little while and then it's all good."

Grace wasn't so sure about that, but pushed her doubts down.

"I know, babe, I do. I wish you had shared this with me, but I get it. At least you have now, so let's forge on." She didn't completely get it but at this point she truly didn't care. His idea sounded good, from what little she knew and it might be the best way forward. That Jack had chinks in the easy-going insouciant armor he always displayed gave her pause, though. The money had been a curse from the minute she'd picked it up so Jack's way made some kind of sense. All she wanted was for him to be the man she loved and could trust. At the same time, she knew neither of them was ever going to be same even after they got out of this situation.

"So what the hell did we stop here in beautiful Twin Falls, Idaho for, Jack?"

It didn't take long to find out.

Jack stuffed $100,000 of the cash into his canvas mic bag and they walked back a block to the main street of Twin Falls, Idaho. They had a serene lunch in a café, and then Jack walked across the street to a pawnshop she hadn't even noticed but obviously was the reason they were even here. It advertised "gold exchange" as well as "guns, guitars and gizmos". Grace ordered cherry pie and another coffee and watched him from the window. He'd said it wouldn't take long, and before she'd finished the pie, he slid back into the booth. He grinned and looked better than he had when they'd gotten to Twin Falls.

"Done deal. Barnett was right. Can't unload too much at one place, though, so on to Boise, where's there's more."

She offered him her fork and he finished the last two bites of pie and she her coffee, picking up the bill the waitress had left on the table. She turned the bill face up and put down enough cash to cover the bill and tip. "Did this guy give you a receipt, or what? How do we access this money when we want it?"

"That's the beauty of it," Jack said. "It's all digital. I have this wallet thing on my phone, and I emailed the info to both of us. That's all we need. If you're worried, though, he even printed out a paper receipt." He handed it to her and she stuffed it into her bag.

It sounded good, maybe too good but then Grace didn't know squat about any of it. She was no techie and while she'd heard about cryptocurrency, she'd have to take his word for all of it, but she'd take Jack's word over anyone's. The whole thing did make sense and Jack seemed nearly back to his old self, like some weight had been lifted from him. He grinned at her as he opened the café door.

"I've got another idea, which I know you aren't going to like," Jack said. He pointed across the street to a beauty salon. "Since it's right here, we need to change up our look. What do you say, Grace? We're too memorable, pretty as we are and all," he laughed, "and our pics are up on the internet. Barry likely told them everything they wanted to know, so we'd be stupid not to change it up."

He was right. She liked this idea even less, but after their transformation at the Twin Falls Cut 'n Curl, she doubted anyone they knew would recognize them at first glance, or maybe even a third. Grace sported a pixie cut in a lovely shade of auburn, and Jack looked like Brad Pitt with a Marine buzz-cut. She figured all the long hair they'd both left behind would fill up the salon's trash cans for the week. They paid the bill and stepped out onto the sidewalk and looked each other.

"Good thing I love you, because with that haircut I'd have never looked at you once, let alone twice." Grace made a face. It wasn't true, but she couldn't resist, thinking about her hair on the floor of that beauty shop.

Jack laughed, putting his arm around her waist. "Maybe not, but with that red hair, you're still gorgeous as ever and I'd have followed you anywhere, sweet stuff."

"Lucky me," Grace said and tried to trip him but he was too fast for her, sidestepping quickly.

They walked back to the car. Jack handed her the keys. "I'm beat, darlin'."

She started the car. "Next stop, Boise?"

"Yep. We got some business to transact there. Might take a day or two, and then, we are headed up country."

She pulled out onto the road. "As in?"

Jack leaned back against the headrest. "Half of Idaho is wilderness, and I know a guy we met on tour a couple of years back. He runs hunters and backpackers into the River of No Return wilderness area, sometimes by plane." He smiled. "I'm thinking that's a pretty good place to hide out. It's warming up and we can get into the backcountry soon. Nobody can find us there. For now, I bet he knows someplace in between we can hole up even if it's too snowed in up there yet."

A cabin in the middle of nowhere actually sounded pretty good for a while, no people to be worried about. She turned onto Interstate 84, and automatically went to push her hair away when she turned her head to check on the oncoming traffic. Her fingers brushed the edges of her weirdly short hair which she hadn't had since third grade. Everything was different now and maybe the hair was a good reminder they weren't in Kansas anymore.

Even wilderness was all well and good but she sure as shit didn't want to spend her life serenading elk and the random grizzly. God knew how long they'd have to lie low and having a lot of money wouldn't do them much to advance their careers in the literal middle of nowhere, even if it wouldn't be forever. At least she hoped so.

Then again, she couldn't help but wonder to what lengths somebody missing nearly a million dollars would go. It might not even mean that much to them, she thought, it might just be the principle of the thing. She'd seen that TV show where Escobar buried money all over Mexico because there was so much cash he couldn't spend it or give it away fast enough. You never could tell about people and they had no idea whose money this even was. Maybe no matter how deep into the woods you hid, there were people who'd sniff you out, track you like wolves and discover you no matter where you hid. After how they'd left that poor bastard back in Utah, it was getting harder and harder for her to figure out exactly who the wolves were anymore.

20

Angel stopped the car beside the gas pumps in the Texaco station off the Twin Falls first exit. It was the most convenient and noticeable with a huge neon sign, and perhaps their quarry had thought so as well. She went inside and handed the clerk $50 for pump #2 which Chang picked up at her nod. She wandered through to the drink section and chose a Coke and a canned iced tea for Chang, which he'd probably detest, but there weren't many options. That man would have to start adapting until they got to a more civilized area. In Chang's mind, that might be a lot of places but certainly wasn't this one.

She went back to the cash register and smiled at the clerk, this time an older man rather than the usual teenage boy. She put the drinks down, along with two candy bars and a bag of trail mix.

"Hey. How's it going?"

He smiled back. "Pretty good. Where you headed?"

She shrugged. "The ocean, so Seattle, I guess." It had worked last time.

He laughed. "Honey, you want ocean, just keep going to Portland and beyond. When you see water, stop."

She laughed too. "I guess that would work, but I have some friends going to Seattle with us so I guess it'll take a little longer." She pulled out some money from her pocket. "Maybe they stopped here not long ago. We got separated a day ago and I hope we're on the right track. A really good-looking guy and a girl, both with long hair? Seen anyone like that?"

"Can't say I have," he said, scratching the stubble on his chin. "It's been pretty slow this week and I can tell you there ain't been anybody stopping by I'd call good-looking except maybe Cal Norton and his girlfriend when they're not high on meth, but they only live a couple of miles from here. They don't look as good as they used to, but that stuff's no damn good for nobody. Don't think they're going to Seattle anytime soon, since they can hardly pay the rent on that trailer of theirs." He laughed. "Not exactly in your league."

Angel chuckled. "Oh, well. Thought I'd ask." She held out her hand for the change and he dropped the coins into her hand. "Thanks, appreciate it."

"Anytime. Drive safe, now."

She climbed back into the driver's seat. Chang was already in the car. She handed him the bag. "I got you iced tea, all they had." She leaned back in the seat for a few seconds and finally realized how bone tired she was. They hadn't stopped anywhere to sleep since this chase had begun, except for naps in the car.

"He hasn't seen them. We're going to have to ask around the town now. But, I tell you, Chang, I need some sleep." She glanced over at him. The dark circles under his eyes matched hers. "So do you. And a shower. I smell like one of Luis's yard goats."

Chang smiled and lifted his lapel, taking a sniff. "Agreed. I doubt there'll be a Hilton here, but I think you're correct, Angel.

It is also true, according to my research, that cognitive abilities begin to slip incrementally in relation to how little sleep humans have had."

He opened the iced tea bottle and took a sip. "There was a study done at MIT by Professor Theodore Lowenstein in 2016, that demonstrated that brain function—"

Angel held up her hand. "I get it, Chang. We're getting a room. Maybe even some new underwear."

"Wait." He got out of the car and went inside. Angel fumed, tapping her fingers on the steering wheel. Now he figured out he had to pee? Within five minutes he was back, a plastic bag in his hand.

"What's in there?"

"Phones," he said. "I've not been thinking as I should've been. Give me yours."

She nodded towards her bag on the floor and he fished it out, and along with his own, took out both the batteries. He stepped out of the car and crushed both the phones beneath his foot and threw them into the trash can beside the gas pumps.

"We should've done that before now, but it is always best not to think back, but only forward. I believe some sleep is the restoration we need to avoid making any more mistakes."

She drove out of the gas station and got back on the freeway. The next exit had a Best Western sign underneath it and she hit the turn signal. "New things all around. I bet they even have a Walmart here and you can get some new undies. I'll pick them out. You want football logos or hearts?"

Chang groaned and downed half his iced tea while Angel giggled. Lack of sleep was making her silly. If she'd ever known a man who freeballed it was Chang. Besides, the chances of finding Versace or la Perla underwear in Twin Falls, Idaho for either of them were worse odds than Chang's needle in a haystack.

DAWN LIGHT FERRETED out a crack in the thick drapes of the Twin Falls Best Western's front window into Room 118 and straight into Angel's eyes, her body curled up into the shape of a conch shell in one of the queen beds. In the other, Chang blissfully snored on as though he didn't have a care in the world. She turned over and stretched out her arms. The digital clock on the nightstand between the beds read 6:00 AM. *Dios mio*, they'd slept like the dead, maybe twelve hours. They'd been running on nothing but quick naps and adrenaline for days, so it wasn't surprising, after all. They'd checked in late afternoon and after a shower they'd fallen into the beds as though they were on the clouds of heaven and were both asleep within minutes, too exhausted to worry about food or even security.

Since they were both alive and unharmed, Angel figured Luis hadn't pinpointed a location yet, but they needed to be more vigilant. Or, perhaps they'd be met with a hail of bullets when they went to the motel breakfast buffet. At least they'd be clean when they were laid out in the morgue, but she was pretty sure they were still undetected, tucked away in this backwater ordinary place.

She glanced over at Chang. He slept on his back, still as a perfect Chinese sculpture, his beautiful face tranquil, eyes still closed. She sat down gently on his bed, wrapped in the towel she'd left beside the bed the day before.

"Chang," she whispered.

His arm went around her neck and buried her face in the mattress before she could even blink. The pressure was excruciating and she screamed soundlessly into the sheets, kaleidoscopic colors exploding behind her eyes, her fist pounding feebly into the arm that held her down. Just before she thought she was going to die, the pressure eased and she gasped a deep lungful of air.

"Angel, I am so sorry." Chang sat up and cradled her into the arm that seconds before had nearly ended her life. "Please forgive me. I have not awakened in a room with another person in some years, only one in which someone had come to kill me. Forgive my reflex actions. Please try to understand I would never hurt you."

Her breath was coming in short bursts and she could feel her heartbeat drumming fast in her chest. She made a conscious effort to slow her breathing as he stroked her back.

He felt warm and comforting, this strange and deadly man, even though he'd just tried to kill her. Many times she had thought Luis was capable of just that, but she'd been careful enough to never anger him. This was something entirely different. As her panic eased, she realized they were skin to skin, her breasts crushed against his chest and she pulled awkwardly away, her eyes meeting his.

"I'm sorry, I should've known better, Chang, I—" his lips gently touched her mouth, the next words unsaid. *This is such a bad idea*, Angel thought, and then for the first time in her life, she discovered what it was to make love to someone.

For that was unexpectantly what it was, perhaps for both of them.

Afterwards, they lay side by side, reluctant to move away from the comfort of closeness and openness, touching each other in gentle caresses as though to make sure they were each still there.

"I have watched you for so long," Chang said. "Wanting to kill that pig for the way he treated you. Wanting to take you away to a high mountaintop in the Wiehan hills of China where we could be together and feed each other teacakes and dumplings and drink plum wine and make love all day."

She reached over and kissed his neck, trailing her fingertips down his chest. "That sounds wonderful. And for a long time now I have watched you," she said. "So correct, so perfect. I would fantasize about you and breaking through that impenetrable façade, to take me away from what was happening every time Luis touched me. I was ashamed and told myself you would never want me after what Luis has made me."

He pulled her into his arms. "You are perfect to me, Angel, and I know Luis was never a lover but only a master."

They missed the Best Western breakfast buffet.

THE TWIN FALLS CAFÉ served breakfast all day, but Angel ordered a sandwich anyway, while Chang was content with his usual poached eggs, fruit and tea.

When the waitress brought their check, Angel smiled. "That was a great sandwich, thanks." She left a twenty-dollar tip and the waitress beamed. "Say, we're traveling with my sister and her husband and they got way ahead of us back in that storm in Utah. Have you by any chance seen a young couple, very attractive, both with long hair, maybe were in yesterday?"

"You know, there was a real cute couple in here for lunch yesterday, don't think they were from around here." She shrugged. "Could've been them. But I don't think they've got long hair anymore, according to Trudi from the Cut 'n Curl."

"What do you mean?"

"After lunch, they went across the street to the beauty salon," she chuckled and nodded towards the window. "My sister works over there. They were both so cute. Got new hairdos from what I heard. She thought they were nuts, but they seemed happy as larks when they left. The customer is always right, eh?"

They stood on the sidewalk outside the cafe and looked across the street. The Cut 'n Curl stood between a hardware store and a pawn shop with a couple of guitars in the window. Chang looked at the establishments with a practiced eye.

"You take the salon, I'll take the pawn shop," Chang said.

"Why the pawn shop?"

He smiled grimly. "I think it is possible our friends might be smarter than we thought. Meet you back at the car."

Angel got back to the car first and slid into the driver's seat, watching as Chang made his way across the street. She started the engine.

"Where to?"

"Boise. Get on the 84 west." He buckled his seat belt.

"If you're wondering what I found out, yes, it was them. They not only cut their hair, both of them, but she's a redhead now as well."

Chang smiled. "Clever. I am not surprised. That's not all they did. The pawn shop man was most accommodating after $100. Jack exchanged a lot of money yesterday, and got the addresses for some places in Boise to do more. They are quite clever, our little musicians, much more so than we thought. Music is not all they know. Perhaps there is even more that we don't know about them yet."

Ten miles out of Twin Falls, Angel glanced over at Chang, who seemed lost in thought, staring out the windshield.

"You know," he said, turning his head and meeting her gaze, "I've been thinking. We've lost some money, yes, but we've gained something infinitely more valuable, Angel. Perhaps we should consider letting our friends go on their way. We may want to concentrate our efforts on eluding Luis's spiderweb rather than finding these two."

She turned her eyes back to the road. "Yes, *mi amor*. This is true. I have been thinking along those lines myself but somehow I just cannot let them walk away from this. We've come too far, taken too much trouble, to toss away not only the money but all our efforts."

Chang was silent but Angel knew he wasn't pleased. As the miles passed, she felt more and more worried, trying to focus on the road ahead instead of her own rising doubts. She had been vacillating on the wisdom of chasing their quarry, not to mention their eventual fate, just as Chang was now. She and Chang had indeed found something much more valuable than money and she felt a warmth inside that she'd never known before. They were following a path that would lead to nothing that would enhance that feeling, but only disturb it.

That they would find Jack and Grace was not what concerned her. Of course they would. What they would have to do when they did was another question entirely. That was the part she didn't want to think about.

And then, of course, there was Luis.

There was always Luis.

21

The small city nestled in the woods and mountains, bisected by the fast-moving green river, was not what Grace had expected, after Twin Falls, Utah, and Colorado. Boise was a little gem out of place in one way, but gracing the tradition of the country it had its roots in. It reminded Grace of what she'd seen on TV about cities back East, not that she'd ever been to any. It had a pioneer flavor, true, but looked as though it had been built and laid out more thoughtfully than the rambling sprawl that was the rest of the west, at least what she'd seen of it so far. In the middle of the downtown area, Idaho's white Capitol building rose up like a sentinel keeping vigil over the buildings and streets of the city.

She drove toward it down the aptly-named Capitol Boulevard, passing stores and restaurants, among them bookshops and music stores, another rarity compared to most of the towns they'd been through, with old stone buildings housing banks and businesses. The architecture looked as though it had been there since the settlement began, along with stately old Victorian houses on the last street before the river. Along here, among the spring flowering lawns and gardens, she pulled over and parked, rolling down the window and enjoying the verdant spring flowers that perfumed the air.

She knew the end of the soothing hum of the car's engine and steady movement would eventually rouse Jack. For now, she leaned back against the headrest and tried to clear her mind, running her hand over the shaggy short hair on her head with a small sigh of regret. On the other hand, she supposed it was smart, a small price to pay for not being dead.

The last few days had been a nightmare, if not hag-ridden, certainly worthy of a good James Patterson thriller. She only hoped she and Jack would get as lucky as some of Patterson's characters managed to. To think just last week, having enough money saved up to record and promote their first album was the dreamlike pinnacle they'd aspired to. Be careful what you wish for, Grace, she told herself. Having too much money was their problem now, and how to survive long enough to spend it were the first and last things on an extremely short list.

Jack coughed, sitting up in the seat and pulling off his seat belt. He stared out the windows blearily. "Where are we?"

"Boise. Looks like a nice town."

Jack nodded. "Yeah, it is. Only been here once but it's a cool place. Little off the mainstream, but for us right now, that's good."

Grace fought off the urge to tell him from little what she'd seen, Boise, off the mainstream or not, looked pretty damn good. It wasn't Nashville, but in a way, it reminded her of it, especially the Capitol, but she and Jack were adaptable and could set up shop anywhere. Anywhere safe was the condition at the moment, but for now, Boise wasn't that place no matter how nice it looked, nor was any city at all, or a place where people congregated. People who could identify them, haircuts or not.

"So where are we going?"

Jack rummaged around in his pocket and pulled out his

notebook, the one he always kept close, to jot down ideas, pieces of music, and pretty much anything else that flitted through his active mind.

"Guy in Twin Falls told me about a couple of places here. OK, on Idaho Street there's a gem store and pawnshop where they do crypto transfers." He looked over at her. "I think it's smart to offload more of this cash, Grace."

He was likely right. She didn't care as much as she had from the first thrill of looking at all that money. Right now she wished it would just go away. She shrugged and started the car. "Just tell me where to go, Jack."

Half an hour later, he came out of store on Idaho Street, waving another receipt at her when he got into the car. "Looking good, babe. Tuck this away. We can do some more tomorrow."

"Now what?" Dusk was falling and Grace was tired and irritated. "Cabin in the woods, Davey Crockett?"

Jack sighed. "Funny, Grace." He leaned over and kissed her cheek. "Not tonight. There's this place a guy told me about back in the day. Moon's Café and sporting goods. All the outfitters go there for breakfast. That's where we'll hook up with somebody to take us up there. But, that'll have to wait until morning since they're closed. I haven't seen any sign of anyone following us or doing anything suspicious, so I think we're safe for now. Let's find a hotel and call it, what do you say?"

Luckily, Boise was not New York. Two people dragging backpacks around here was not an unusual occurrence, even in what purported to be the "best" hotel in town, and the parking garage was free and security monitored for guests only. Paying with cash rather than a credit card took a hefty deposit, but the clerk was happy to do so, especially with an extra $100 for his kindness. Room service was an assured given, with a restaurant on the premises.

Grace stood in the shower, washing the lavender-scented

Crabtree & Evelyn shampoo and conditioner out of her short hair, a little red dye disappearing down the drain, while Jack waited for the room service waiter with their steaks. *If we die tomorrow*, Grace thought, *at least we'll die well-fed.* She had no idea who was on their trail, but she knew, just as Jack did, that someone was. While there hadn't been any sign at all except for the brief TV transmissions of occurrences now far behind them of things happening that might be related or might not, depending upon your level of paranoia, there was that phone text. Besides that, it didn't mean their pursuers had given up, only that they were invisible now, which in a way was even scarier. They couldn't afford to let their guard down for a second because anybody that was looking for that kind of money wouldn't be kind to them.

Still, here they were, sitting ducks. Grace turned the water off and stepped out of the glass shower, pulling on the plush terry bathrobe. They'd always been sitting ducks, but even ducks got hungry and the smell of grilled steak enticed her out of the bathroom. She sank into a chair at the table where Jack sat waiting in front of two silver domes. It was almost as though the last few nightmare days were far behind them. He poured red wine into two glasses and handed her one.

"Hey princess."

"Hey yourself." Candlelight was kind to his new boot camp haircut and likely to her pixie cut as well.

"Dinner looks great. Man, I could get used to this."

"You might as well, since I'm a princess now, I command it."

"To Wilder and Grace." He lifted his glass and she clinked hers on it.

"I was thinking Grace and Wilder." She wasn't really but she couldn't resist, especially after the cryptocurrency thing.

Jack raised an eyebrow and took a sip of the wine. "Yeah, I can see that."

Dinner was great.

THE SMELL OF BACON, the sweet tang of maple syrup with pancakes and coffee was thick in the air, but pleasantly so, as they entered the cafe and looked around. The restaurant area was crowded with people, all talking and eating at a record pace at a record volume.

Moon's was a throwback to the 1950s, sporting a formica-topped lunch counter, well-worn red leather booths, and tables, with a black and white tile floor, all housed within a sporting goods store, but not just any commonplace sporting goods store. At Moon's, you could buy black powder and horns to keep it in, animal traps, hand-tied designer trout flies, elaborate creels and fishing rods and an array of top-of-the-line backwoods gear Grace had never imagined existed, along with the requisite guns of all types, some even that looked like 1800s replicas, and compound and recurve bows.

There was even a counter with a taxidermist ready to stuff your hapless prey as a trophy for your pride and posterity for years to come, the lives of the huge salmon, antlered deer, elk, moose and snarling bears on display proved it. Grace didn't want to look at them.

They sat down at two empty stools at the counter, broken up every two feet or so with a most efficient holder that housed napkins, salt and pepper shakers, sugar, strawberry jam, ketchup and carafes of cream and maple syrup. Men and some women, dressed in everything from three-piece suits with briefcases at their sides, likely heading to the Capitol building right across the street, to those in buckskins, Carhartt jackets, jeans and boots, likely heading to the woods. All were happily eating with great enjoyment and many were ordering the special, so Grace and Jack did too.

This was truly a restaurant of the people, by the people, and for the people. She felt right at home, except for the taxidermy, which there was no point in mentioning because she knew Jack didn't care. Jack liked the place too, his shoulders relaxing as though he knew it somehow fit them, even the newcomers they were.

The fast-footed waitress filled their coffee mugs and flitted away to the other end of the long counter. Grace and Jack silently exchanged glances and sipped their coffee while listening to the flow of conversation around them. It was only 7 AM, but the sign on the door said Moon's opened at 5:30.

"Hope we haven't missed Charlie," Jack said. "Here I thought we were up too early."

Before Grace had taken five sips of coffee, the waitress briskly placed two huge platters of food in front of them, along with wrapped silverware, and hustled away again to the pass-through from the kitchen to grab more orders.

"Holy cow," Grace said, staring at the food in front of her. "Even lumberjacks couldn't eat this much."

Three eggs, bacon, hashbrowns, sourdough toast and a slab of something covered in cream gravy covered every inch of the plate. Grace stuck her fork into the gravy-covered mass.

"What the hell is this?" She whispered to Jack. "Doesn't look special to me."

Jack grinned. "Chicken-fried steak, I think. I've seen billboards about it since we passed the state line. Local favorite, served in all the best diners."

Grace sawed off a bite, chewing slowly. "Wow, that's really good."

They applied themselves to the task of demolishing the breakfast special, which proved to be easier than they'd thought, but they tried to take their time, unlike most of the other patrons. Still, even as slowly as they tried to eat, every seat that emptied was quickly filled by new arrivals. Jack glanced at each one, looking for his friend, but by the time the waitress had refilled their coffee three times, he was looking anxious. He had reason to be because it was clear Moon's didn't tolerate tourist dawdlers, and disdain was likely to be followed swiftly by a "please leave and give your seats to other customers" request.

"You have a number for this guy?"

"No," Jack said. "Met him at a show I did here back in the day, he was a pal of Dave Murray's from the Ramblers. We talked a while about Idaho's backcountry and stuff like that. All I know is he mentioned this place where he said everybody hangs out at breakfast in the mornings."

Grace lifted an eyebrow and stared at him.

"I know, I know, it's kind of a long shot," Jack said wryly, "but I figured it was a place to start, rather than just wandering through the countryside. We could use some luck."

"It's okay." She was pacified by the chicken-fried steak and couldn't work up her usual sarcasm.

The waitress came by, slapped down a check and snatched up their empty plates. "More coffee, guys?"

"Please," Grace said but she could tell the waitress wasn't too pleased about it. Fast turnover was the name of the game at Moon's. Time was running out.

She was starting to worry about caffeine overdose but took another sip of coffee just as Jack stood up, waving at someone who had just entered. "Hey Charlie!"

The big bearded man in the flannel jacket looked confused as he ambled over to Jack. "Do I know you, man?"

"It's Jack, Jack Wilder, Dave Murray's friend," Jack said. "We met one night a couple of years ago when the Ramblers played at the Rooster Tavern."

Charlie looked blank and Grace felt worried. Then he broke into a smile. "Oh yeah, the guitar player guy. Man, what the hell happened to your hair?"

Jack laughed. "Long story, but my girl here wanted me to try something new."

Grace could've kicked him but she smiled. "A slight miscalculation, I agree. Hi there, Charlie, I'm Grace."

"Pleasure," Charlie smiled, and she could tell he meant it. They always did, pixie cut or not.

"Let us buy you breakfast," Jack said. "We could use some advice."

CHARLIE WAS a godsend of advice and much more. Jack's initial idea of the River of No Return Wilderness Charlie shot down in seconds.

"It's still snowed in up there, man. If you're looking for peace, quiet, and somewhere not to be bothered, you can't get in there for another month at least. Since you guys need a place right now to make music with no company or distractions, I've got a better idea. There's this ski resort, Bogus Basin, just up the road, maybe twenty miles, and the season is pretty much over. I know a guy who has six ski cabins up there, really nice ones. They go empty in the summer, no skiers, no lake to draw the summer people, just some occasional hiker-type tourists from Seattle or Los Angeles and really, not many of those unless it's word of mouth. He'll give you a good deal because this is his slow time. It's still close enough you need anything, you can just tool down to Boise for supplies."

It sounded perfect, but it was going to take a day while Charlie got in touch with his guy, which they spent wandering around Boise, waiting to hear from him. It was a nice town, big enough but not too big, and Grace liked it. Another night at the hotel made them both nervous, but the car was out of sight, they looked completely different, and they'd seen and heard nothing that led them to think danger was close. For now, that had to be enough.

Charlie called very early the next morning, and Grace

threw on her clothes and hit the coffee shop while Jack packed their stuff. The only other person up and about was a dark-haired woman, another customer getting stuff for her husband or boyfriend, doing the same thing Grace was. Within ten minutes, much to her relief, they were on the road.

They met with Charlie's real estate friend the minute the office opened, got the keys, and stopped off at a supermarket on Bogus Basin Road where they stocked up on supplies and drove up the highway towards the ski resort. There were no signs, but they'd been warned to look for three large pine trees close together at the fifteen-mile point marker. It was just a turnoff that led to the promised log cabins, all empty with no cars in their driveways.

It was perfect, secluded cabins nestled in the woods. It hadn't hurt that Jack gave Charlie an extra $200 and that Charlie was soon heading out to guide some hikers on the Snake River that afternoon and wouldn't be back for two weeks, so no one could question him if they came looking and somehow discovered his existence. They didn't want any more casualties on their consciences. All Charlie knew was that they were looking for a quiet place to compose an album and he had no reason to suspect they were on the run from anyone. From what he said, he'd be long gone anyway and that made both of them feel a lot better. They didn't need another Barry on their consciences, even given that Charlie looked a lot more able to take care of himself.

When Jack parked the car beside number six, the furthest cabin down at the end of the gravel road, Grace opened the car door and took a deep breath of the fresh aromatic smell of pine trees, their new growth of pale green needles wafting in the early spring breeze.

"This could be heaven." She raised her arms over her head and took a deep breath. When she did it again, Jack smiled, shook his head and started unloading the car.

Before long, groceries put away, and bed made with the ample linens and fluffy comforter stored in the cabinets, along with a supply of thick white towels, Grace was starting to feel as though they'd landed in Wonderland, instead of just a place to hide out. Jack brought in some wood and lit a fire while she bustled around like a goodwife from some pioneer movie. She started giggling at the very thought, but all those Little House on the Prairie books she'd devoured as a kid kept surfacing no matter how she tried to tamp them down.

The log cabin was small, but nicely appointed, if you ignored the elk head mounted above the stone fireplace, which Grace managed to do, concentrating instead on the flames flickering over the oak logs below. The kitchen was small, but fitted with new stainless-steel appliances, even an Illy coffeemaker, and the whole décor was half big city skier, half mountain man plaid, from the couch she sprawled upon to the down quilt in the bedroom. Jack emerged from the kitchen, carrying a bottle of Cabernet and two glasses, the garlicky aroma of simmering marinara on the stove, one of the culinary delights he'd truly mastered.

"What do you think? Good place to hole up for a while?"

"I really love it," Grace said, "Charlie's a good man. Even if he thought we were bullshitting, and I'm pretty sure he did, if we can't write an album here in the deep dark hidden forest, we can't write it anywhere. More importantly, it feels like we're safe, and that's the best thing. You did good, Jack." She held up her glass.

Jack leaned over and kissed her, touching his glass to hers. "To us, to safety, and to luck, darlin'. So far, so good."

22

─────────

Angel stood at the window at looked at the small city below. They'd checked into the downtown hotel purported to be the best in Boise last night and had enjoyed room service and an evening together even better than their first one. Making love with Chang was like nothing Angel had ever known before. Many things had changed in a very short time, and Angel felt anticipation for a future she'd never dreamed she could have. That Chang was an integral part of that, as long as it lasted, was what made it truly special.

It was a beautiful clear day, the sun rising with possibility. She tightened the belt on her bathrobe and glanced over at the bed. Chang was still asleep, sprawled on his stomach like a leopard hanging on a tree branch, and just as beautiful and dangerous as one. She wasn't sure exactly what she felt for this man. Love wasn't a word in her vocabulary that had surfaced for years now. Certainly not for her family, those she'd trusted and thought had loved her, the same people who had given her to Luis without a backward glance, her mother as desperate as her father, sacrificing their oldest daughter to feed her little brothers and sisters. She didn't hate them for it anymore. There was just an emptiness inside, along with the sure knowledge she would care for any children she'd have with her life and all the love she could provide, never sacrificing them to the fate she'd endured.

Chang was different altogether. There was fascination, a curiosity and truly, lust with no shame, but after the first time, she'd wondered if it would last, that unfamiliar passion that had unfurled within her. If this was love, there would be time to explore that territory buried and betrayed for so long.

So far, and she smiled in remembrance, last night had been the same as the first. She watched him for a few minutes, basking in the aura of whatever this was, but it was too new and untried and she was far too wary to believe in fairy tales anymore, much as she wanted to. Still, it was magical and enticing and she never wanted this feeling to end.

She'd let him sleep for a while, he deserved it. She threw on a tee shirt and jeans and headed down to the hotel's coffee shop for coffee and hopefully, some green tea for him. Looked to her untried eyes as though this was the sort of place that would have it and Chang would be happy. Best to get started early, since they had a lot of area to search.

Chang's needle in a haystack adage was exactly right this time. Angel wasn't sure Jack and Grace were in Boise, but she just had that instinctual hunch that had served her well so far. If they were looking for a place to hide, the Idaho wilderness was certainly that, from what she'd seen in the guidebook she'd picked up, and they'd have to contact someone who knew the wilderness to get there, she surmised. They were from back East and didn't know the territory any more than she and Chang did. Boise was the starting off place. Even if the couple had been here before, half the damn state was wilderness and nobody, no matter how desperate, could head into that without some guidance and information. These forests and mountains frightened her a little and she knew instinctively she was correct in that feeling, not if you wanted to survive nature itself, an infinitely more dangerous foe than anything else, just as the desert could be.

She and Chang would have to track wilderness guides, back country rental agencies and real estate offices. On the other hand, if their quarry had traveled on to Portland or Seattle, Chang's comment would apply and it could be fruitless. They'd lose them quickly in a big city and she knew they'd been very lucky so far. She'd give it a day, maybe two, as little as they could afford that. Even now she couldn't help but look over her shoulder, just thinking about Luis.

He was indeed the spider with a large web, one with nearly invisible strands, which Angel knew only too well. So far, they'd been lucky, or at least they thought they were. This was the first time they'd spent any amount of time in one place besides Twin Falls, which was probably why she was nervous. As long as they'd been moving, through the countryside with no prying eyes, they were relatively safe. Cities were dangerous for them, but Boise looked innocuous, like the perfect little city, but Angel knew how looks could deceive, and that the cartel had a long reach into the most unlikely places. Every city had its dealers and contacts and this one, while relatively small and remote, wasn't any different. Junkies were everywhere and so were those who supplied them.

She gave the barista her order and sat down to wait in the empty cafe. It wasn't Boise's booming tourist season, since the ski season was over early with the low snowfall and it wasn't warm enough for the hikers and summer tourists to have arrived yet. Apparently, what guests had checked in were not early risers. As she picked up her cardboard tray of cups and croissants, another woman entered and came to the counter to stand beside her.

"Good morning. Two Americanos, please, and two bear

claws. Those were delicious yesterday," the woman said, glancing over at Angel, still smiling.

Angel froze. There could be no mistake. Short red hair in a pixie cut just as Twin Falls Trudi had described, but the beautiful face was still that of Grace Whitney, just like in the promo photos Angel had seen on the CD liner. Could they possibly get this lucky?

She strolled nervously out to the lobby and dawdled around, looking at the kiosk of Boise area attractions. There weren't any that interested her but she took a few pamphlets anyway. Soon the red-haired woman came out of the coffee shop carrying a tray with cups and a waxed bag of pastries similar to Angel's. She headed to the elevator area and Angel trailed casually behind her, watching as the redhead pushed floor five. Angel and Chang were on six, the penthouse.

Angel followed her into the elevator and smiled at her as though she was meeting a celebrity, glad her fingers were holding the coffee tray that disguised their trembling. "Six, thanks."

Grace punched the six button and smiled at her. "No worries."

The elevator stopped on five and Grace turned right and walked down the hall, while Angel veered left, slowly, looking back as the woman inserted her card into a door and disappeared. Angel crept back down the hallway, noted the room number, and returned to the closed elevator. She pushed the garage button. Just to be sure she wasn't imagining things, she wanted to see their car.

The garage was dark, lit only by the overhead security lights. There were only a couple of dozen cars and it didn't take her long to find the white Honda Odyssey, right in the first row. She didn't recall seeing it the night before. Still, here it was. They must've been blind to have missed it, or maybe they'd checked in late. She hurried back to the elevator, punching the number six button over and over, shaking with impatience, especially when a couple with two children showed up, and she had to hold up the elevator for a few minutes, dragging in their excessive baggage and chasing after their unruly offspring.

"Wake up." She stood two feet away from the bed where Chang was still asleep.

Chang sat up like a marionette as though a puppet master had pulled his strings, eyes alert and arms rigid.

"Stop it, it's me," Angel sighed. The guy was a killing machine. They'd have to work on this morning routine. She couldn't help but wonder about his ex-girlfriends if there were any still alive.

He blinked and focused on her. "Angel."

"Yes." She handed him the cup of green tea. "Drink it and get dressed. They're here."

He took the cup. "Here?"

"What I said. They're in room 523. We can go see them right now and that'll be the end of it. Let's get this over with."

He went to the bathroom, shutting the door, and Angel began stuffing their few clothes into the small suitcase she'd bought the day before, waiting impatiently to get the toiletries out of the bathroom. Chang finally emerged and dressed while she took everything and shut the suitcase. She even checked the wastebasket. They couldn't afford to leave anything behind that Luis or his people could find. She tapped her foot restlessly while he put on his shoes, sipping his tea between each shoelace.

"Stop it."

Angel glared at him. "Hurry up, *cabron.*"

Chang sighed. "You said she got coffee and pastries, just like you. She has no idea who you are and she's in no hurry. I have learned that calm is a great asset, Angel, a habit I sense you do not practice but may need to employ. They will not escape us."

She wanted to throw what was left of her coffee at him but she took a deep breath. "Let's go."

The lone elevator took forever to arrive. They stepped out on the fifth floor, and knocked on the door of Room 523. No response.

She knocked again and then again.

"Garage," Angel snapped. She ran back to the elevator and Chang kept pace. The door opened immediately and she punched the garage button. The doors opened onto the dimly lit space but it only took Angel a few seconds to see that the parking space where the Honda Odyssey had been shortly before was now empty.

CHANG WENT to get the car while Angel returned to the lobby. Angel had wanted to scream in frustration and berate Chang for his slowness, but she knew it would do little good, and likely incite a lecture about chi or calmness, and then she'd truly lose her temper. Even given their new relationship, she knew that wouldn't be a good idea. Instead, she took some deep breaths and stopped at the front desk. The clerk was a friendly young man, although not the same one they'd seen the night before. This must be the day guy. She crossed her arms and leaned on the counter.

"Hi."

"Good morning," he said, blushing a little. "How can I help you, ma'am?"

"Well," Angel smiled, "let me count the ways." His cheeks got pinker.

"Sorry, just kidding. Seriously, I need your help. We wanted to surprise my sister because it's her birthday in two days, so we didn't want them to know we were here, you know?"

He nodded vigorously, clearly eager to be of help and disguise his embarrassment.

"But ...she and her boyfriend must've headed out for a romantic retreat in the mountains or whatever because I noticed their car is gone. They were in Room 523. I was hoping you could help me figure out where they went so we could still meet up. Could you look and see if they checked out?"

"Sure, I can do that." He ran his fingers over the computer. "Yeah, they did check out, just a few minutes ago. You just missed them. Sorry."

"Oh no. We've come all the way from Denver hoping to surprise them. I knew I should've called her but I didn't want to ruin the surprise. By any chance, did they ever say anything or ask you anything that could help me out here?"

"You know, early yesterday they asked me about Moon's and how to get there, I remember that. Got the impression they were meeting somebody there."

"What's a Moon's?"

"It's a restaurant and sporting goods store. Real popular place. A lot of outfitters and river guides hang out there, so maybe they were going into the River?"

"River?"

"River of No Return Wilderness Area," he said. "Could be, but it's not a good time of year quite yet. Course, if they were looking for a short stay retreat sort of thing, there's lots of other options not that far."

"Such as?"

He ticked them off on his fingers as he talked. "Idaho City, Sun Valley, lots of places down on the Snake River, Birds of Prey area, even Bogus Basin now that the skiers are gone."

"Guess we'll be staying another night, given that. Don't want to be going off in the wrong direction. "Tell me, where is this Moon's?"

Early as it was, Moon's was a busy place. As they stood there taking it in, a couple departed, leaving open a small table, and they wasted no time in sitting down at it, dirty dishes and all. A waitress bustled up with a tray and efficiently removed all of them, wiping down the table and plopping down two menus. "Be right back," she said with a smile.

Angel stifled a laugh at Chang's expression and handed him the menu. "You'll find something. I have faith in you."

He flicked a forgotten crumb off the table and accepted the plastic folder, his face blank. It seemed he'd given up complaining about restaurants, at least for a little while.

She glanced around. Dead animals hung from the walls in an artful display of antlers and teeth. Given the wares on display on the other side of the half wall that separated the restaurant from the store itself, she wasn't surprised. Guns, guns and more guns, along with bows, knives and every sort of hunting, fishing and camping gear lined the shelves and racks. Americans sure loved to get out in the woods and kill things. She supposed it was better than what she'd grown up with and seen, as Luis and his men only killed people. At least these creatures got their heads nobly displayed on a wall instead of hanging from an overpass.

"So, what'll you have?" The waitress was back, holding her green and white pad and pencil like a shield and sword, at the ready. She didn't look all that friendly.

"Ah, well, two eggs and..." Angel looked belatedly at the menu, "and sausage and biscuits?" She wasn't sure what the hell that was, but it was all over the listings on the menu. She was growing fond of American food.

"Sure, whatever. Scrambled?" Angel nodded. "And you?" The waitress looked at Chang and it wasn't friendly at all.

"Tea. Two poached eggs and toast. Do you have any fruit?"

"We got orange juice," she said flatly. This wasn't going as well as Angel hoped it would. They clearly thought Mexicans were field laborers but Asians seemed to be a different thing altogether unless they were working on a railroad or making dumplings. What kind of place had they landed in? It'd looked friendly when they came in, but you never could really tell. Maybe it was just this bitch having a bad morning.

Chang shook his head but Angel said brightly, "I'll have some orange juice." The waitress smiled at her and left.

"Jesus, Chang, make an effort here," she said. "Blend, you know? We are weird enough for this place. The only Mexicans they're used to seeing have been probably been picking strawberries and they've likely never seen an Asian man in an Armani suit in their lives." She looked around and snorted. "Rephrase. They've never seen an Armani suit to start with. Boise's out of the way but this place is out of place and time."

He stared placidly at her and shrugged.

"It is fine, Angel. The world is full of places like this and more. I have been to many working for Luis. Be thankful it is not Florida. Calm, as I have said. Breathe."

There was no point in engaging with him on this, possibly because he was right. Her nerves were strung tautly and the only thing that would help was finding their elusive couple.

She glanced around at their fellow diners. A lot of flannel, boots and brown jackets were scattered around the room. How to engage any of them in conversation about out-of-the-way cabins or wherever Grace and Jack had gone was the question, but she knew they'd come here and instinct told her this was where they'd pick up the trail. The conversational noise level in the place was high, and she could pick up bits and pieces now and then, but nothing useful.

The waitress brought their plates with a bright smile and Angel was surprised to find she had an appetite. Chang seemed to be enjoying his poached eggs after his initial suspicion and after she stuck a fork in the gravy-covered mounds in front of her, she was surprised at how tasty they were.

"Fruit?" She handed Chang her glass of orange juice and he took a sip, nodded, and drank half the glass, handing it back with a half-smile.

Angel laughed softly. "You are so funny."

The waitress stopped back and put their check on the table.

"Wait a sec, please," Angel said. "I know you're busy, but have you seen a pretty girl with short red hair in here, maybe yesterday?"

"Not that I can remember," she said, somewhat dismissively. "A lot of people come and go in here, honey."

"Thanks," Angel smiled but she hadn't wanted to. It was getting down to that needle in a haystack, and going quickly. She couldn't let Chang's pessimism get to her. They were so close to finding Jack and Grace, she could almost smell them and she wasn't ready to give up now.

A bearded man stopped by their table, chewing on a toothpick, his friend beside him. "Say, y'all wouldn't be movie people or something, would you? I heard they're making that new Kevin Costner western around here."

Angel flashed back to the diner in New Mexico. Attractive people who dressed and looked different were suspected of being in the entertainment business for some reason. America was a strange place. Luis had at least been right about that. This might be useful. She smiled brilliantly at him.

"And here we were, hoping to keep a low profile but I guess you've found us out," she said, shaking her head in mock consternation.

The man smiled and his friend nudged him. "Damn, Cody, you were right."

"I knew it," bearded guy beamed, elbowing his friend. "Say, you wouldn't be looking for local actors, would you? Cause if you are, you couldn't find a better wrangler than Cody Ralston, right here," he slapped his chest, "and my friends ain't bad neither."

"How convenient," Chang said, chiming in smoothly, as though he'd been born for this role. "I'm the casting director and you two look just like what we're looking for." He looked them up and down and smiled with approval. "See, honey, I told Mort we didn't need any tired Los Angeles actors for this."

Angel nearly choked on her coffee. Chang had just morphed into Mr. Hollywood and even she believed it.

"Not only that, but I'll tell you a little secret," Chang continued, "we just got in late last night and we're looking for a place a little out of the way to finish up pre-production. I'm sure you understand. Somewhere with some peace and quiet, so we don't have people pestering us."

He lowered his voice and the two men leaned in conspiratorially. "Not you guys, of course, I can see you know the ropes, but you know how word gets around. We don't want a bunch of lookie-loos."

Cody nodded and grinned like he'd just found the mother lode. "Sure, man. In fact, I heard Charlie talking to somebody about these ski cabins up the road that might be just what you're looking for. I'll ask him."

Chang shook his hand. "Cody, I think you're going to be my go-to guy here. I'm going to put you down as a point contact with the studio. You got a phone?"

"Sure," Cody said, "but Charlie's sitting right over there." He pointed to a table nearby. "The one in the Carhartt."

Chang gave one of his rare smiles and it was like the sun had come out in this crowded basement café. "Introduce me, would you please, Cody? And don't forget to give me your phone number. Make sure you give it to my assistant here. I think we will have business to discuss. How fortunate we happened to meet today. We certainly could use a guy like you to help us out. Local talent that really knows the area is exactly what we're looking for."

Angel finished the orange juice and watched as the mesmerized Cody took Chang over to the man he'd pointed out before. She stood up and threw two $20 bills on the table.

Chang. She should've known better. The man was a chameleon. He hadn't survived this long on luck alone.

23

Mario pulled the pillow over his head to muffle the shrieks from Luis's bedroom, but he knew already it wouldn't be enough tonight, just like it hadn't been the nights before. He breathed heavily into the mattress and finally threw the pillow across the room.

This time, he was done. He threw open the door to the main room where Tomas and Jose were watching some naked blonde woman with impossibly large breasts dance a tango with a boa constrictor, both men stuffing salsa-loaded chips into their mouths and delighting in the woman's fake moans. When they saw him heading for Luis's room, their eyes widened.

"No, Mario, no, no, este es suicido," Tomas, the brighter one, said. Mario ignored him and flung open Luis's door.

Luis was straddling the naked bloody woman on the bed and raised his fist to hit her again when Mario grabbed his wrist.

"Jefe," he said softly, "she is not Angel nor will she ever be. Let her go."

Luis stared at Mario, his eyes wild. Several tense seconds passed and he rolled off the woman and lay panting on his back on the other side of the bed. Mario nodded at the sobbing woman and handed her a fistful of $100 bills. She wiped the blood from her face with the sheet and scrambled up, throwing on her dress and shoes and running out of the bedroom. He heard the outside door slam shut.

For days now, Mario had been charged with acquiring and excessively paying off hookers, all of whom had the requested long dark hair and slim build. He knew this could not continue, no matter how much money was spent in payoffs. Luis's anger and turmoil were directed towards only one, but she was the one he could not touch, at least not yet.

"I will kill you for this," Luis rasped, sitting up.

"Perhaps, *jefe,* but listen to me before you do," Mario said and sat down beside him, carefully avoiding the blood spatters.

"Even for Las Vegas, the police are starting to take notice," he said. "Even you cannot do this anymore. We are lucky none of these girls has died or known someone who would try and come after you, but soon one of those things will happen. This is not Mexico, but even here, law enforcement steps will be taken. They value their whores in Las Vegas because it is part of their tourist industry needs. You know this, Luis. It is my job to keep you safe and this must stop, or even I and our many friends cannot fix this."

Luis shrugged but his eyes bored into Mario's. He was listening, but Mario knew only too well that even drunk as he was, Luis could move as quickly as a rattlesnake towards the Glock he always kept under his pillow, bodyguard or not. Mario's muscles tensed, ready to strike or run when Luis rolled over and patted him on the shoulder. His eyes were glassy, and he blinked slowly but purposefully, heavy lids closing slowly, like a snake's after eating its prey.

"Perhaps you are right, Mario," Luis said. He rose slowly and staggered towards the bathroom. "I will forgive this transgression, but only if you do the rest of your job."

"Of course, anything you ask." Mario had nearly forgotten how to breathe for a few seconds.

"Find that little whore and that Chinese traitor. I can wait no longer. Only then will I be at peace."

MORNING BROUGHT breakfast and the dawn, but not yet the information they were looking for. Luis decided to substitute gambling for hookers, and they all spent the day wandering around Caesar's ground floor, gambling, eating, and drinking, with occasional forays into the shopping area, where the fountains, changing skies, and actors greatly amused Luis, as did the magic shop, designer boutiques and jewelry stores.

As evening approached, they headed for Amalfi, a restaurant Luis much preferred over Gordon Ramsey's or the Bacchanal buffet.

"Gordon Ramsey is a buffoon," Luis pronounced and Mario couldn't disagree. "If I wanted to eat food made by a clown, I would go to the circus. At least Senor Flay knows how to cook seafood."

If it was up to him, Mario would've headed to Lindo Michoacan and great Mexican food, but it was never up to him, much as he tried. Even with the lures of dolphins or faux Paris, Luis seemed reluctant to leave the fantasy confines of Caesar's and there was no question about venturing a contrary opinion. Perhaps soon Luis would want food from his homeland and wish to venture further afield where he would find new people to either praise or condemn, but it was not this night.

It was later that evening at the roulette wheel that Luis's cell phone chirped with the call he'd been waiting for. He motioned to Mario to take over his bets and moved away from the table, listening intently. Mario had just won $300 when Luis grabbed his shoulder.

"Let's go. Finally, they have a lead on our thieves."

Mario wasn't sure whether he felt elation or dread, but either way, this crisis would soon be resolved and they could go home. He had no particular grudge against either Angel, unlike Luis, or Chang, whom no one really knew, but it didn't matter. He was a *soldado* and he would do what was necessary. He nodded at the croupier and gathered his chips.

The four of them sat in the living room of the suite, Luis on the phone intermittently, sometimes listening quietly and at others, more loudly, berating the caller when he didn't agree with what he'd said. Mario, Tomas and Jose were quiet as mice, because they knew the way of things. That they would leave in the morning was all he was sure of, but Mario wasn't sure of their destination.

"What the fuck is Twin Falls?" Luis shouted into the phone. "Is there even an airport there?"

Finally, he slammed the phone down and poured more tequila into his glass. "So. Tomorrow we go to this place they grow potatoes, this *norteamericano* state called Idaho."

At last, there was a destination and this journey would soon be over. Mario settled Luis in his bed with a half a bottle of El Mayor while Tomas and Jose watched "Cooking with Bambi", one of their favorites which involved a voluptuous redhead wearing only a chef's toque doing a variety of things with raw vegetables and kitchen utensils, none of which involved cooking.

He poured himself a tequila and went out to the balcony. The dazzling lights of Las Vegas greeted him and he sat down on a chair, sipping slowly, and imagined the lives of all those below and trying hard not to think of the fates of the two people they were leaving to find tomorrow. Mario knew his place and he was prepared to fulfill his duties. There was no time for reflection or imaginative scenarios. Luis was his *patron*, and that was all there was in this world.

24

———

After they returned from Moon's, Angel paced around the hotel room while Chang sat by the window, sipping his tea and staring out the window. He looked as though he was just looking at the view but she knew he was noting every person and car that passed on the street below, as they waited for Charlie's real estate contact to call. They'd given Charlie $500 and asked that he forget he'd ever seen them, using the movie business paranoia as an excuse, and asking for an out of the way place where they could do their preparations without disturbance.

Charlie had seemed very amenable but when Angel had asked about properties and off-season ski cabins in particular, he'd said he didn't know of any, and she was well-practiced enough to know a lie when she heard one. Still, he gave them a contact and Angel didn't press it. When the real estate man called, she'd figure it out. No point in alerting Charlie or making him suspicious enough to contact Jack and Grace, who had in all likelihood been there the day before she and Chang had shown up. Charlie was only a step on the road to someone who could really help them, especially when he was paid well.

She ventured out to a large department store and picked up some clothes that seemed more Idaho-like, leaving Chang to his surveillance. She asked him his sizes but he never bought clothes off the rack so the best he could offer was his shoe size. Angel guessed and bought jeans, boots, and the ubiquitous Carhartt jacket for Chang, so he'd look a bit more like everyone else in Boise. No more designers for that man until they were out of this place. She debated when she passed a hat shop, drawn by the black Stetson in the window. He'd blend in with that hat but she was pretty sure he'd never put it on. For herself, she also purchased some jeans and a couple of sweaters, and a pair of cowboy boots she liked.

They should've taken the time before now to camouflage themselves better but at least they'd accomplished it now and she hoped it wasn't too late. Luis's tentacles could reach every-where. She got back to the hotel, dumping her purchases on the bed. Chang was still in place at the window.

"There's a guy."

Angel peered over Chang's shoulder. A man stood in front of a coffee shop across the street, holding a paper cup. He was white, shaggy brown hair, dressed casually in jeans and a jacket, his phone in the other hand.

"He's been there for about five minutes. Before that, he was in front of the pharmacy on the next block. Maybe harmless, but he's been lingering and so far there's no reason for it."

"I don't like it," Angel said.

Chang didn't answer but as they watched, a ponytailed blonde girl in a green pickup truck pulled up to the curb and the man jumped in, putting his phone in his pocket. They drove off.

"False alarm," Angel said. "His sweet little honeybunny was late."

Chang raised a skeptical eyebrow, but shrugged and went back to his station. She brought him a cup of tea and a cheese sandwich, but he barely acknowledged her although he managed to consume both mindlessly.

Even after her shopping trip, it wasn't even noon. Angel changed into some of her new purchases but paced restlessly around the room until her phone rang. The real estate guy. Go time. She looked at Chang and picked up the bag they'd packed earlier.

Chang punched the elevator button for Garage but Angel hit Lobby.

"Why?" Chang raised that eyebrow again.

"You get this stuff into the car, I'll meet you in the garage. I want to give the desk clerk a reason to forget he ever talked to us, *comprende?*

Chang smiled. "*Si, jefe.*"

She laughed. "I think that might be you at this point, but thanks."

She was still smiling when she walked to the front desk and the clerk smiled back. He was same one as yesterday. She hadn't noticed before, but his name badge said 'Michael'.

"Hi."

"And hello to you, Michael," Angel said, sliding $500 across the counter. "We'd appreciate it if you could forget you ever saw or talked to us, just in case anyone asks. Can you do that?"

He looked a bit stunned, but recovered swiftly and pocketed the money. *How quickly we adapt*, Angel thought with a tinge of regret. Innocence was so quickly destroyed.

"Of course, I can." He looked down for a second and then back at her. He smiled. "For you."

"Thank you, my friend," Angel said, and leaned over the desk and kissed him on the cheek. "One more small favor? There may be some people looking for us and there is one especially that is a very bad man. He travels with other bad men. If he comes here, could you call me, just in case? It would mean a lot to me. I hope to see you again, Michael."

"Yes, I can do that," Michael smiled and pocketed the slip of paper with her phone number. "Safe travels."

Heels clacked on the floor behind her as a gust of cold air blew into the lobby. A pretty blonde girl, ponytail bobbing, came to stand at the desk, eyeing her impatiently, fingers tapping on the marble countertop. Angel waved goodbye at the blushing clerk and headed for the elevator banks. Could this be the same girl that had driven the pickup truck? She pressed herself against the wall around the corner.

"Hey," the girl said. "I'm looking for my friends that I'm pretty sure are staying here. Have you seen a dark-haired girl and a big Chinese guy?"

Angel held her breath. Hopefully, Michael was worth the money.

"No, nobody like that," the young clerk stammered, "I'd sure remember that. We don't get a lot of Asian people around here, you know?" He got bolder, earning it now. "I mean, it's Boise."

Angel didn't wait to hear any more but strode off and ran down the stairs to the garage. Chang stood by the Escalade and she motioned him over.

"We're made. The blonde in the pickup is up there right now." She started towards the car but Chang put out his arm.

"Wait."

It wasn't two minutes later the elevator chimed softly and the blonde girl stepped out of the elevator, staring out at the cars while her eyes adjusted to the dim light. It was a moment too long.

"Cartel?" Chang came out of the shadows and gripped her arms from behind. She snarled at him, struggling to get out of his grip.

"Just say it and this will be over."

"Fucker." She wriggled out of his grasp, the small knife in her hand whipping across his stomach. Chang never flinched, but his displeasure and pain were evident when he silently snapped her neck and dropped her to the concrete floor.

"Well." Angel picked up the knife and stuffed it into the girl's waistband. She eyed the thin red ribbon blossoming across Chang's white shirt. It looked fairly shallow, but painful.

"I did say life and death, didn't I? Good thing I bought first aid stuff this morning, it's in the bag. I'll drive while you patch up. You were right, as you always are. Luis is closer than we thought. Let's put her in the Escalade, we can dump her somewhere later."

There was no sign of the green pickup once they were out on the street but Angel kept checking behind them. The real estate agent's office was only a couple of miles away but she circled the block three times before she parked. There was no sign of the pickup or anyone else out of the ordinary. Luis's people were minor league types up here, as Boise was not a big city, likely not as sophisticated in surveillance as other places might be. Chang had checked and found no tracker on the car. Even so, they needed to get this business over with quickly.

She parked and looked over at Chang, who had busied himself on the short drive with the supplies she bought. The cut didn't look deep enough to need stitches, but it was a good five inches long and messy. He'd very efficiently bandaged it with gauze and tape, smiling bleakly as he buttoned his new jacket over the telltale bloody shirt.

"Rock and roll, as the Americans always say. It's not that bad," he said. "You're doing most of the talking this time anyway."

She kissed him. "Did I mention I love you?" She could not believe those words just popped out of her mouth but they seemed right.

"No." He opened the car door. "You don't have to."

Angel smiled to herself. No matter what happened, there was this and this was more than she'd ever had.

The real estate office was in a strip mall, tucked between a coffee shop and a bail bond outfit. They opened the door with the sign that read "Sonderville Properties".

"Hey there, good morning." Hand out waving like a flag, the man advanced on them like a hound on a scent and Angel had to stop herself from recoiling from his limp sweaty handshake. "Ben Sonderville. You can only be the people Charlie mentioned. Goodness gracious, you two are something special all right."

Chang shook his hand, his smile closer to a grimace, pressing his hand to his carefully buttoned suit coat.

"Todd Miyaki, nice to meet you, Ben. This is my assistant Marlene. She usually handles the business details."

"Nice to meet you both. Happy to be of service," Ben said, waving them to the chairs in front of his desk, while he settled back into the swivel chair behind it. His pomaded hair smelled of some rancid citrus scent. With his brown plaid sport coat, he looked like every salesman Angel had ever seen on American TV shows. Sometimes fiction was just as true as real life.

"So I hear you're looking for a fairly, shall we say, private place to do some business," Somerville winked, "and I think I've found a few choices for you. I'm happy to be of service on this, and I sure hope you'll keep me in mind when the rest of your associates arrive, Todd."

He spread out a few plastic sheets of properties in front of them.

"Now, here's one in the Highlands, up at the end of Harrison, very exclusive. It's gorgeous, lot of glass, very modern, secluded at the end of Highland View Drive, and that drops into Hull's Gulch. Views you wouldn't believe. It's got six bedrooms, and an electronic gate and security system. It's known to be unapproachable, so there's no traffic or curiosity seekers, if you know what I mean," he smirked and pointed to the next one with scarcely a pause for breath.

"This one here's out in Idaho City, and you know, it's a drive, but hey, maybe that's what you want. It's a log cabin, but a sweet and very fancy one, I gotta say. Again, good size with all amenities, of course. I heard it was rented to Mel Gibson before."

Before Angel or Chang could react, he launched into his next pitch. "Now, this one here, it's out in Star, it's a horse ranch, but the owner is some weird Hollywood guy," he paused and looked up, "whoopsie, no offense, you know. Anywho, he's never around and rents it out most of the time. Fabulous place, open beams, four bedrooms, gourmet kitchen. You don't even have to feed the horses, there's people for that. Most of the time, I hear, the wind's out of the west, and horse corrals are east, so no aromas disturbing your dinner, you know what I mean? Gotta think about these things, am I right?"

Chang put his hand over Ben's before he could flip over the next plastic sheet.

"Ben."

Angel wasn't sure if it was the tone of his voice or the touch of his hand, but Ben's torrent of words halted in midstream.

"We were sort of thinking something much more low-key. A mountain cabin, nothing fancy, but of course with comforts. Say, a cabin, maybe fairly accessible in winter as well as in the warmer months, for instance. Something simple but nice, but out of the way and not far from downtown Boise and the airport. You have anything like that?"

Angel smiled. "We'd be happy to pay you extra for your efforts, Ben. You seem like a man who knows his business and takes care of the needs of his clients and we know that's worth a great deal. We can keep secrets too."

She was quite sure good old Charlie had deliberately steered them away from anywhere Jack and Grace could have gone and had alerted Ben to do the same.

Ben looked down at the listings on his desk and then back at them, as though he was measuring his options. And, as

Angel well knew, he was. Ben didn't look it, but it was clear he knew an opportunity when he smelled it. Angel slid $500 across the desk. Ben nonchalantly picked it up like it was something he saw every day, and put it in his desk drawer. Angel couldn't help but wonder how many people on the run showed up in Boise. Maybe more than she thought. Somerville sat back and smiled at them, the first genuine thing he'd done since they'd walked in the door.

"You know, now that you mention wanting something smaller and unobtrusive, there's this place up Bogus Basin Road that could be just what you're looking for. I think it's perfect for you two. They like to sort of vet the people they let in there and keep it quiet, you know, friends of friends, and that could be perfect for you. I think we can work something out."

Angel smiled. "I'm quite sure we can, Ben."

"Let me make some calls," he said. "There's a coffee shop three doors down, other side of the hair salon. Why don't you get a cup and a sandwich, and I'll have some good news for you soon."

Angel thought about giving him more money but he seemed eager enough.

"Great. Half an hour, then?" Chang said.

Ben beamed. "That should do it."

The coffee shop wasn't as bad as it looked, given its location. Two surprisingly tasty almond croissants later, they were back in Ben's office and in possession of a map and a set of keys. Chang was in considerable discomfort, Angel knew. She wanted to only get to a safe place so she could take better care of him.

Ben waved goodbye as they drove out of the parking lot.

"He's a loose end, Angel. We will come to regret this." Chang was clearly aggravated.

She jangled the keys in her hand. "Stop worrying. I told him to go to Las Vegas for a couple of days," she said. "It wasn't a suggestion and I think he knew it. He's stupid, but not that stupid. Hope he doesn't waste much time."

Chang shook his head. "As do I. I'm not at my best, but I don't want to come back here if your compassion proves to be wrong. And if Luis sniffs him out, it isn't just Ben that will regret his tardiness, it's us."

25

———

"I thought I just saw some lights," Grace said, peering out the front window. "Goddamnit, I hope nobody else has rented a cabin up here."

"Well, it's not like we're the only people in the world, Grace," Jack said from where he sat beside the fire, tuning her guitar. He'd gotten pretty sanguine about the whole thing since they'd gotten to the cabin. Maybe it was the pine trees, but the serene quiet hadn't yet affected her. She was nervous as the proverbial cat.

"Listen, I took a walk out to the road this morning. There's other cabins and places up here besides this one, I'm sure, and people that work at that ski resort up the mountain. We're going to see reflections from the road as they go by and maybe people turning in on the wrong road. None of these side roads up here are exactly clearly marked, remember?"

He put the guitar down. "I think we're safe, for a while. I feel good about it, like I can finally take a breath. Charlie knows not to let anyone know we're here, and he's a standup guy, so probably it's just a turnaround. Worst case, some other real estate guy could rent one of these cabins to a hiker or something, Charlie said that could happen, even though they aren't really on the usual real estate radar screen." He glanced at the gun on the table beside him. "Try and stop worrying."

He poured her another glass of wine. "Come on, let's finish this song. The woods seem to be agreeing with you. It's melancholy, but that's sort of what we do, and this is the best song we've written in a long time, babe."

She couldn't disagree with that. It was a good song, probably reflecting some of the feelings of the last few weeks. She looked out again but only the faint outlines of the trees met her gaze, standing sentinel against the rising moon. Darkness fell swiftly here, even more so than in the backwoods Tennessee town where she grew up. In a weird way, it made her feel at home. She was glad Jack felt better, but she was still having a hard time relaxing herself.

Jack handed her the guitar and took out his lap steel, doodling around with the tune, and she joined in, humming along. She sang the first verse, Jack nodding and filling in. By the time she launched into the chorus, with Jack harmonizing, it was really sounding good. She blathered nonsense words for the last two verses, they'd come up with something, and they were both grinning by the time they launched into the final chorus.

"Girl, that was...something," he said. "Holy shit. We got us a hit here, god willing and the creek don't rise, as every Southern grandma since forever has said. And it's not the only one."

She laughed. "Yeah, I think maybe we do." She put down the guitar and kissed him. That hard piece of ice in her chest was finally melting and she finally drew in that first deep breath.

"I guess all this shit got my brain working as an escape from thinking about getting hunted down and ax murdered or whatever these people might do. Right now, all I care about is this music, and you."

Jack moved his lap steel over and pulled her into his lap. "Well, there's music, but you are the most important thing in my life, Grace." His hand cupped her face. "No matter what tomorrow or any other day brings, I thank whatever gods there are for you. We'll get through this together."

Grace knew they wouldn't get any more music written that night but as Jack said, there were more important things and she couldn't argue with that.

She got up early, just as the sun was creeping over the nearby peaks. Jack was snoring softly and she didn't rouse him, softly shutting the bedroom door, a long-time habit and not just on this trip or their run from the devil, as she had come to think of it.

She opened the window to let in the scent of the pine-scented air and stood in the kitchen, waiting for the coffeemaker to do its work, as she always did. She'd dreamed of more songs and the guitar lines were running through her head like newly formed earworms that were driving her nuts and she had to get them out. She poured a cup and took it to the couch, picking up her guitar.

It wasn't five minutes and one cup of coffee before she had a plaintive guitar line to go with the song in her head and she smiled in delight. Jack was right, the woods were good for them. She got up, refilled her coffee cup and grabbed the notebook she always carried from her old backpack. She sat back down and began scribbling lyrics on the paper. The image of those trees against the moon last night had struck her, as had the mountains they'd seen for the last week, still snowcapped. Something about the bleakness and the perfection of both crystallized in her, along with the desperation she'd felt for days.

By the time Jack shuffled out towards the kitchen, smiling blearily at her and pouring himself some coffee, she had three more songs down, at least in their infantile stages. She played one for him and he looked at her as though she was the sun rising.

"Grace, good god, girl. You are amazing. To keep up with you and pay my half here, I'm going to have to get busy, aren't I?"

"Yep. But I know you're up for it." She looked at his pajama bottoms and snorted. "So to speak."

Jack rolled his eyes and left for the bathroom. Grace chuckled and went to the kitchen to make some eggs. This mountain air was good for a lot of things.

It turned out to be one of the best days they'd ever had making music together. Maybe adversity and sheer terror struck a chord of creativity, or just that they were so glad to not have to listen to the Southern Mavericks anymore they felt compelled to combat that mediocrity with music they loved. By 4:30 the sun was starting to go down and Jack put down the lap steel and stood up, stretching his back and working out the kinks

"Let's talk a walk before it gets blackout dark the way it does up here," Grace said. "After the sun sets it gets pretty cold still, but it's perfect right now." She stood and stretched as well. "With the lights from the cabin, we can still see enough."

Jack threw on his jacket anyway and they headed out. He hesitated for a second when he pulled the door shut, eyeing the keys on the kitchen counter.

"I don't think we need to lock it, either," Grace said. "Nobody but bears coming calling, far as I can see."

"Bears?" The look on Jack's face was priceless. "They got bears up here?"

Grace laughed. "I'm sure they do, but we're fine. Don't know about you, but down to the main road and back is about all I'm good for. Come on, it'll be a short walk and we can see the place all the way. I'm looking forward to that wine."

"Funny, Grace. Fucking bears," Jack muttered. "I ever tell you how much I hate bears?"

"Now that you mention it, no," she said. "Childhood camping horror?"

He glared at her. "Something like that. You know, for some people it's sharks, snakes or spiders? Me, it's bears."

"You want to talk about it?"

"Not really. All I'll say is my dad had this still up in the hills, you know that, and a little cabin with just an outhouse up there." He paused, and looked at her. "Thing is, when I was about eight, I was in the outhouse and this bear came by. Good thing I was already sitting there inside but he thought coming in was a good idea anyway. Must've liked the smell. I started screaming so hard my throat hurt for days. My dad scared him off after what seemed like hours, but it was only a few minutes. Ever since, well...bears."

Grace tucked her arm into the crook of Jack's elbow when she noticed he kept staring intently into the trees and even turned to look behind them twice.

"It's OK, I get it, and that must've been really scary."

He shot her a look and she giggled.

"Thanks for your support, Grace."

Now she doubled over, laughing outright. "I just keep thinking of you sitting in that outhouse while the bear was trying to batter down the door. Good thing you were already in the right place, so to speak."

"OK, OK," he said, and began to laugh too. "It was a ridiculous situation, I'll give you that. But it traumatized me as a kid."

They ambled past the empty cabins when Jack stopped dead, staring at the second to last one. There was a car parked on the other side of the cabin and there was a light on inside.

"There's something really scary, Grace, and it's no damn bear."

Company, just what they feared could happen. Grace's

stomach plummeted to what felt like her toes, and she tightened her grip on Jack's elbow. They slowly turned around and went back down the lane, her legs moving like stiff boards. So much for the serenity of making good music.

"I want to run," she whispered in Jack's ear.

"You can't," he said, gripping her arm like a vise. "Casual, babe, casual. It could be nothing. Let's just get back to the cabin and we'll figure it out. No panic."

"Did you bring the gun?"

Jack looked at her. "Hell, I didn't even lock the door, remember?"

Dusk was quickly turning to full dark, and in this place with no streetlights, that was very dark indeed. They walked back to their cabin as though they were robots, and once on the porch, ran inside and bolted the door. Jack immediately checked and the gun was exactly where he'd left it, along with everything else. Nothing had been touched.

They looked at each other.

"What do you want to do?" Grace said.

"Hell, I don't know." Jack started to run his hands through his hair before remembering he didn't have any. He stared at her, the scar on his pale chiseled face standing out with no long blonde waves to soften it. "What do you think?"

Grace took a deep breath and blew it out. "First thought is, pack the car and run. Second is, calm the fuck down. Third, we don't know who the hell these people are, so let's find out. It's getting just as dark over at their place as it is here. Let's reconnoiter and see if we can find out who they are."

"Whoa there, Grace, what are you, some movie heroine? This is the real world."

Grace sat down on the sofa, feeling mildly insulted. "No, and don't be an asshole. Thing is, I'm goddamn sick and tired of running like scared rabbits from some people we don't even know exist for sure, Jack. Could be whoever's in that cabin is just some tourist wanting to hike the mountains instead of the bogeymen we're so worried about. So,let's find out. You don't look as though that Glock is a stranger to you. Nor doing what it takes when the chips are down."

She feinted a mock punch at him and he grabbed her arm. "What do you say?"

"You're right, I'm tired of running too. And, it's not like I haven't done my share of spying on my cheerleader neighbor back in junior high, so I have some expertise in this arena." He grinned.

"Besides, we can always scamper back like rabbits, pack our shit and haul ass if we don't like what we see. Especially after I take the fuel pump out of their car and slash their tires."

26

Mario Valenzuela doubted the Inn at 500 in Boise often had guests like Luis Reynaldo, to say nothing of Tomas and Jose. He'd fruitlessly searched for a hotel that had large suites, but there simply weren't any here, not of the quality of this place and with its own restaurants, another of Luis's essentials. In the end, he'd booked the largest suite the Inn had and the two adjoining rooms on either side of it. It was close to the last place their people had caught a glimpse of Angel and Chang, and even though they were in the wind now, they wouldn't be for long.

The desk clerk eyed him suspiciously, to say nothing of his companions waiting in the lobby, but an additional $200 had made him smile, if a little nervously, before he handed over the plastic cards in their folders.

"Welcome to Boise, Mr. Valenzuela," he said, "please do not hesitate to contact me for anything you need." Mario always carried a large supply of $100 bills. They were like a magic ticket for getting people to do what you wanted.

"Thank you," Mario said. "It is good to know," he peered at the clerk's name badge, "Michael. I may do that."

He slid another $100 across the counter. "We may have some acquaintances show up soon, and I'm sure you will show them the same courtesy as you have me, as you seem to be a very observant young man."

The clerk smiled. "Of course. Thank you, sir."

The rooms were on the top floor, and that was high enough for the mountain town, the view not competing with many other buildings of this height. Luis had ensconced himself atop the king-size bed in the main suite, a frosty glass of El Mayor in his hand, by the time Mario returned, depositing Tomas and Jose in one room and his bags in another.

"So, my friend," Luis said. "We wait. Our informants are on their way?"

"*Si, jefe,*" Mario said, turning to the window. The mountains were still snow-capped and the setting sun glittered off their peaks in a pink and lavender glow. It was beautiful, as nature often was, much more beautiful than some of the creatures that inhabited its environs.

"And then," Luis said, sipping his tequila, "we will find our little rats on the run. They think they have escaped. That only makes this all the more exciting to me."

He sipped some tequila. "You see, Mario, even though I am a man who is beset with problems, a man with a hunger for justice, I am also a man of patience. You have been kind enough to support your *jefe* and school him with temperance during these trying days. You are a brave and thoughtful man, Mario, and I am fortunate to have such a one as you beside me."

Less than an hour passed before a knock on the door came, and Mario opened it to a thin brown-bearded man in his twenties who stood nervously fingering the collar of his jean jacket. Mario gestured for him to come in, and he did so, stopping a few feet from the doorway as Mario shut the door behind him.

"I'm Jim Blanchard, uh, the guy who's been watching for that couple like you wanted. I work for Teo."

Mario nodded and escorted him to the bedroom where Luis had sat up from the pillows and stared avidly at the newcomer.

"So, you work for Teo, *si*?"

Jim pushed his long brown hair from his face. "Yessir, I do."

"A good man, Teo. So, tell me, where have our little birds flown?"

"Well, sir, that's the thing. My partner has disappeared and she was the one who went into this very hotel to find them. She thought they were staying here. I haven't seen her or either of them since."

Mario wanted nothing more than to disappear into the floor. This kid must be suicidal.

Luis said nothing for a long minute. "That is unfortunate. Explain."

Jim swallowed audibly. "There's not much more to tell. She texted me she was on them and was coming inside. The last thing she texted was she was going down to the garage and that's the last thing I've heard since. I waited down the block, and then drove around, you know, thinking I'd find her, or them, or something."

Jim gave a dry cough. "We're pretty sure they're driving a black Escalade, but you know, there's a few of those around, well, you know, not that many, since pickup trucks and soccer mom vans are the norm around here, but still enough so that I'd notice, but I guess I must've missed them because I've been down to the garage to check it out after driving around a few blocks, and there was no black Escalade, and there was no sign of Brittany since either, and I'm pretty damn worried about her."

Jim visibly slumped, as though the torrent of words had exhausted him. He looked at Luis apprehensively.

Luis reached for the bottle of El Mayor and poured more

tequila into his glass. He sipped slowly, glanced at Mario, and returned his gaze to Jim. Mario closed his eyes briefly. He knew what was coming. It would be difficult to clean up in this place so he fervently hoped Luis would restrain himself at least this once.

"So, Jim," Luis said. "What you are saying to me is that your partner is missing and so are the people you've been assigned to watch for me?"

"Uh, yessir, I guess that is about it."

Santo Christo, Mario thought. This kid was beyond stupid. Did he have a death wish? He should've disappeared into the wilderness around here and hoped for redemption or at least short memories.

"I am disappointed, Jim. I do not like to be disappointed, *comprende?*"

"Uh, yessir, I am sorry."

"Oh. You are sorry? Well then." Luis smiled. "What shall we do now? Have any ideas, *Jim*?"

"I will find them, sir."

"Yes, Jim, you will." Luis sipped his tequila. "Or, you will die. Do I make myself clear, or do I need to phone Teo?"

"No, no," the kid said, his face paling. "I'll find them, sir. I swear."

"Excellent." Luis gestured to Mario. That little interview was over, much to Mario's relief. He took Jim to the front room and opened the door. The sound of the bottle of El Mayor hitting the wall behind them made both of them jump a little.

Jim looked at him, eyes wide. Mario grabbed his arm.

"*Cabron*, you just got really lucky that your brains aren't splattered against that wall instead of a bottle of tequila. You better get a lead on them fast. I do not normally give advice like this, but you're in way over your head. If you don't find them, do not come back here. You show up empty-handed and you won't be leaving a second time."

Jim nodded his head up and down and walked very fast towards the elevator. Mario watched him go and sighed. It wasn't going to be a very pleasant evening. Even their so-called award-winning chef wasn't likely to make a dent in Luis's frustration and Mario was pretty sure the supply of hookers in Boise wasn't up to Las Vegas standards, if there were even any available here at the Inn at 500. Any snow bunny skiers looking to make lift money had long gone.

The desk clerk had seemed as innocent as a boy scout, even though he was very good at pocketing bribes. Unfortunately, Mario was likely to find out just how innocent by the time the night was over. That Blanchard kid better come up with something if they had to spend much more time here in delightful downtown Boise. If he didn't, Mario would have to deal next with Teo, who was a certifiable maniac.

27

"I like it here," Angel said, standing in front of the fireplace. "It's just like the frontier cabins in American western movies, don't you think, Chang?"

Chang unpacked the grocery bag in the tiny kitchen and rolled his eyes. "Only movie I've seen with a cabin like this was a Tarantino film, Crazy Eight or something with cowboys and it didn't end well for most of them."

He gazed around, taking in the log walls, open beams, the cozy-looking plaid furniture and suppressed a shudder.

"I prefer a lot more glass, mixed with steel, preferably twenty stories up. Still," he pulled her close, "I am happy you find it charming, Angel."

She kissed him and spun away to the small kitchen and looked through their purchases. "I'll make you some tea and you'll be much happier. Better to make plans after some tea with you, I've found. You're less cranky. People die when you're cranky."

She put most of the stuff in the refrigerator, leaving the tea and coffee out. They hadn't bought all that much, not planning on being here long enough to need much, but there was the tea

Chang wanted, along with fresh chicken, vegetables, rice, eggs, and Coke, which Angel loved. She eyed the chicken and vegetables suspiciously, placing them in the refrigerator. Chang had been insistent he would cook a decent meal and they would have an evening together before facing off with Jack and Grace. A shiny red teakettle sat empty on the stove and she filled it with water, turning on the burner.

They hadn't been entirely sure they'd find Jack and Grace here, and they'd had to pay Somerville more than necessary to divulge that the place even existed, and Angel had sighed with relief when they quietly pulled onto the small pine needle-covered road, rolling quietly into the first cabin, not wanting to alert their prey, and the Honda Odyssey visible, parked beside the cabin at the end of the lane. No other cars were here, which was good. The last cabin was a good distance away, and they'd taken care to be as quiet as possible when they'd arrived, unpacked the car, and opened the cabin. Angel saw no point in haste which only led to easily avoided mistakes.

It would take Luis some time to find them here, a lot more time than it had taken for them to find Grace and Jack. Luis had no thread to follow except that obviously someone had spotted them, but they hadn't had that problem, following a thread Luis didn't know existed. The girl in the trunk should give them a respite and he'd have to start over with his informers.

Besides, for all she knew, Grace and Jack had no idea just who was after them, although by now she didn't think they were dumb enough, especially after that foolish text message she'd sent, to think that no one was, hidden away as they were. They just had no idea who that might be. Even if they noticed them, they could be just some nice couple up for the week to do some hiking or get some mountain air rather than some desperate gun-carrying lunatics.

Chang came back with their bag of clothes and toiletries and put it in the bedroom. A quick glance had told her that room was full of more plaid and she stifled a laugh. He was going to have to get past that but she had no doubt he would. If she'd learned nothing in the last few days, it was that Chang was a very adaptable man.

"Let me." Chang's hand came down on hers as she reached for the teakettle. "It's just bags, but even so." He looked down at her. "Would you like some?"

Angel smiled. "Yes, I think I would. If you like it so much, there must be something to it."

She opened the windows to get some fresh air into the cabin that had been closed up for some time and loved the scent of the huge evergreen trees that surrounded the place. She heard the plaintive guitar right away, carrying well through the crystal-clear mountain air, and then Grace's lovely voice, soaring on the high notes, with Jack's lower one harmonizing. She stood very still and drank in the music, Chang quietly watching her. Their music was beautiful and just as their songs she'd listened to in the car, it touched her like no other music had before. She was dangerously close to thinking of them as friends. She'd never had any but whether this foolish doomed couple knew it or not, their music had bonded them to her.

They settled into the chairs in front of the fireplace and he placed the mugs of tea on the table between them. The aroma of the jasmine tea filled her nose as she picked up the cup and took a sip. Tea wasn't a usual thing for her but he wasn't wrong. It wasn't just the tea, but more than that. The tea embodied a sense of warmth and contentment along with that enticing smell. It was a calm she badly needed.

"Thank you."

He inclined his head slightly. "It will be a shame to see that talent die, Angel. I can see how much you like what they do."

"Maybe they don't have to die, Chang. We take back the money and we all disappear, even them, poor again but breathing, before Luis knows they even exist. What about that idea?

Yes, I was angry at first but now, I am thinking differently than before."

"Angel. You are becoming sentimental. I have seen how people of your heritage do that, all flowers, music, and passion. We cannot do this. Loose ends, remember?"

Anger flared in her and she knew he'd see it in her eyes. She sipped her tea and quieted her thoughts. She hadn't thought to leave one tyrant for another, especially this one who had shown her what love could be.

"They are not loose ends, Chang, if Luis never knew they existed, and how could he, except for us?"

"What you say could be true," he conceded. "We will see how today and tomorrow unfold."

"Yes," she said. "We will."

He smiled at her in that Chang way and her heart lurched. How had she gone so long without knowing what it could feel like to feel this way? She took another sip and kissed him, the taste of jasmine on his lips as well as hers.

"We don't have time for this," Chang said.

"If we don't have time for this, we should never have started this journey," Angel said. "But we did, and now I have found that this is what truly matters."

The sun was still shining when they stirred atop the plaid comforter, the glowing light sifting through the high green pines. Angel turned, her eyes meeting Chang's.

"You have given me acceptance and serenity, Angel," he said. "That is something that has eluded me for years now, a contentment I thought to never find again."

He ran a fingertip gently down her cheek. She took his hand and kissed his palm.

"As you have done for me," she said. "Kindness where I have had none and from someone where I least expected to find it."

"As you have for me," he said.

"Do you trust me enough now, to tell me how you came to be working for Luis?" She knew she was taking a chance, but she wanted to know everything about him. For a minute, he said nothing and she knew it had been a mistake. But then, he put his hands under his head, rested back on the pillows and turned towards her.

"I grew up an orphan on the streets of Hong Kong," he said, "stealing from tourists and the food vendors to survive are my first memories, aside from a prostitute mother that died when I was four. I can't remember anymore what she looked like. By the time I was thirteen, I knew there was no future for me on the streets except to join the Triad. I would do whatever was necessary because I already had." His face was impassive and his eyes fathomless when he stared at her. "So now my higher education began. I stole for them, killed for them, and worked my way up to learning to be an assassin, and I was especially gifted, and so of greater value. I was alone, and that was how I liked it because I'd always been alone. I earned my reputation and the prestige it brought me. Then one day I met a girl." He stared up at the ceiling and she knew he was lost in his memories.

"She was the daughter of the head man and off-limits to one such as me. She was destined to be the wife of a banker, or even a banker herself. She was beautiful and innocent and we fell in love. We were so careful, but not careful enough. She became pregnant and before we could make plans to escape the country, her father discovered this and knew exactly who to blame. He killed her for shaming him and tried to kill me. I had an old friend in Macao who smuggled me onto a ship bound for Mexico. There I found Luis. What I've done for him is no different from everything that I'd always done.

"In many ways, Angel, this situation we are now in, reminds me of that one. I will do anything to protect you. I have never told this to anyone but you. I thought I would never care for anyone like that again, but I find it is not so. You have given me back the ability to care for another."

Tears ran down her cheeks, and she cradled his face in her hands. "I love you, and I never knew what that was before. I will be grateful for you every day of my life to come, *mi amor,* and we will have many more of those." She nestled into his arms, breathing in his sandalwood-scented skin and he buried his face in her hair. They fell asleep, free and unburdened with any lingering doubts the past had given them.

Much later, Chang sat up and nudged her shoulder. "I am sorry, but we have a job to do, Angel, before it gets full dark. I hope it is the last time we have to do such a thing. We must bury that girl that's in the back of our car."

She groaned. "Maybe we should just take a drive and dump her over the side of the road once it gets dark."

Chang raised an eyebrow. "Maybe. However, they rent these places to hikers and these American hikers are a special breed. I'm not sure what motivates them. Mountain climbing is a sport I understand, it's a challenge and leads to a personal conquest. But these hikers just ramble around in places that people haven't yet built things on, and they go into the ravines and gulches off the side of the road, Angel. Sometimes they stumble upon all sorts of artifacts." He reached down and pulled on the boots she'd bought him. He seemed to be fond of them.

"Also, you may not be aware of this, but Americans are crazy about dogs, and they take them everywhere, especially on vacation. They are almost like their children, something I find quite peculiar. A dog could find the scent of a dead body in no time. We dump her off a cliff, she will be found, sooner or later, maybe even within a few days and I don't think we want her found that soon. I would prefer never, and there's only one way to do that."

He pulled on the other boot. She knew he was right.

She also knew she was losing her edge, that honed blade

sensibility she'd cultivated for so long. Maybe it was just that she was free after such a long time, maybe it was the music Grace and Jack played, that kept running through her head, or maybe it was Chang and the feelings he roused in her. Whatever it was, she knew she would need to go back to being the person she'd been if they wanted to survive this situation. Everything else would be a reward for when they were safe.

"Sorry," she said. "Really I am. Let's get it done."

They heard the music again even clearer now, the second they stepped out of the cabin door. Angel stood and listened and even Chang paused for a second before he went to the Escalade and opened the back door.

He hauled out the blonde girl's body and she plopped onto the pine needle-covered driveway like a rag doll. Angel recoiled at the sight but she knew this had to be done. Chang gave her a few seconds, but then nodded to her and she picked up the girl's feet while he took her shoulders. They carried the body behind the cabin and into the woods a few yards, putting her down softly on the forest floor.

"I saw a shovel beside the woodpile," he said, "could you grab it, please?"

Angel retrieved it and handed it to him, watching as the shovel bit into the ground. After the first few loads of soft dirt, Chang had to push firmly. The ground was colder and harder the deeper he dug.

"Do you want me to help with that?"

"No. You are not strong enough for this."

She didn't argue. She sat down on a boulder and watched him. The music wafted through the trees, occasionally stopping and starting. She couldn't make out the words but Grace's voice, then joined by Jack's tenor in harmony, was fascinating. Sometimes the guitar was louder, as though he was testing the volume. It was mesmerizing.

Chang dug. She sat. The music stopped and Angel felt as

though a light had gone out. Time passed and she shivered. The sun sat quickly up here and the temperature dropped accordingly.

"Ready?"

She looked up. Chang had put the shovel aside and picked up the blonde's shoulders. "Get her feet, like before."

It was getting quite dark. She grabbed the girl's feet and they slung her into the hole. It wasn't six feet, but it was close enough.

"Want me to get a light?"

"No, I can see enough," Chang said, grasping the shovel. "Let's just get this done."

Angel kicked dirt into the hole while Chang shoveled.

"Ever do this before?" Angel said.

"Once. That was enough. I don't ever want to do this again. Any of it."

They scraped mounds of pine needles and debris over the freshly turned earth. They would check in the morning but it seemed good enough for now.

Chang picked up the shovel and took Angel's hand. "This is the life we are leaving. Luis would be the only exception."

She squeezed his hand and leaned into him in the soft dark. "We knew it wouldn't be easy, Chang, but it will be worth it. We can create the future we want. We have the freedom and the money, and most importantly, we have each other. We were thinking down the wrong paths and maybe it's time to change all of it."

"We could use a new path. Tomorrow we will make one."

They walked back to the cabin to the warmth and the softly welcoming lights.

28

They didn't follow the road but instead went through the woods behind the cabins, creeping soundlessly, or at least as soundlessly as they could, given the size of Jack's boots.

"You should've taken off those boots and just gone in your socks," Grace whispered. "So much for that Cherokee blood, 'moving silently through the night' crap."

"That was most likely my great-great-grandmother, long diluted by berserker boot-clomping Highlanders or something," Jack hissed. "Stuff it, Grace. The pine needles muffle the noise, for Pete's sake."

They'd reached the back of the second cabin when they heard the clink of a shovel scraping dirt or rocks. A man's voice said "any of it" and then something about "Luis."

Grace clutched Jack's arm but she could barely make out his face in the gloom. Man, this had been a dumb idea. Her legs were trembling and she hated it.

"Is that them?" she whispered in Jack's ear and he jumped a little.

"Don't do that, Grace, Christ I'm nervous enough," he whispered back. "The hell should I know? Maybe they're burying a body."

She stiffened. "Not funny, Jack."

"Ssshh."

They crept closer, hidden by the trees. The light from the cabin windows was all the illumination there was, but enough to see two people, one carrying a shovel, walk around to the front porch of the first cabin, the one where the car was parked.

They heard the door open and quietly close.

"Christ, another ten steps and we would've been on top of them," Jack said, grabbing her hand. "Come on."

He pulled her further back into the darkness of the trees and Grace had no objection. They were both breathing like they'd run a marathon but it was fear, not exertion. From where they stood hidden by the trees, they had a clear view of the cabin outside, but far enough away they couldn't see much of anything going on inside.

"What do you want to do?" she whispered.

"I don't know," Jack said. "That was close. For all we know, they were digging a hole for trash, maybe they do that in the mountains. Because of bears or something?"

"I doubt that," Grace said, her stomach churning, "but I admit it's kind of a leap to burying a body. We need more intel. Isn't that what spies say before they jump to conclusions and get the wrong guy?"

Jack chuckled softly. "OK, so?"

"We watch and see what they're doing and who they are, for starters," she said. "That should tell us something."

"Lead on, MacDuff."

They were already wearing dark clothing, but Grace grabbed a handful of dirt and rubbed it on both their faces before Jack could protest.

"They look out the windows for any reason, they won't see white faces looking back," she said.

"You've seen Braveheart too many times, Grace, but you're getting the hang of this pretty fast."

They crept out from the cover of the trees behind the cabins and closer to the lighted windows. A man was crouched down, lighting a fire in the fireplace, and they could hear some noises from the kitchen area and a woman's voice. The window beside the fireplace was open and they could hear every word.

"You know I can't cook," she called, "I've never learned to do anything like that. Since you bought this stuff, you need to get in here." Her words were accented.

The man smiled. "Angel, I will do everything. All you need to do is have a tequila and watch." He stood up and gazed at the windows and Grace had a sudden urge to drop to her knees, pulling Jack with her.

"We have plenty of time," the man said. "After the chopping is done, once I start cooking, it goes fast. You can watch." He was Asian, unusually tall, and very handsome.

"He looks like a giant Jackie Chan," Jack whispered. "I wonder what she looks like."

They didn't have to wait long. Long dark hair framed a face made for the movies and she moved like a dancer, handing the man a glass.

"I know you prefer tea, *mija*, but you have spent enough time with Luis that you appreciate this as well, *verdad*?" She stretched up and kissed him. "For me?"

He took the glass from her and sipped it with no noticeable change. "For you, but it is...acceptable."

She sat down in front of the fire and sipped her drink, leaning her head back on the cushions while he headed to the kitchen. "You know what would be nice? If we just pretended for one night that our whole world is right here inside this cabin, together, without worrying about anything or anyone else."

The tall man came out of the kitchen, leaned down, and

kissed her upturned face. "Maybe we can do that, Angel. At least we can try."

He went back into the kitchen and they heard the clang of pots and pans, and within minutes, the aroma of sizzling onions. There was no more conversation, the woman silently sitting on the sofa, drink in hand.

Grace squeezed Jack's hand and jerked her head towards their cabin. They silently blended into the trees, going back the way they'd come. She breathed a sigh of relief after they came through the door and bolted it.

Jack went to the kitchen and poured two glasses of 1776 Pepper whiskey, handing one to Grace.

"We got some decisions to make."

"We sure do," Grace said, still shivering. She downed half the whiskey. "I'm thinking the run like rabbits option is about right."

Jack had that thousand-yard stare that he got sometimes. "Maybe." He focused back on her. "Maybe not. We still don't have any idea who that couple is. I didn't see any guns or hear any intent to swoop down and slit our throats. They don't look like the Hollywood version of cartel drug types to me, but what do I know?"

"True, but we have no idea whose money I stole, do we? Could be our pretty couple is here just for us. Can't judge a book by its cover. Maybe they robbed a bank in San Francisco, for all we know."

"Again, maybe. They could be some outdoorsy types from the Silicon Valley, more tech money than common sense. They didn't seem to be in any hurry to hunt us down. Sounded like they were planning a romantic evening. Maybe that's why they came here in the first place, little hiking, good food, fireside sex, a getaway."

Grace rolled her eyes. "They don't have to be in a hurry. If they've followed us this far, they know we're not exactly dangerous terrorist types. We're sitting ducks, Jack, is what we are, here in our little cabin, thinking we're safe as chickens in their henhouse. If we hadn't gone for a walk, we still wouldn't know. They have plenty of time to cook their fucking dinner and then come kill us later, all fat and happy."

Jack poured more whiskey. "Still, they didn't look all that dangerous to me. We've been looking for a safe haven and I don't want to keep running anymore, just because we're spooked."

Grace slammed her glass down. "Did you get a good look at that guy or are you fucking blind?" She went over to the fire, holding out her hands to the warmth.

Jack followed her and put his arm around her waist. She turned around to face him and tucked her head under his chin.

"I'm sorry. It's just I've got a bad feeling about them. I keep thinking I've seen her somewhere before. Then again, I'm suspicious of nearly anybody I see any more."

"I know," Jack kissed the top of her head. "You're not the only one. I do trust Charlie, though, and he wouldn't give us up. Besides, he was leaving town, remember?"

"True," she said. "I sure would like to finish that damn song. I've got even more rolling around in my head, and I think you do too.""

Jack cocked his head and looked down at her. "I do. Something about this place..."

"I know, I feel it too. In spite of that, this is a risky idea but I'm damn tired of that car too. Maybe our imaginations are getting the best of us. You have the Glock on you?"

He pulled it out from where he'd stuffed it in the waistband of his jeans and she nodded. She went to the bedroom and came back with the rifle they'd bought at Walmart before they left Boise, along with a box of shells.

"I'm damn tired of running, just like you are. Maybe we're just spooked like some kids telling ghost stories and if the cat knocks over a bottle, everybody freaks. Still, if it wasn't for that damn text, I'd feel a lot better. So, what really makes me feel better is this rifle." She loaded the gun and set it on the kitchen table, patting it reassuringly.

"Let's make dinner, I'm starving. You know what they say in the Marines or something?"

"No, can't say as I do," Jack said. "What do they say?"

"Eat while you can, because you never know when you'll get the next chance." She went to the kitchen. "Something else they say? You're not paranoid if they really are out to get you."

"We'll take turns keeping watch tonight, just in case our neighbors aren't truly the city elitist hiking type. I'll go first. We won't get a lot of sleep. But, first thing in the morning, we can leave if we're still not sure."

"Hoo rah," Grace said. "You want fries with that?"

29

The day had passed into night so slowly that Mario felt as though each second had stretched into infinity. No word had come from any of their sources, not even the hapless Mr. Blanchard. In Mario's opinion, if he was Jim Blanchard, he'd be halfway to the Canadian border but he didn't think the man was that smart. He shrugged and took a sip of his own glass of tequila. People never ceased to amaze him in their abject stupidity. In his line of work, there were a large number of them. It was the relatively smart ones you had to be careful about.

"Mario," Luis yelled from his bedroom. "Still nothing?"

Mario went to the doorway. "*Nada, jefe.* He eyed Luis, lolling on his pillows like some Arabian pasha, his shirt open to his hairy chest, eyes bloodshot. Not a man that inspired confidence at this moment, but Mario knew how fast that could change. Luis hadn't gotten where he was by being soft. The man could strike like a cobra, even when you least expected it and he was never to be underestimated, as many dead men had discovered at the moment of their last breath.

"*Mierde.*" Luis sat up. "We will go to this Italiano restaurant and see if their chef is as good as advertised. I doubt it, but I am willing to be surprised. I could use a surprise, eh Mario?"

Fifteen minutes later, the four men were led to the best table in the half-full restaurant, Luis resplendent in his Versace suit. No one would suspect the man had been through a bottle of tequila that afternoon. Tomas and Jose were unusually respectful and quiet for them, as though they knew Luis's temper was fraying rapidly. Mario carefully reconnoitered the other diners as well as the wait staff he'd seen so far and all seemed normal, at least as normal as he assumed Boise usually was.

The place was nicely laid out, candles and wall sconces glowing on the white linen, crystal glasses and silver set on the tables with fresh flowers. Classical piano music on a low volume floated softly through the large room. They were ensconced in one of the large booths beside the windows, not that downtown Boise at night was a very exciting street scene but at least it was relatively dark. The mouth-watering aromas of garlic, caramelized vegetables and roasting meats that wafted through the dining room were enticing.

Luis ordered half a dozen appetizers and two bottles of wine while they perused the menus to decide upon entrees. He was not a man for delayed gratification and Mario prayed they didn't dawdle, or this wasn't one of *norteamericano* pretentious restaurants where they picked their own herbs from the rooftop gardens or thought people were more grateful for their food when it arrived an hour after they ordered it because the chef was some celebrated pseudo-genius who took his time and had a soon-to-be-forgotten cooking show on HGTV. The few times he'd had to experience that nonsense annoyed Mario even more than it did Luis and today was definitely not the day for it.

Fortunately, the appetizers arrived swiftly and were excellent, as was the wine. Entrees were ordered along with a healthy dose of solace, at least for Mario.

"So, another day of waiting looks to be our fate," Luis said, spearing a perfectly charred octopus tentacle. "I do not like this, but it gives me even more time to think of suitable punishments for our two little friends when we find them, and find them we will."

He bit voraciously into the octopus as though it was a piece of Angel herself. Mario looked away and put his fork down. He'd never been fond of octopus anyway.

Tomas and Jose didn't seem to mind, but they never did. For years, along with Mario himself, they'd done whatever Luis asked, becoming the most trusted of his associates, which was why they were with him now. Mario had watched them saw off women's heads and throw those mothers' babies into the adobe bricks of the houses they raided without the slightest qualm, set people on fire and watch them burn and other atrocities. He'd done similar things himself in the early days, before he had people like Jose or Tomas to do it for him.

It was the way it was done. Terror and intimidation were the keys to ruling a cartel and the people in it. You learned that or you became one of those casualties yourself. It became a part of you. Mario had come to think lately that there was a better way to do business, but with Luis, new ideas were not welcomed and those who suggested them did so at their peril. New ideas or innovative suggestions were seldom adopted. It would take time, but Mario knew there needed to be changes eventually.

A busboy efficiently cleared their depleted appetizer plates and subtly whisked the crumbs away. Within minutes, their entrees arrived. The waiter stood by to ascertain all was as hoped for, and two more bottles of wine arrived and were poured. With a nod of approval, the waiter left them to their feast.

The food was delicious. Mario had ordered the rabbit, and it was expertly cooked and presented with a spicy mustard sauce and the requisite Italian polenta. Luis, who had been expounding upon the future fantasies of how he would punish Chang and Angel, became absorbed with his tomahawk steak and conversation lagged as Mario realized for the first time that day that he was hungry.

As they were ordering desserts, the hotel desk manager appeared at Luis's elbow. He seemed a little unsettled.

"Please excuse the intrusion upon your dinner, sir," he stammered, "but there is a gentleman here who insists upon speaking with you."

Luis sat back in his chair and waved languidly at the man. "Bring him in, *por favor*."

So, Jim Blanchard had returned, Mario thought. *Hopefully with good news but at least it was a public place so his timing was good if he wanted to live another day.*

But it was not Jim Blanchard, but Teo Martinez who walked up to their table wearing a feral grin. He wore a suit but it was clumsily tailored, the jacket let out enough to accommodate his thick torso but not cut well enough to disguise it.

The man was built like a gorilla and Mario did not remember him fondly. The man was also a thug and a bully. Those attributes, which Luis championed, had led Teo to the Northwest US two years ago, building a distribution network that rivaled but still gave allegiance to Luis's vast one in the Southwest. Mario sat up in his chair, wishing he'd not had that last glass of wine. He was hoping he wouldn't ever cross paths with Teo again.

"*Hola, jefe,*" Teo said, inclining his head towards Luis, his eyes scanning everyone around the table. "Mario, it pleases me to see you again as well. I have some good news to share with you."

"Ah, Teo," Luis said, waving at the waiter. "Please, bring a chair for my friend."

Teo sat and Luis poured him a glass of wine. "What do you have for me?"

"Even though our initial operatives lost their trail and bungled their jobs, we have discovered those you seek were here, and asking around for out-of-the-way places," he said. "They have said they are making a movie and want to be discreet."

He laughed heartily as did Luis, accompanied by Tomas and Jose while Mario managed a grim smile.

"Maybe they are thinking they will be movie stars," Luis said. "Maybe they are thinking it will be the next "Sicario", but it is most likely to be "Texas Chainsaw Massacre". He laughed heartily and so, of course, did everyone else, especially Teo.

After that bout of hilarity, Teo gulped half his wine and continued. "So, after interviewing a few of our local real estate representatives, they have provided us with some information. They are probably in one of three places, if they have stayed in this area, but that is all we learned before the information was...exhausted, so to speak." He shrugged. Collateral damage was not a term Teo was well acquainted with, but torture was as familiar to him as his victims' pleading breaths. A change in location had not made any difference in Teo's workstyle or ethics, Mario was sure.

"Tonight, we will continue our search and find which of the three bears the fruit, *comprende*? As soon as we find any trace of them, the knowledge will be yours as well, *jefe*. My gift to you. What more can I do for you?"

Luis patted Teo on the shoulder. "You have done all I've asked, Teo. That is all. They are nothing we cannot handle on our own, but I respect that you have asked. Depending on what we find out, I may have need of your services, so I may call upon you."

Teo nodded and finished his wine. "Anything you need. We should know where they are sometime later tonight or early tomorrow. As soon as we learn anything, from my ears to yours, *jefe*."

Luis was in a much better mood after that. The tiramisu and grappa arrived and were demolished in short order. Before they left the restaurant, he whispered in Mario's ear.

"That blonde at the bar? See how much she wants. I know a *puta* when I see one. She has been watching me all night. This could be a bargain, no?"

He laughed and patted Mario on the back. "I know I can trust you to get the job done, just as you always do."

He wasn't wrong. Certainly not about the whore. But soon all of this would be over and they could go home.

30

The persistent chime of the burner phone on the nightstand woke her, the unknown number glowing in the dark. Angel had given the number to only one person. Beside her, Chang snored on softly. That man was clearly not used to tequila. She picked up the phone, her heart racing.

"Speak."

"Angel?"

"Yes."

"It's Michael from the Inn at 500. The man you spoke of, the bad man. He is here, with others. People have been here to see him. I was not on duty after noon yesterday or I would have called you sooner. Now, they are on the move and have just left for the car. I thought you should know."

"Thank you, Michael."

She put the phone down and nudged Chang. His eyes flew open but he didn't respond with a killing strike. Progress.

"Luis is coming," she said and that was all she needed to say. Chang moved pretty fast for a guy with a bit of a hangover.

Within five minutes, their small amount of luggage was

loaded into the Escalade. Chang started the engine and she put her hand on his where it rested on the gearshift. He raised an eyebrow.

"Go down there and park the car on the other side of theirs. This will only take a minute. Yesterday, I was ready to leave them alone but if Luis is so close we're not leaving a million dollars with those two, I don't care how good their music is. We might need every dollar. Besides, we could be in New York or Paris right now if it wasn't for them."

Chang glanced at her, a half-smile on his lips. "You become very unforgiving when you don't have your coffee, Angel. I will need to remember this."

GRACE JERKED AWAKE, not sure exactly what had roused her. She'd tried so hard to keep her eyes open. It was her turn on watch and she'd fallen asleep, the rifle beside her. It was still dark outside, and the glowing embers of the fire gave off a faint illumination. As her eyes adjusted, the outlines of the furniture and the walls came into focus. The second knock on the door galvanized her, and she jumped to her feet, clutching the rifle. Whoever was outside, it couldn't be a friend, since they didn't have any. Godamnit, they should've packed up last night and gotten the hell out of here. *Stupid, stupid, stupid,* she thought, her heart banging like a bass drum with every word.

"Jack," she yelled, not caring who heard her. She pressed close to the door and she jerked back like it was on fire when the knock came again, even more insistent this time.

Jack staggered out of the bedroom in his pajama bottoms, clutching the Glock in his hand. "What the hell?"

She waved him away. "We've got company and I don't think it's the fucking Welcome Wagon."

"Open the door, Grace," said a woman's voice. "Don't make this harder."

They knew her name. Her stomach lurched and she threw a panicked look at Jack. He nodded and slid behind the bedroom door frame. "We don't have a choice, let's just get this over with and see who they are. I got your back, Grace."

Grace unbolted the door and swung it open, stepping back and pointing the rifle at the open doorway.

Even in the dim light, she recognized the couple from Cabin #1. They surged into the room and the Asian man slammed the door behind them. An AR-15 was slung over his shoulder.

Grace backed up further towards the kitchen and quickly flicked on the light, putting her hand back on the trigger. How could she have missed it last night? Maybe it had been too far away, but something had eaten at her ever since and now she knew what. It was the woman she'd seen at the hotel coffee shop in Boise, that last morning right before they left. This was no coincidence and these people were sure as hell not just some weekend hikers.

"Stop right there or I swear I'll shoot."

The woman gave an amused smile. "We're out of time, *mija*. Give me the money and we'll leave you alive. And don't give me some shit about you don't have it. I know you do so let's make this simple."

"Get out," Grace said.

The woman looked at her companion and sighed. "One last chance."

"Out," Grace screamed and raised the gun.

She couldn't believe how fast the tall man moved, but the word had scarcely passed her lips before he grabbed the rifle, spun her around, and held her fast, his arm pressing on her throat. Jack's shot went high, the bullet thudding into the ceiling beam above Grace's head.

"Drop the gun, Jack," the woman said calmly, "or Chang will break her neck. Your choice. Cute jammies, by the way."

How did they know their names, Grace thought, realizing right then that she and Jack were so far on the losing end of this standoff they might as well be standing on tiptoes over the abyss.

"Do it, Jack," she croaked. Hopefully, they both wouldn't end up dead, but she was pretty sure if he didn't, they both would be in the next minute.

Jack stared at them for a few seconds. "Is this what they call a Mexican standoff?"

The woman rolled her eyes. "Put it down, *cabron.*"

He put the gun down on the floor. "You want me to hold my hands up like they do in the movies? 'Cause, shit I can do that, too." The scorn in his voice wasn't lost on their intruders.

"Not necessary," the woman said, stepping over and scooping up the Glock.

Chang loosened his hold and Grace stumbled over to Jack, who put his arm around her.

"Give us the money you stole and we're out of here," Chang said, flicking his eyes to the woman. "Time is pressing."

"Well, this is no time to argue. But, the thing is, we don't have it anymore, well at least not most of it and not here."

"How is that?" the woman said. "You either have it or you don't."

"Well," Jack said. "What happened is, I put most of it into cryptocurrency as we went and the rest in a safe deposit box in Boise. Got a couple thousand here, for, you know, traveling money, but, yeah, the rest is, how do you say, inaccessible? At least at the moment, for anybody but me."

He was lying, Grace knew. He'd put some into digital currency, but there was still at least $300,000 in her old guitar case. It didn't matter but it might give them some time.

The Asian man looked at his companion. "I warned you,

Angel, they were smarter than we thought. Remember Twin Falls?"

She glared at him and turned back to Jack. "So, you are the only one who can authorize getting this money, from whatever," she gave Chang another scowl, "and that safe deposit box?"

"Well, that's about it, yeah." Jack was visibly shaking. Grace wasn't sure if it was because he was half-naked in the freezing room or sheer terror. She wasn't in any better shape herself.

"If you want to live, you have two minutes to get your clothes on and get in our car," the woman called Angel said, pointing the gun at them. "You will set this right. That is our money you stole. Now, my friends, we are all out of time. *Andale!*"

They ran to the bedroom and threw on some clothes, stuffing their feet into boots. Grace looked wildly around the room, wondering what else she could take, but there wasn't enough time to decide, except for her purse and the burner phone in it.

"Don't bother to take anything else," Angel said, watching from the doorway with the pistol. "There are much worse people than us on their way here right now. You see, *mi amigos,* that money you stole? What you don't know is that we stole it first, from a drug deal that went very bad, so we could escape this animal. Now he's out for revenge as much as he's out for money. They will not just kill me and Chang, but you as well, since they will think you are our friends. The worst is, they won't kill us before they cut us up alive and do worse things than you can imagine. They are fond of power tools and blowtorches. You will either come back to your little cabin poorer but wiser to sing another day or we'll all be dead and that will be all there is."

She gave them a grim smile and turned on her heel. "By the way, the new hair styles are unfortunate but you may live to grow it back. If you listen."

Grace was trying hard not to panic. They'd always known the money wasn't clean, but if Angel was telling the truth, this was worse than anything they could've imagined. Jack grabbed his wallet and threw a jacket at her, throwing on his own.

"I swear to God, Grace, we're going to get out of this, I promise you," he whispered, "not sure how yet, but we'll think of something. They haven't killed us yet at least. Maybe they'll just take the money and leave us."

She gave him a look. "And they lived happily ever after. Sure. We'd better think of something, because if we don't, we're as dead as that mouse we found in the woodpile the first night. He was just looking for happiness too, and look what happened to his ass."

"Nothing opens until nine, and it's zero dark fucking thirty out there," Jack grunted and bent over to lace up his boots. "We got three hours to talk them into not killing us, or get the hell away from them somehow." He stood up and hugged her. "We can do this, Grace."

"We have to. There's no options, Jack."

"I know. Believe me, I know." His face was grim as he took her hand.

"Good," Angel said as they came out of the bedroom. "Let's go."

Jack and Grace had taken three steps when Chang opened the cabin door and a barrage of bullets stitched smoking holes into the back wall and the cushions on the plaid sofa. He slammed the door shut.

"Down." He yelled and none of them needed any urging. Jack and Grace had already flattened themselves on the floor.

"Luis is here." Angel said. "*Madre de dios.* You got an extra clip for that thing?"

"Of course." Chang gave her a baleful glance. "In the car."

Grace nudged Jack and cocked her head at the back door in

the kitchen. They began crawling towards the kitchen when Angel pointed the Glock at them once more.

"Oh no, rabbits. The real big bad wolves are here, and you will face them as we do, *amigos*. You brought this on yourselves."

"Who the fuck are these people?" Grace said, not only scared but angry now. "You brought them down on our heads."

Chang didn't even turn his head. "Fate has a way of finding us all."

"Who the hell are they?" Jack said.

"Sinaloan cartel," Angel said tersely and Grace's blood ran cold. "That is Luis Reynaldo out there. He is a very bad man to cross or steal money from but we all did. If we want to live, we fight together."

If Grace was scared before, now she was nearly paralyzed with fear. Even she knew who Luis Reynaldo was. The American public had been enamored for years now with drug trafficking and cartel drama series. Escobar, El Chapo, and Reynaldo's names had been splashed around for some time. Grace hated those shows like Narcos, that glorified the murdering bastards, but people seemed to have an endless appetite for them. For a second, she closed her eyes. If they didn't figure this out, they'd be the featured body bags in the next season on Netflix. She wanted fame but not that kind.

"Listen fast," Chang said. "Are you any good with a gun?" He looked at Jack, who nodded. "This clip is all there is, so aim well. It's set on single-shot."

Chang slid the AR-15 across the floor to him, then looked at Grace, and handed her the rifle he'd taken from her earlier. She reached up and grabbed a handful of bullets from the box on the table and stuffed them in her pocket. Angel kept the Glock, and Jack tossed her an extra clip. They all looked at Chang.

"There's a butcher knife in the kitchen," Grace said to him. He gave her a little smile.

"I'm better with my hands," he said. "We must be very quick, you understand? Far as they know, it's just me and Angel. They may think there are more people, but not dangerous ones. I think there are only four, maybe five out there, but I can't be sure. They will come in, we cannot stop that but it is better if they're inside. That is when we know how many and that is when we kill all of them."

He sounded very sure and Grace didn't doubt him for a second. She couldn't afford to. She'd never shot a gun in her life until two days ago when Jack had shown her how to load the rifle and practice shooting tree branches outside the cabin. He said she had good aim. She sure hoped that was true.

"Make no mistake," Angel said. "You must kill them or they will kill you."

"Got it," Jack said and picked up the AR-15, crouching down behind the shredded sofa.

The door burst open, and a young white man stepped in, pouring rounds into the room, most of them too high to get to them on the floor but it wouldn't take him long to readjust. From behind the kitchen counter after the initial hail of bullets, Grace took aim and shot the man in the chest, surprising herself. He went down but two more men entered the doorway firing assault rifles, stepping over his body. The noise was deafening and she ducked back down to wait for the next opportunity for a good shot. Adrenaline coursed through her body and she found she had no remorse whatsoever about shooting another human being who was intent on doing her or Jack harm. All those days of worry had come to this and she felt more alive than she ever had in her life.

Chang sprang up behind the door and took out one of the gunmen with a throat strike but the other man was only inches away and had already turned his gun on Chang before Grace could get a clear shot. Angel's bullet went wide, as did Jack's. As fast as he was, Chang couldn't move fast enough before the third man shot him. The big Asian man wavered for a second and looked back regretfully at Angel as he fell to the floor.

Angel screamed in anguish, almost as though the bullets had hit her as well, and shot wildly at Chang's killer, who simply laughed and pointed his gun at her. Before he could pull the trigger, Jack stood up and took the man down with two shots from the AR-15.

Grace looked at the three bodies on the floor in disbelief. She couldn't be sure they were dead even though they weren't moving but nothing was certain anymore. Her hands were shaking but she aimed the rifle towards the door anyway.

For a minute, it was quiet. The cabin reeked from the acrid smell of gunpowder and the coppery stench of blood. Grace wanted to cough but she was afraid to make another sound.

"Angel, I am disappointed in your defiance. Still, *mi dulce amor*, there is time to come to Luis," a voice called from the porch outside, "if you don't resist me, and be the good girl you've always been, I promise a quick death. If not, well, that would be *desgraciada* for you, *traidoras puta*. There are worse things than death, I promise you this."

Angel looked behind her and her eyes met Grace's. "We must kill him, Grace. Your fate will be little better than mine, I promise you."

Grace didn't doubt her for a second.

"Which one is Luis?" she said to Angel.

"The fat one," Angel said. "The one who looks like Antonio Banderas let himself go to shit. You will know." She edged further into the kitchen closer to Grace and the cover of the cupboards. "The other one, who looks handsome and nice but is definitely not, is Mario, his right hand."

Grace glanced over at Jack and gasped. The front of his jacket was stained with blood and his face was pale, but he grinned at her and gave the AR-15 a pump before crouching back into his position behind the sofa.

"Whatever we got to do, darlin'. They figure I'm dead already anyway. These guys don't know shit about us Tennessee boys."

More than anything else in this world, Grace wanted to be beside him but she knew that was suicide at this point. Her mouth was so dry it felt like sandpaper. She resolutely lifted the rifle.

Two men, both Mexican, peered around the doorway but they were far more cautious than the last two, peering in quickly and pulling back to the safety of the thick log walls. She sighted the rifle, waiting for a shot. It stayed quiet, as minutes passed and that worried her.

Behind her, the kitchen door blew open with a blast of gunfire, and Grace's back and legs were peppered with a hundred hornet stings, splinters of shattered wood protruding from her skin. Angel fared no better and staggered beside her, then spun around and fired the Glock wildly at the large man who lunged inside. He laughed and lifted the gun from her hand like it was a toy, Angel's bullet hitting the ceiling. He pitched it behind him, and drew Angel close to his chest, heaving the shotgun on its sling behind his shoulder while he held a large knife to her throat with his free hand.

"Luis," he called. "I have her." He glanced over at Grace. "And her *puta* friend."

Before Grace could turn the rifle on him, he kicked her hard in the stomach and she fell to the floor but propped herself up on one hand, reaching towards the rifle she'd dropped, now a foot away from her hand.

"Bitch, I will slit her throat if you move one more finger toward that rifle." His voice rose. "If there is anyone else left in this cursed cabin, put your guns down now or both these whores die."

Jack did not materialize. Wherever he'd hidden, Grace was glad of it and hoped he'd stay there for the moment, at least.

Her stomach hurt badly but she barely registered it. Just trying to stay alive was more pressing. Angel's eyes met hers in a bleak stare. At that moment, they became sisters in the effort to survive, the ties of instinct and need more important than blood or money.

"Ah, my Angel, how pretty you look for Luis. I was worried you hadn't kept yourself up to my standards." A large man wearing a black suit strode into the cabin through the front door, his very presence seeming to take all the air out of the room. He was accompanied by a tall Mexican man who held a pistol. They both came closer, stopping only a few feet away from where Grace lay.

"Teo, it was a good thing you and Blanchard came along," Luis said to the man who had come in the kitchen door, now holding Angel in his grip. "Tomas and Jose were useless, as you kindly noticed, and sorry about your man, although he was pretty useless also. You may need some more demanding recruiting parameters, my friend. Perhaps this day I did you a favor, eh?"

He looked down at Grace. His eyes were dark and had all the emotion of a shark inspecting his prey. "And who do we have here?" He propped up her chin with the toe of his boot and after a quick inspection, dropped her like she was filth staining his boot.

"She will be entertaining later, for as long as she lasts. For you, my Angelita, I have some very special things planned and she can watch so she will not be surprised when it's her turn. Teo has been kind enough to supply me with some necessities. You know how much I like to play with drills and this place you have found to hide in is ideal for my purposes, so far away no one will hear your screams. How thoughtful of you to have found it, but then you've always been so attendant to my needs, haven't you?"

He laughed heartily at his own words. The sound echoed

around the cabin walls and Grace was more frightened than she'd ever been in her life. This guy was a certifiable maniac. She never thought her life would end here on this bloody floor in a place nobody would ever think to look. She futilely wished, for perhaps the hundredth time, she'd never seen that fucking backpack.

"You can let her go now, Teo." Luis said to the man holding Angel. "But first, cut her just a little, to give her a preview of what will come."

The man called Teo smiled and drew his blade over Angel's left arm and then took a swift shallow cut across her stomach. She stayed silent for the first one but couldn't help but cry out at the second. He dropped her to the floor, laughing and licking her blood from his knife.

"*Bastardo.*" She clutched her stomach, her shirt already soaked with blood. Grace swallowed heavily, bile heaving in her stomach. She'd never seen this woman before two days ago but whoever she was, she didn't deserve the fate they had planned for her, any more than Grace herself did.

She'd never wanted to kill anybody before but she'd sure gotten a taste for it this morning. These depraved people didn't deserve to draw breath in this world. She eyed the rifle lying on the floor just a foot away and her fingers twitched. It might as well have been a mile. She felt herself giving to despair as much as she tried to think of a way out of this. But Jack was probably dead, and she and Angel wouldn't be breathing for long if these animals did what they said they would.

She weighed her chances of grabbing the rifle before one of them shot her, glancing back at Teo just as his face exploded, blood and brain matter spattering over Grace, Angel, and the kitchen walls. Jack stood in the kitchen doorway, clearly unsteady but steady enough. Eyes wild, he pointed the AR-15 at Luis and the man next to him. The tall quiet man touched the large turquoise stone in the bolo tie around his neck. He silently raised his pistol and shot Jack in the leg before Jack could pull the trigger again. Jack fell groaning onto the kitchen floor beside Grace, reaching towards her.

His eyes closed.

She could hardly breathe but she could feel the tears running down her cheeks. She reached over and grabbed Jack's hand, raising her eyes to the handsome man with the gun. She wanted to look into the eyes of the man who would kill her as he had Jack.

He looked back at her appraisingly and then his eyes flicked to Angel, lying silently next to her on the bloody floor. He turned to the smiling fat man beside him.

"Luis," he said, and for the first time, his face portrayed emotion. "I've been thinking for a long while that it's time for new blood."

He shot Luis Reynaldo in the face and twice more in the chest before the big man fell heavily to the floor. From where she lay, Grace watched in silence as Luis Reynaldo's blood pooled in a crimson river, mingling with that of the woman he'd loved and had come so far to kill.

31

Mario Valenzuela had always been a patient man. He'd waited a long time for his ascendancy. Over the years, he had come to thoroughly detest Luis Reynaldo and the needlessly brutal methods he employed to make his business work the way he wanted. He was no different from the other cartel lords, that was true. But in Mario's view, that way of thinking was on an outdated downward trajectory that was not sustainable in this business. Times were changing.

Mario had known from the beginning there was a better way, but he learned early on in his association with Luis that a man who expressed different ideas was a man who had just filled out his own death certificate.

Mario was a businessman, and he was not looking for redemption, because that was something he could only ask God to give him, given the business he was in but he knew with all his heart and soul that this cartel could be run without the viciousness that Luis seemed to crave.

His long association with the man had taught him the ways in which it should change. He wasn't a fool. Death always rode on his shoulder, but it wasn't necessary to subject innocents or even the people who worked for him to mindless violence to ensure his success. Mario was a businessman and one who knew how to reward and respect value, especially in people.

He had always cared for Angel, and so many others like her. Mario was a man who paid his debts, all of those he could make right, and even many of those that were not his to pay but those he could make right.

Surveying the wreckage Luis had wrought in this remote cabin in the woods, he knew this was the first debt he owed as *jefe*. There was no one left alive that would tell a different tale. First, he made some calls for help to those he knew he could trust. Then he gathered up the weapons as Mario was a very thorough man.

By the time the sun set on this long bloody day, much had changed in the little cabin in the pines. Bodies disappeared as though they'd never existed, floors and walls were scrubbed clean, bullet holes were erased and casings were disposed of, carpenters had hung a new back door and a new plaid couch, just as ugly, had been delivered. The refrigerator and pantry were stocked with food. Everything looked much the same as it had the day before.

Most importantly, while all that was happening, a very well-paid and discreet medical team arrived quickly, headed by a surgeon, accompanied by nurses and medical equipment. An impromptu OR was set up in the bedroom and they immediately went to work on Jack. Mario monitored it all, and as the surgeon and his team went to work, another PA stitched up Angel and Grace, bandaged them thoroughly and administered oxycontin.

Grace was reluctant, worried about Jack and, Mario suspected, possibly had a former bad association with said drugs. She was also afraid of him, he knew, although she didn't need to be. However, based on the events of the day, he understood. She had watched him shoot the man she loved. He took her hand in his.

"You need to do this for yourself, *senorita*." He stared into her eyes. "I hope this is the worst day of the rest of your life. At this time, you are in pain, and do not let the bad things this drug can do in the hands of some stop you from the relief you need today. It will not last, I can assure you of that, both the physical pain and the drugs. For more solace, the only remedy is time." He shrugged. "And perhaps prayer, if you choose."

She stared into his eyes for a few seconds, then took the cup from the nurse while her eyes moved back once again to the surgeon still busy beside Jack.

The surgeon and his team finished their work and after he disposed of his gown and gloves, he came over to Mario, while the nurses busied themselves making Jack more comfortable on the gurney they'd moved in, hooking up an IV. He would be unconscious for some time.

"He'll make it." The doctor wiped his forehead and leaned back on the cushions of the new sofa. "He took two bullets in the arm and one high in the chest, and then another in his leg. Missed all major arteries and the lung, and he's a lucky young man. Barring infection, he should be up and around in a couple of weeks, but it'll take quite a bit longer for him to be back to normal. He may have some damage to the leg even after it heals, but that may alleviate over time. I'd say your friends should plan on spending at least some of the summer up here."

"Yes," Mario said. "I have already made those arrangements."

The doctor stood up. "My nurse will stay and monitor him closely for a day or two, and I'll leave detailed instructions with her and his girlfriend on what to do and what to watch for. She will keep in touch with me for the next few days and will be on call if needed. Nice doing business with you, Mr. Valenzuela."

Mario shook his hand and handed him a well-stuffed

manila envelope. "Thank you for your assistance and discretion."

"Of course. Please feel free to call on me any time, *patron*."

It was dark by the time the cabin was quiet, and everyone had left except the nurse. The only sound was the quiet beeping of the machines monitoring Jack, whose condition needed constant surveillance.

There had been no choice but to shoot the young man to stop him from killing Mario as well as Luis, but Mario had aimed as carefully as he could. It was the earlier shots in the chest that were most worrisome. Still, Mario had done all that he could. It was in God's hands now.

The moon was rising over the tall pines and the ambient light from the fireplace and the glowing Tiffany lamps inside the cabin were all the illumination he wanted. Mario sat outside on the porch and sipped a glass of Grey Goose citron, the ice cubes clinking in his glass. Despite his heritage, he'd never really been all that fond of tequila. One of Teo's men, no, now one of Mario's men, sat in a Tahoe SUV outside on the road, likely listening to music but the sound didn't carry and Mario didn't care anyway. There would be no one coming. He wanted to be sure all was well before he left this place where Luis had done his best to destroy four people. One of those four had not been so fortunate, which Mario regretted because he'd always liked Chang, sensing something tragic in the young man but at least he had done all he could to assure the other three were alive.

"Mario." Her voice was soft. She was wearing the hospital gown the medical team had brought and her feet were bare. She came outside sat next to him on the other Adirondack chair, her dark hair falling over her shoulders, her beautiful face pale.

"*Gracias, patron.*"

"*De nada,*" he replied. "I am no longer your *patron*, Angel.

You are free to live your life now, the life that has been long denied you."

She was silent for a moment. Then, she took his hand. Hers was trembling.

"Do you mean that, Mario?"

"Yes," he said, and squeezed her cold fingers in his. "I will take the drugs away because that is a curse you don't need and I know you and Chang only kept them for insurance. As for the money, I don't care about that, Angel. You deserve every cent of it. There is a packet on the kitchen counter for you as well. It has a passport, and a birth certificate that says Tucson, Arizona. They are authentic," he smiled, "well, as authentic as the best forgers in the world can make them, which are likely better than the US State department can do. My gift to you."

"*Gracias*. I will never forget what you have done for me. And," she gestured towards the open door of the cabin, "for them. They didn't deserve any of this. *Vaya con Dios*, Mario."

She leaned over and kissed his cheek, and got up and drifted back inside, her hospital gown a pale floating ghost in the moonlight.

Mario finished his vodka and went to the car. He was eager to see Evangelina and his children. There was much to do.

32

The late afternoon sun filtered through the pine trees. Grace leaned back in the Adirondack chair, basking in the warmth. Full summer was not far away now. Nearly three weeks had passed since the morning when Angel and Chang had knocked on their door. Three weeks in which her ribs had mostly healed, Angel's stitches had been removed, and Jack's condition had improved dramatically, albeit with a couple of scares that had been quickly managed. Three weeks that were the longest of her life. She felt like she'd been through a war, and really, she supposed she had been. It was a war of her own making and the guilt she carried was a heavy burden every time she looked at Jack. Since the first day, she'd been at his bedside, sometimes holding his hand even when he was unconscious, to reassuring him when he was awake. His wounds were serious and she'd become an expert nurse, if an uncertified one, one who cared more than anyone else ever could.

She sipped at the glass of pinot noir she'd poured. Mario's minions had been thoughtful and generous with their grocery stocking. She'd watched that man shoot Jack and kill Luis as though the fat man was a cockroach but Mario's help and kindness overrode her initial fear of him. He'd done what he had to do, just as she, Jack, and Angel had. She felt no remorse for the deaths of Luis's men, and neither did Jack or Angel. Everyone's feelings on that were very clear. The deaths of some others in both their desperate flights were not so clear and for Grace, and she knew for Angel as well, they were a source of remorseful nightmares. There was nothing to be done about that, now or ever.

She and Angel had drifted around the place like zombies, caring for Jack, who had been fairly out of it most of the time. They hadn't really talked about anything of any real import, except for the usual 'hey, want some coffee' or 'done in the bathroom' stuff, even though they shared the queen-sized bed in the bedroom beside Jack's makeshift one on his gurney. All the little wolves healing up from their adventures, Grace thought cynically, tucked in like family. Although there'd been many a night when she'd woken to find her hand curled into Angel's, not really sure how it had happened.

While awake, though, it was like they were strangers who'd been through a hurricane and were wandering around a debris-strewn beach looking to pick up the pieces of their lives. To probe too deeply and ask questions that might throw them back into the maelstrom had been territory studiously avoided by all of them.

"*Hola*." Angel stepped outside and sat down on the other chair, tilting her head back and closing her eyes. Grace hadn't exactly been Miss Conviviality herself, but she was starting to be concerned about Angel. The brash and confident woman she'd first seen had disappeared almost completely. Instead, she seemed consumed with grief and guilt over Chang, drifting listlessly around the cabin and wandering through the woods like a wraith. Grace empathized, especially every time she looked at Jack. If he had died, she wasn't sure she would've wanted to live herself.

"Jack asleep?"

"Yes, which is good. He is much better, Grace, especially in the last few days. He will be up and walking soon."

It was quiet, the only sound the soft whispering of the pine trees in the gentle breeze.

"We haven't really talked, Angel, about anything," Grace said. "You know, all this shit." She waved her hand in the air.

Angel nodded. "That is true. But, you know, Grace, maybe it's better to just leave it. We went through hell together and now I think of you and Jack only as my friends, as *compadres* that banded together and survived. That is all I need to know, and all that matters to me."

Grace stared at her for a minute. Maybe she was right. Even so, she felt a need to try and explain and couldn't stop herself.

"When I saw that bag," Grace said, her eyes on Angel's face, "I wanted it and I can't make any excuses. I *needed* it. No more shame, no more going without, no more yearning, no more dealing with the Barrys of the world. I knew it was a risk, but it was one I thought I was ready to take. I was wrong. It led to this, to Chang getting killed and Jack nearly dying, and there is no amount of money in this world that is worth that and I have to live with that for the rest of my life."

Angel reached over and lightly touched her arm, the first time they'd ever consciously touched each other since that day when they'd held hands on the bloody kitchen floor.

"You must not berate yourself, Grace. You were not alone in wanting a different life and doing what you must to achieve that. Chang and I did the same. We made terrible mistakes on this journey and people died. We all saw an opportunity we needed and we took it. We are just people who took a chance to have the life they want. I have learned that takes a level of ruthlessness that is not usual, but it is not one I must seek repentance for anymore. Nor should you. We cannot go back and change anything. It is done and we live with it."

Angel lifted her hand and Grace handed her the glass of wine. Angel took a large sip and handed it back.

Angel's eyes were direct but unfathomable. "*De nada mi amiga*. Now it is my turn. I will tell you a short story and it never will be spoken of again."

"Once upon a time, in a small village in Sinaloa, a father sold his fourteen-year-old daughter to a rich man. She didn't cost much, this insignificant girl, but she was pretty and a virgin and that was all the *jefe* wanted, but strangely he became obsessed with the girl and she became part of his life for many years, having everything except her freedom, the most precious thing there is. She also didn't know what it was to love some-one, because those she thought loved her had thrown her away."

Grace swallowed the last of the wine in her glass. Word-lessly, she refilled it from the bottle beside her chair, and handed it to Angel.

"*Gracias, amiga*. One day not long ago, the man amused this girl, who was a grown woman now, by allowing her to go on one of his business deals to the United States, accompanied by two of his best *sicarios*. The world of drug dealing is a dangerous place and even though this particular meeting was assumed to be simple and amiable, things went very wrong. After the shooting stopped, there was no one left alive but the woman and one of the *sicarios*, whose name was Chang. There were other complications there is no need to speak of, but that is how we came to pursue you and Jack."

She gave the glass back to Grace, her eyes never leaving Grace's face. "At first, I was angry and vengeful and had no thought for anyone but myself and Chang. But as the miles passed, I came to feel like I knew you and Jack. I listened to your music, saw your pictures, and I think came to understand that you wanted that same freedom. I came to have this yearning to see you face to face, but I never thought it would come to..." for the first time, her voice broke, "this."

Jesus wept, thought Grace. *There were a lot worse things in the world than growing up in a backwoods trailer park.*

"What we have now is not just your burden, but mine as well, for being selfish and making you and Jack targets for Luis's wrath and nearly getting both of you killed. I am responsible for Chang's death, which I must live with. That said, *gracias*, Grace."

"For what?"

"For talking." Angel sat back, and for the first time in weeks, Grace saw the confident woman who had come through her cabin door three weeks ago. "For helping me remember who I am."

Grace stared at her for a minute. "I will say the same to you, Angel. All the time we ran, not knowing who we were running from, I came to only want to face you and have this end. With Jack and I coming out on top, of course." She grinned ruefully. "That didn't work out as well as it could've, but here we are. We're alive."

"Ladies." Jack stood there, leaning heavily on the door-frame, his face pale. "I did my part, too, for pretty much the same reasons you both did: the freedom and opportunity to live our lives the best way we can, which that money could provide, besides the fact that I'd do anything for Grace. Of all of us, I should've known better than either of you the terrible price that taking money like that could levy, and of the violence that could rain down on us.

"We left some heavy collateral damage in our wake, that's a fact but one we can't change. Maybe I'm too cynical, but it's helped me to see this whole debacle more clearly. It's going to take some time, but time is luckily something we have that the people we've left behind do not. For them as well as ourselves, we need to make every day count."

As the days passed after that, things got better. The tension eased and they became comfortable with each other, talking and drinking into the wee hours of the night occasionally. They watched movies from the interesting collection of DVDs stored on the shelves, along with board games. Jack taught Angel how to play poker, which she loved and it didn't take long for her to gleefully clean him out of chips at five card stud.

Occasionally Grace wanted to practice shooting guns, a lingering paranoia, but every time she looked at Jack she discarded the idea. Besides, Mario had taken them all away, which was an even better one.

Jack and Grace read out loud a lot, a habit they'd picked up on the road, preferring their own voices over books on tape, which they hadn't had anyway. They liked the sound of their own voices better, finishing their John Irving collection and moving on to Cormac McCarthy, Jack's favorite. Angel loved this idea, and soon she began taking a turn too. Her favorite was Hotel New Hampshire, especially the bear and the motorcycle part, which cracked her up. They avoided thrillers and crime novels, even though Grace had loved them in the past. They'd had enough of that shit in real life.

Since neither Grace nor Angel could cook much more than scrambled eggs, they had no choice but to learn. However, more than one dish found its way to the trashcan and frozen pizza appeared in its place. Jack was a better cook, but he tired easily, reduced to being a couch coach and issuing instructions, accompanied by dismaying groans when they occasionally ignored him.

The days got longer, the sun not setting until late in the

evening, summer languidly settling in. Occasionally one or two of the other cabins had weekend visitors, but they kept to themselves, and mostly they were alone on their piece of the mountain. Grace and Angel occasionally took the Odyssey into town and bought groceries, since their initial supplies were nearly depleted. Even though Mario had assured them they were safe, they avoided restaurants and anything other than the supermarket and farm stands, and only once ventured to a bookstore they found. They felt like refugees, survivors of a war, and in fact, they were.

What they all avoided was talk about the future. How they got to this place had emerged, but how to leave it was deliberately sidestepped for the time being. Maybe because they weren't sure how to assimilate back into a world that for them, was completely different than the one they'd known some weeks ago, at least in perspective. They'd never be the same people they'd been, but they all knew they were slowly assimilating their experiences into the people they'd become.

The one thing that was missing was music, and Grace knew it was beginning to wear on Jack especially, whose arm was slow in its healing, although it wasn't his arm that stopped him, it was his thoughts, just like Grace's own trauma stymied her desire to pick up her guitar.

One rainy July afternoon Jack set up his guitar and played some of the chords and the solo from the last song he and Grace had written the day before everything changed. Grace was in the kitchen chopping vegetables and she put down the knife and stood still as a statue. After a minute, she walked slowly into the living room and when Jack started up the song again, she sang along with him.

"Nowhere to run, nowhere to hide,
You got to depend upon yourself now
Ain't no one out there on your side
You're lost, babe, and you ain't sure how."

"We have to finish this. Are you ready?" Jack said.

Grace smiled. "I think I am. It's time we got to work, Wilder."

Angel came in from the porch. She picked up Grace's guitar from where it was propped beside the fireplace, covered with dust. She looked at Grace and cocked her head.

Grace nodded back. *Why not,* she thought. *Give her something to do. They could work around it anyway.* Angel set to work tuning the guitar, paying no attention to either of them.

Chorus done, Jack gave Grace a smile that reminded her of the old days and started noodling verses and a bridge, while Grace mused words aloud. Then an acoustic guitar line came in, a counterpoint to Jack's. When Jack stopped, Angel continued, fingers flying over the strings.

"Where the hell did you learn to play guitar like that?" Grace said.

Angel looked up and gave a tentative smile. "I taught myself. There was a lot of free time at Luis's ranch. Is it any good?"

Jack rolled his eyes and shot Grace a look. "Well, well. I suppose you can sing, too?"

"*Un poquito.*" She held up her thumb and forefinger, shrugging.

Jack launched into Townes's "Waitin' Around to Die," and Grace's soprano soared through the first verse. By the time the second chorus rolled around, Angel joined in and the harmony was perfection. When the last note died away, they looked around at each other.

"Ladies, get the whiskey. We been lying around here like whipped dogs that never sang a note. That shit's over and I'm calling it right now. We got us some work to do." He looked at Angel. "You in?"

"Why not?"

So it began.

Music once again became Jack and Grace's world, and

Angel stepped through that same looking glass into a universe that she wholeheartedly embraced. All through that summer and into the fall, they worked together, although none of them thought of it as work, but simply what they wanted to do. They had a dozen new songs ready and polished, and a dozen more in different stages. They had a sound, the three of them, unique, plaintive, different than anything out there. Angel added in a Latin flavor with some of her guitar work, as well as Spanish lyrics to a few of the songs, similar to Ryan Bingham's style in Boracho Station. Somehow, it melded into an Americana roots fusion sound that was uniquely their own.

"We got something special here," Jack said. "Nearly getting killed is doing it the hard way, but it puts a flavor on it we didn't have before."

One day after they'd decided to wrap up, Angel put down her guitar, a battered but great-sounding Hummingbird she and Grace had picked up in a Boise music store when they went to buy new strings.

"Listen, guys. We need to talk about the money," Angel said. "I don't want to, you know, disturb our creative run here, but I need to know more about this whole business. I need to know how much it costs to make a record, or whatever you are planning, and all the things that go with it. How do we do this? Do we need a studio, or do you already have one back in Nashville? What about a manager or a record label, if we even need to have those things? I know nothing here. If we're in this together, I'm the only one who doesn't have that information."

Jack looked at Grace. They should've realized Angel had no idea what she was stepping blindly into. "Yeah, sorry. I mean, it's your future too, Angel, and I should have realized how new all of this for you."

"How much was in that backpack you found in the bathroom, Grace?" Angel said.

"Uh, around $750,000," Grace said. "We've spent some, on

the car and this and that. Groceries, whatever." She looked over at Jack. "Some of it's in digital currency, but most of it's here, in cash, stashed in that old guitar case we keep the cords and mics in. We lied about the safety deposit box. Sorry. It was a bad morning."

Angel stared at them for a second and then laughed. "I knew you were lying. Just waiting for a chance to bolt or shoot us at an opportune moment, or the minute we got to the bank. I would've, too, given the circumstances."

"Still," Jack said. "It's way more than enough to get back to Nashville, get settled, hire a publicist and a manager, maybe even get label interest or better yet, put out a first-class album on our own. I'm way in favor of establishing our own label and doing it that way, and getting other new artists we like to sign on with us. It's riskier, but we have to believe in ourselves and our music. I think we've got enough money to do that. It came at a high price, but that's all the more reason. What the three of us have here is pretty fucking great. I think we all agree everything that went down needs to mean something, and this is how we do it, you know?"

Angel nodded. "Oh yes," She sat very still, all traces of amusement erased from her face. "I think from what you say, I will like Nashville, at least if I'm with both of you."

Grace glanced at Jack and raised an eyebrow. Angel was acting a bit strange this afternoon. She'd been doing well but she did have episodes of melancholy, and even the occasional temper tantrum, usually over as quickly as it'd come.

"There's something you need to know," Angel said.

Oh shit, Grace thought. *Here it comes. I don't need any more surprises.*

"Remember those two backpacks of mine Mario brought in from the Escalade?"

"Yeah, sort of," Grace said, not sure where this was going.

"Well, they weren't full of clothes. I lied, too."

Angel looked at them. "What I'm saying is that if money can help buy success, we don't need to worry about that. I still don't know much about the American music business, but it sounds like a good investment and it's what I want to do. Besides, I have no desire to go to medical school." She grinned. "I have another two million dollars in those backpacks. Courtesy of Mario Valenzuela. I could use some new underwear, but it's not like I'm itching to go to Paris to get it, *verdad*?"

"Holy shit." Jack looked as though he was about to pass out, and Grace choked on the sip of water she'd just swallowed.

Angel just smiled and picked up her guitar.

ON THE MORNING they woke up to the first snow flurries, Grace knew it was time to go. Angel was enchanted, having never seen snow before. She got dressed and went outside, letting the snowflakes fall on her outstretched arms, face to the sky.

Grace and Jack watched her from the porch.

"Nashville better get ready for that one," Jack said. "I sure wouldn't want to be some club manager that tried to tell her what to do. You two are a lot alike, now that I think about it. I could be in real trouble here."

Grace ran her hand through his shaggy hair, now just past his ears. He looked like a twelve-year-old, hair falling over his forehead. She loved it. "Don't worry, you're holding your own, country boy. I just want to go home, make an album and get back into the world. Not a lot of the world, but a little. See if it's changed as much as we have. You?"

"Oh, hell yeah. Looking forward to Barnett's house with more than one bedroom, too, until we find a place of our own."

"No more than I am."

"You have any idea just how unbelievably fucking lucky we are?" Jack said. He pulled her close.

"Every day, Wilder, every damn day." She watched Angel circle around. She put her head on Jack's shoulder.

"Lucky is the understatement of the century, Jack. It also took grit and we all have that. You said it first. It needs to be worth it. We have to make sure every single day counts," she said. "Now we can afford to do what we want, and give back too."

"Oh, we will, darlin'. That's a promise. Wilders never break a promise."

Oh, Grace knew that. She'd always known that.

They'd make it worth the risk, all three of them. She knew that too.

ABOUT THE AUTHOR

Kathleen Morris is an award-winning writer, an aficionado of American and Western history, is a graduate of Prescott College in Arizona and lives and writes in the desert Southwest. Her debut novel, The Lily of the West, the story of "Big Nose Kate" Haroney, was published in 2019 to critical acclaim and was awarded "Best First Western Novel" from Western Fictioneers. Her second novel, The Wind at Her Back was published in November 2020, and The Transformation of Chastity James, a Western Writers of America SPUR Award Finalist in 2021. Fallen Child, a novel of revenge followed in 2022. Visit her website www.KathleenMorrisauthor.com for more and to see what she's currently working on.